BOTH SIDES NOW

Moving to Britain Guide

Compiled by the
RTE *Both Sides Now* team
Puts the vast experience of this team
at your disposal.
**The most complete guide
to Working and
Emigrating.**
All the information you will need
gathered over several years of working
with emigrants and emigrant groups.

*IF you are already in Britain, this is the
essential book for you.
IF you or your family are thinking of
going – this book is a must.*

It will save you money time and hardship.

BOTH SIDES NOW
Moving to Britain Guide

Cés Cassidy

and the Both Sides Now team

Cartoons: Donald Teskey

An RTE publication
in association with
B&I Line

THE O'BRIEN PRESS
DUBLIN

First published 1990 by The O'Brien Press Ltd.,
20 Victoria Road, Rathgar, Dublin 6, Ireland
in association with RTE.

British Library Cataloguing in Publication Data
Cassidy, Cés
Both Sides Now: moving-to-Britain guide ,
1 Immigration. Great Britain.
I. Title
325.41
ISBN 0-86278-231-7

Typesetting and layout: The O'Brien Press
Cover design: Steven Hope
Cover Photograph: Peter Harding. Photo page 13: RTE
Printed by Leinster Leader Ltd., Naas

ACKNOWLEDGEMENTS

My grateful thanks to Packie Bonner, Shay Black, Geraldine Hickey, Shaun
McCarthy, Philip Chevron and to the following for their assistance and
encouragement while I was preparing and writing this guide: *In RTE* Kevin
Healy, Dir. of Programmes; Cathal MacCabe, Head of Music and Variety;
Producers Peter Browne and Tom McGrane; Producer/presenter Aonghus
McAnally; BAs Sharon Murphy, Carol Kelehan, Pauline O'Donnell, Orla Fagan.
In transit B&I Line, Aer Lingus and Ryanair; *Irish Advice Services* Triona, Mary
and Kate in Emigrant Advice Service, Dublin, and everyone in the listed emigrant
centres around Ireland.
In London Seamus McCormick, Federation of Irish Societies, and Seamus
McGarry; Seamus Troy, Council of Irish Counties Association; Geraldine Vesey,
and everyone at Brent Irish Advisory Service; Kevin, in Housing Advice
Switchboard; Reena and everyone in the Piccadilly Advice Centre; Marcus
Ravell and Angela Hickey, Citizens Advice Bureau, Greater London Office;
Mary Cribben, Cricklewood Homeless Concern; Brendan Mulkere and all at
Brent Irish Cultural and Community Association; John Fahy, Maria Maguire,
Irish In Greenwich; Gerry, at Irish in Islington; Jim O'Hara, St Mary's College
of Higher Education, Strawberry Hill; Fr Jim Kiely and Sr Carmel McGowan,
Hammersmith Irish Advice Centre; Fr Tom Scully and all at Camden Irish Centre;
Sr Joan Kane and all at Haringey Irish Centre; Sr Carmel Keegan, South London

Irish Welfare Bureau; Geraldine Hickey and all at London Irish Women's Centre; Hilda McCafferty, ILEA; Nick Hardwicke, Centrepoint, Soho; Pete Husbands, The London Connection; Kate Hoey, MP for Vauxhall; Olive Ahern, Atlas Employment Agency; Maria Doyle, Accurate Appointments; Martina O'Donoghue, Alpha Numeric; Linda, at Computer Staff; Mary Devitt, Hibernian Nursing Agency; Anne and Tom, Migrant Training Schemes; Julie Hamilton, Safe Start; Rob Saunders, TUC; Tony O'Brien Construction Safety Campaign.

In Manchester Clare Wynn, Manpower Agency; Anne Pierce, Citizens' Advice Bureau; Julie, Manchester Chamber of Commerce; Sr Elizabeth Cahill, Manchester Irish Community Care; Michael Forde and all at the Irish World Heritage Centre, Cheetham Hill; all at the Irish Association Club, Chorlton; Liam Bradshaw, St Brendan's Centre, Old Trafford; all at North West Housing Aid; Laurence Graham, BBC Manchester.

In Leeds Blue Arrow Personnel Services; Richard Norton, Anne Blair, Citizens' Advice Bureau; Tom McLaughlin, Leeds Irish Centre; Everyone at First Stop Centre; Stuart Ross, Leeds Chamber of Commerce; Stephanie, at Leeds Housing Welfare.

In Bradford Beryl Cassidy, Bradford Irish Music Association (and Seán!); Margaret Fielded, Bradford Citizens' Advice Bureau; Bradford Infromation Centre; David, at Bradford Chamber of Commerce.

In Liverpool Tomny Gibbons, Employment Service Jobcentre; Phil Farrelly, Liverpool Irish Centre, Mount Pleasant; Tommy Walsh and all at Liverpool Centre; Breege and Mavis, Irish Community Care, Merseyside; Cheryl Lang, Liverpool Chamber of Commerce; Dominic McVey, St George Hotel; Angela Heslop at the Basement Project; Max Tsu, Liverpool University Irish Centre.

In Birmingham Fr Joe Taffe, Plunkett House; Alice Davis, Irish Welfare and Information Centre; Pat McGrath and all at Birmingham Irish Centre; Pierre Watson, Birmingham Chamber of Commerce; Shelter Housing Aid Centre; St Francis Centre, Handsworth; St Dunstan's Centre, King's Heath; St Anne's Centre, Birmingham; Citizens' Advice Bureau (Ms Matthews and Ms George).

In Coventry David Cairns, Council House; Mary Dawson, Council House; Brian Willis, Coventry Chamber of Commerce; Coventry Citizens' Advice Bureau (MS Sue Darling).

In St Albans John Doyle, St Albans Irish Association; Pat and Diane Judge, St Albans Comhaltas Ceoltoiri Eireann; Citizens' Advice Bureau, Upper Lattimore Rd.; St Albans Tourist Information Centre; Roger Osborne, St Albans Council.

In Luton Sr Eileen O'Mahoney, Luton Irish Advice Bureau; Pauline, at Luton Chamber of Commerce; Luton Council. And to all those unsung heroes, omitted from the above list for space reasons, our grateful thanks!

Irish Community Statistics: The figures given for the Irish communities in Britain are estimates based on the 1981 UK census updated by current figures at the Irish CSO. We are aware that next year's UK census figures may show considerable change in the population estimates currently available.

Contents

Chapter 7 Liverpool *151*

Chapter 8 Birmingham and Coventry *176*

We're Irish right down the line

When you choose to sail B & I you're making an important decision.

You're travelling with an Irish owned company. A company that instinctively understands the value of a warm welcome and friendly, good-natured staff.

You are also choosing a company that is committed to providing a comprehensive service, with unbeatable value from both Rosslare to Pembroke and Dublin to Holyhead.

And B & I is a company that welcomes innovation – like the unique 'FlexiFares' service.

Brand new fare systems, (exclusive to B & I) that abolish restrictions on departure and return dates. So you can plan your trip the way it suits you and come and go as you please.

So don't just cross the Irish Sea this year. Make a B & I Line for Britain and you can rest assured that the company is Irish all the way.

For booking details and fare structures contact B & I at Dublin (01) 679 7977, Cork (021) 273024, or talk to any travel agent.

B&I LINE

ROSSLARE – PEMBROKE   DUBLIN – HOLYHEAD

Foreword

At two minutes past ten on the evening of Monday 6 June 1988, I switched on my microphone in Studio 3 in the radio centre and welcomed listeners to the first 'Both Sides Now' programme. I think it's fair to say that two years later I am still overwhelmed at the response to the show, both here at home and from the Irish community all over Britain. Each week, the letters come pouring in, with information, queries, requests for family and friends across the water, success stories and also poignant reminders of how bad it can be when things go wrong.

We've travelled to most parts of Britain, broadcasting the show from places like London, Birmingham, Manchester, Leeds, Liverpool, Luton and Glasgow. And no matter where we go, one thing always strikes me: the incredible difference between those Irish people who made adequate preparations for emigration (whether it was enforced or voluntary) and those who went off with 'a few bob' in their pockets and a vague notion that finding work and a place to live in Britain would be 'no problem'.

Sadly, it can be a very major problem, compounded by the complete change in environment and culture. So often people have told me about their failed attempts to chat to a fellow passenger on the London Underground. I doubt if many coaches bringing Irish folk home to Wexford, Cork, Kerry, Galway or Donegal would ever travel in such stony silence! However, it's still a shock to the system to realise that you may have to start anew and make friends in what will be, for quite a while, an unfamiliar culture.

And unless you've got a job to go to, or you're lucky enough to find work very soon after arrival in Britain, the money will run out fast. And then it's just a matter of time before your options also run out. Forgive the pessimism, but this is exactly what happens.

So I suppose this guide is all about passing on the experiences of those who've seen the two sides of The Irish Sea; and how to give yourself the best chance of making your time in Britain as successful as possible, both personally and professionally.

The many hundreds of Irish people I've met around Britain while working on 'Both Sides Now' – people who have contributed to this book with both practical advice and helpful contacts – are themselves a great source of support for you, wherever you meet up with them. They remember well what it was like when they first went to Britain, looking for work and a new way of life. And they'll help you out in many ways. But it's wise to remember that they can only help out to a certain extent... How you'll fare in Britain basically comes down to your own planning and preparation before you leave Ireland, as well as your own sense of motivation when you get to Britain.

I sincerely hope that you will find this book useful, whether you are just about to leave Ireland, or have recently settled in one of the cities mentioned in it.

But a final reminder – forewarned *is* forearmed. There is no substitute for preparing properly for emigration. Believe me, you'll be very glad you did.

From myself and Cés, a heartfelt thanks to producer Peter Browne for his guidance and encouragement. And many thanks also to producer Tom McGrane for his help and sound advice.

Take care!
Aonghus McAnally

CHAPTER 1

Before You Go

*Talking to emigrants on the 'Both Sides Now' programme
has led Aonghus McAnally to believe that preparation is
all-important. Here he passes on his suggestions.*

We were over in Manchester one weekend last spring to broadcast
'Both Sides Now' from that city and on our travels we met up with a
man from Donegal, Terry Connolly.

Terry had left The Rosses in the early seventies and he spent ten
tough years working as a chef in hotel and restaurant kitchens all over
the north-west before going on to open his own restaurant. The
business prospered and Terry was in Manchester to meet up with his
two younger brothers, who have also done well in the construction
industry in Britain. Aonghus asked Terry how was it that all of his
family had made a success out of the emigration road.

'Well, you could say that the luck of the Irish had something to do with it,' Terry answered. And then added dryly: 'About one per cent I'd put down to luck and the other ninety-nine per cent had to do with decent planning put in at home before going, as well as, I suppose, a fair bit of effort when I first came over to Britain.'

Terry's father, it transpired, had spent many years working in Scotland back in the forties. So he knew the emigrant road and he used to counsel his sons: 'Do all the ground-work you can before you go and it will carry you through the first rough months over there. And after that, boys, it's just a matter of plain hard work!'

'And he was right of course,' Terry said. 'You can never depend on your luck, but good fortune usually follows on the heels of hard work anyway. It's not so much the luck of the Irish – more the luck of the perspiring!' Sound advice from someone who has put in more than his fair share of perspiring over hot stoves in his time!

So, keeping Terry's experience in mind, let's take a look at the planning and preparation side of things.

It's a fact that Irish people heading off to live in Canada, Australia or the USA will spend six months or more thinking about their decision to go … putting together references and setting up advance accommodation and a job to go to.

Their destination as emigrants is so far away, geographically, that they know they've got to get all the details right first time. They can't nip back home every second weekend just to collect birth certificates, or sort out their social insurance.

In the same way, although Britain is so much nearer home, you'll hardly be in a position to come back to Ireland during your first month or two there, simply to collect references or some other vital item that you forgot to bring with you. It's wise to adopt the same approach as the long-distance emigrants: give yourself several months to weigh it all up and to prepare yourself well for a new way of life in Britain.

So where do you start? Well, thought comes before action – think about the following:

*How will you live there? (Remember, if you're unemployed, social security benefits are harder than ever to get, and accommodation will be scarce).

*What about your own capabilities? Have you ever lived away from home before? Could you last out a tough couple of months at the beginning, when everything is new and you're missing friends and family at home?

*Are you sure that there's nothing you can do here at home? Check

14

out all the alternatives to emigration. Are there any training courses or job possibilities in your area? Talk to FÁS staff. Visit your local Community Centre. Explore every avenue that might lead to job skills and work here at home.

To help answer these questions, call into your nearest emigration advice centre. These centres carry a vast range of helpful information and staff can advise you on everything from job prospects to taxation, medical care, your rights and entitlements. They can also help you assess your particular circumstances and give solid support as well as level-headed advice on how to make Britain work for you. Their advice is free and a visit will save you time and money in the long run. So check the list on p.29 to find your nearest advice centre.

The Government's FÁS centres should be another port of call. Obviously it's not FÁS policy to promote emigration, but for those set on going, it offers a one-day briefing session that includes video information and 'fact packs' on Britain. And if job seeking is your only reason for going to Britain, FÁS will also tell you about SEDOC, the European Placement Service, with job possibilities in other European countries, to suit all skills.

If you've been to the advice centres for information and you've talked over your emigration plans with family and friends and decided that going to Britain is right for you – then the next thing to consider is where in Britain you'll do best. Don't settle on London as your destination simply because of the 'bright lights/big city' syndrome.

The vast majority of Irish emigrants head for London when they go to Britain. As a result the Irish Centres there are finding it desperately hard to cope with the numbers calling on them for help with finding work and somewhere to stay. The demands on their hostel accommodation are enormous and in a city of seven million people, it's getting tougher all the time to find work.

The pressure of living in a fast-paced city is also something you should consider seriously: there's little time for the kind of community life we have here in Ireland and it can be frightening and very lonely at first, particularly if it's your first time away from home, friends and family. And even if you do know some Irish people living in London, remember that your accommodation may turn out to be on the other side of the city from them – and tube travel can be expensive if you are on a budget.

On the other hand, cities with long-established Irish communities like Manchester and Leeds have a lot to offer. We've met many emigrants, now settled in places like Bedford, Coventry and Luton, and most of them are very happy with their lifestyle. A good number of them had relatives or friends already living in these areas, but many had lived in London for a while, found it tough going and left to seek better work opportunities and a greater sense of community.

So before automatically deciding to make London your destination, look at the possibilities other places in Britain might hold for you.

On one visit to Leeds this year, we met a Corkonian, Davey Power, who had exchanged the Leeside for Leeds some thirty-five years ago – and reared grandchildren as well as children there. He loved Leeds and told us that he was 'lucky, first go' with his choice of city. He said he believed that, for an emigrant, 'Half of success lies in settling on the right place to emigrate *to*'. And there's truth in that.

If you've taken time to think about all the implications of emigration (things like how you'll cope with the reality of leaving home, perhaps for the first time ever, to live and work in a totally different culture), and you feel it's the right step for you, then the next stage is to take some practical action on the preparation front. Have a look at the list that follows and see what you can do about each area. The more you can manage to set up in advance from here, the easier it will be for you when you arrive in Britain.

ADVANCE ACCOMMODATION: TEMPORARY

Whatever your destination in Britain don't leave anything to chance when it comes to organising somewhere to stay. A roof over your head and somewhere safe to leave your possessions is the most basic requirement when you are in unfamiliar territory. So try to line up somewhere for at least a month. You'll need that amount of time to find your own flat or lodgings.

Don't settle for an offer from pals to 'Put you up for a night or two.' It's not any real help to you if you're going to have to move bags and baggage somewhere else every couple of nights. And we've learnt ourselves (through hard experience) that heartfelt offers from friends to 'stay with us whenever you're over' rarely work out that simply. Remember that friends regularly (a) Go on holiday, (b) Move flat, (c) Move cities, (d) Have other friends to stay.

So if you don't check out their current situation before you leave Ireland, you could end up paying for hotel rooms at prices that will eat into your budget.

RELATIVES

If you have relatives in the city you are going to, then check to see if they can let you stay for a couple of weeks. And if they can't manage this, they may know of friends or neighbours who would take you as a lodger for a month or so, or on a long-term basis.

FRIENDS

If you intend staying with friends in Britain, write to them or call well in advance to make certain they can let you stay. Many landlords in London will no longer allow their tenants to take in friends. And keep in mind that your friends may well be living in pretty cramped circumstances themselves. Sleeping at the foot of their bed may seem like a homely arrangement to you, but it's a surefire recipe for losing your friends! So try and find some alternative and hang on to your friends.

IRISH CENTRES

Staff at the Irish Centres in Britain usually know of good lodgings in the local Irish community. Write to the manager of the nearest centre before you go, asking for a list of places you might try. You'll find the list of Irish Centres on p.220.

ADVANCE ACCOMMODATION: HOSTELS

In London and in many other cities around Britain, there are organisations that run hostel accommodation. But these can vary greatly in terms of conditions and how long you are allowed to stay, and many are designed to provide only a short-term option, while you are looking for a flat or bedsit.

Others, like St Louise's Hostel in Medway Street, London SW1, will decide on the individual needs of the women who come to them. Some are allowed to stay for up to a year. St Louise's accommodates 133 women in the 18-24 age group; single rooms cost from stg£40 a week; doubles are from stg£35 – rent is payable one week in advance. The kitchen and bathroom facilities are shared between eight women and you need to write in advance for a place.

St Louise's is one of a number of such hostels catering for first-time arrivals in London, but it's not 'typical'; each hostel differs according to the particular job it's trying to do. Some hostels are less 'supportive', i.e. there may not be anybody on hand to advise you about job-seeking, flat-hunting or money problems, and conditions range from comfortable to depressingly basic. Prices can range from stg£40 to stg£100 per week. Check the list of hostels on p. 55. Write to Irish Centre staff for advice. Then write to several hostels to apply for a place. Remember that demand for hostel places is heavy, so write well in advance of arrival.

ADVANCE ACCOMMODATION: YOUTH HOSTELS

YMCA

There are YMCA (Young Men's Christian Association) and YWCA (Young Women's Christian Association) hostels throughout London and all around Britain, catering for short-term or long-term stays. The prices vary from one hostel to the next; for instance, one London YMCA charges between stg£70 and stg£90 a week. For details and a full list of hostels, write to *The National Council for YMCAs,* 640 Forest Road, Walthamston, London E17. Phone 03081-520-5599.

YOUTH HOSTEL ASSOCIATION

The Youth Hostel Association also has a number of hostels in London and around Britain. It's a members only organisation, which means that you must buy membership (cost stg£7.50) to stay in their accommodation. After that, it's approx. stg£7.00 a night, with a maximum of four nights' stay. For details write to *The YHA*, 14 Southampton Street, London WC2. Phone 03071-836-8541. (You can also join International YHA from Ireland through An Óige.)

UNIVERSITY BED AND BREAKFAST ACCOMMODATION

Universities in Britain provide B&B, or self-catering, short-term accommodation during the summer and from mid-March to mid-April, as well as from late December to early January. There are fifty locations to choose from. Ask for details from individual universities. For brochure and details write to The General Secretary, *British University Consortium Limited,* Box B89, University Park, Nottingham NG7 2RD. Phone 03-0602-504571.

OTHER ACCOMMODATION

THE WORLDWIDE BED-AND-BREAKFAST ASSOCIATION

This association offers rooms in London and right around Britain . It's not a particularly cheap option – prices start from stg£20 a night, and obviously it's not long-term accommodation. But it is another option if you're stuck for a roof over your head. Phone 03071-3515846.

BED-AND-BREAKFAST HOTELS

Bed-and-breakfast hotels in London are generally nothing like our B&B accommodation in Ireland and nothing like proper hotels anywhere. They are usually run-down hotel buildings, used mainly by unemployed single people or families who are waiting for council accommodation. The conditions range from poor to dismal, with people sharing rooms and bathrooms and no cooking facilities at all.

The amount of money local authorities will pay to help with board and lodging costs is very small and this is what drives so many people to stay in these cheap hotels. They have little alternative. Try to avoid having to use this kind of accommodation by finding somewhere to stay before you arrive in Britain.

SHELTERS

London and some of the bigger cities in Britain have shelter accommodation. This ranges from the small, friendly and clean kind to the large, institutionalised sort of shelter. They are usually closed during the day and conditions are basic: single-sex dormitories, mass-produced food, rules and regulations – and strictly short-term accommodation. Shelter accommodation is for emergency circumstances, when all other alternatives have been tried.

SQUATTING

A squat is not secure accommodation. You can be evicted very quickly once you are discovered. You will have no furniture and no facilities (getting gas or electricity connected is extremely difficult) and you leave yourself open to all kinds of problems. It's not recommended as an accommodation option, but if you are decided on it, then you need to know exactly what you are doing and what your rights are. Contact *The Advisory Service for Squatters*, 2 St Paul's Road, London N1 2QN. Phone 03071-359-8814. (Mon-Fri, 2pm-6pm.)

IDENTIFICATION

It is vital to bring proper identification with you to Britain. It doesn't matter if you are a direct descendent of Brian Boru, or even closely related to someone in U2. You must have ID. And that means having at least two acceptable forms of ID, for example a driving licence, a cheque book and card, a medical card, your birth cert (original, not a photocopy) and your passport. Although your passport is not required for travel to and from Britain, it is an invaluable identification document and it is accepted as one of the two forms of ID required if you're claiming social security benefits in Britain. To apply for a passport you need: your birth certificate, the completed passport application form, plus two passport-size photographs all signed by a garda at your local station.

The Dublin Passport Office is in The Setanta Centre, First Floor, Molesworth Street, Dublin 2. Phone 01-711633. In the busy holiday season, two thousand passports are issued daily, so expect to wait your turn. Remember to allow up to fifteen days for the application to be processed.

The Cork Passport Office is based at 1A South Mall, Cork. Phone 021-272525.

The Belfast Passport Office is based at 47 High Street, Belfast BT 12QS. Phone 08-0232-232371.

BIRTH/MARRIAGE CERTIFICATES

Baptismal certificates aren't accepted in Britain as valid ID. You must have a state birth certificate. You can get this from the *General Register Office*, Dept. of Health, Joyce House, 8 Lombard Street East, Dublin 2. Phone 01-711000. The full version of the birth certificate costs IR£5.50. A marriage certificate is often required for tax-claiming purposes, as well as additional ID in DSS (Department of Social Security) offices. It also costs IR£5.50.

Certificates by Post

The Register Offices at Joyce House gets up to 100 postal applications per day. There is a delay of about a month with postal applications, however, so it's best to get certificates from the office before you go.

REFERENCES

Decent references increase your job-seeking (and indeed flat-seeking) chances. Get these from ex-teachers, or ex-employers, bank-staff, your local community centre manager or local clergy. Bring certificates of exams passed, or courses completed. Take along a dozen copies of your CV. Bring your last two wage-slips, if you've been working in Ireland, and bring your P45 as well. And if you've a trade, then don't forget to bring your tools with you.

ORGANISING A JOB IN ADVANCE

This is the tough one. Organising a job in Britain before you actually move there obviously isn't an easy matter, but it is possible if you've got good job skills, or training and work experience. You have nothing to lose by contacting recruitment agencies there. See p.69. Employment Agencies, London; see also agencies listed under 'Employment' in chapters on Manchester, Leeds, Bradford, Liverpool, etc.) Send the agencies your job history (CV) to date. This should be well-thought-out, no longer than two pages and complete with copies of references. Also include a brief covering letter informing them when you will be arriving in Britain , your address there and a daytime phone number if possible.

* Check the Irish Sunday newspapers for English job advertisements.

* Check *The Irish Post* and *The London-Irish News* (on sale in the major newsagent chains here).

* Call to Emigrant Information centres here for information on the employment scene in Britain. (Many stock *The Irish Post* and *The London-Irish News.*)

* Check your local library for English newspapers and trade journals.

* Ask relatives and friends in Britain if they know of any job openings in their area. Make it clear that you don't expect them to turn up a job out of thin air for you, but that you'd appreciate it if they'd keep their ear to the ground.

MONEY MATTERS

HOW MUCH WILL YOU NEED?

The thorny matter of how much money you'll need to take with you depends, of course, on just how much cash you can manage to call on after paying travel costs. But whether you are single or travelling as a family, there is an absolute minimum you will need to tide you over the first couple of weeks in Britain.

If London is your destination we'd recommend that a single person should take stg£700 and a family stg£1,000. This might seem like a lot but look at the breakdown of basic expenses for a single person:

Bedsit: stg£50 per week. You'll be asked to pay a deposit of stg£200, plus a month's advance rent. This means a total of stg£400 for accommodation costs. Now assuming it takes you a week or two at the very least to find that bedsit (and it will), then you'll need another stg£50 to stg£90 per week to pay for temporary accommodation.

Daily food, travel, newspapers and other basic costs will amount to approx stg£90 per week. So, even assuming that it takes you just two weeks to find your bedsit, and keeping costs right down to basics, your expenses will total stg£670 to stg£700.

If you are planning to base yourself in Manchester, Leeds, or any other city outside London, the cost of living may be less expensive, but you shouldn't risk taking much less than the stg£700 (or stg£1,000 for a family) advised above, because it's during the first couple of weeks, when you are new to a city, still job-seeking and looking for long-term accommodation, that spending is heaviest. And if you are claiming social security in Britain, remember it will be several weeks before the money comes through.

TRANSFERRING BENEFITS

If you have been claiming unemployment benefit in Ireland for at least four weeks, then you are entitled to transfer those payments to Britain, where they will continue for a period of up to three months (provided you have that amount of benefit left). Inform your local employment exchange at least three weeks ahead and give them your forwarding address. They will make the transferral and give you a form to take along to the DSS dealing with your area in Britain.

If a husband is going to Britain, and his wife is staying behind, the Department of Social Welfare will transfer the full amount of benefit to be collected by the husband and he will send it or part of it, back to his wife in Ireland. If this fails to happen, then the wife should notify the local exchange and she will be able to claim supplementary welfare.

If you have been on unemployment assistance in Ireland, that stops when you leave the country and you can apply for Income Support (social security benefit) when you get to Britain. Income support payments are usually made two weeks in arrears.(For details of signing-on procedures, see Ch 2, p.75.)

INCOME SUPPORT

Current Rates of Income Support Payment in Britain, 1990-1991: In general, under-eighteen-year-olds will not be able to get income support except in certain specific circumstances (e.g. if you are a single parent, or if you can show that you would 'otherwise suffer unavoidable, severe hardship'). You are expected to register for the Youth Training Scheme programme instead, which pays a training allowance. (See p.79 for details of the YTS.)

Single person, aged 18-24: stg£28.80
Single person aged 25 and over: stg£36.70
Lone parent, under 18 years: stg£21.90
Lone parent under 18 years (higher rate): stg£28.80
Lone parent, 18 or over: stg£36.70
Couple, both under 18: stg£43.80
Couple, one or both over 18: stg£57.60

If you have dependent children you will receive per child –

Under 11 years of age: stg£12.35

11 to 15 year of age: stg£18.25
16-17 years: stg£21.90
18 years: stg£28.80

In addition to this, a family can claim an extra stg£7.35 family premium. A single parent can claim an extra stg£4.10 lone parent premium, as well as the family premium. And there is also a child benefit payment of stg£7.25 per child, per week (usually paid every four weeks). Those eligible for income support should also get housing benefit (help with 100 per cent of the rent cost and 80 per cent of the poll tax charge.)

The process of claiming benefits, and working out what benefits you may be entitled to, can be complicated when you are new to the British social security system. You should first seek advice at your nearest Irish Centre (listed in each chapter under 'Advice') or your local Citizen's Advice Bureau, a nationwide free advice service. You'll need to bring details of your Social Insurance record.

Form E 104 should be given to your DSS office if you are claiming sickness or maternity benefit.

Form E301 should be submitted if you are claiming unemployment benefit.

These forms can be obtained from *The Department of Social Welfare,* Gandon House, Amiens Street, Dublin 1. Phone 01-726333.

For further information, contact *The Social Welfare Department,* International Division, Store Street, Dublin 1. Phone 01-786444 extn 2500.

MEDICAL MATTERS

When you are planning to live and work in another country, the availability of medical services there must be considered. In Britain, the National Health Service gives free GP and hospital services, without any national insurance qualification, if you are 'employed, seeking work in, or ordinarily resident' there.

You must register with a local GP as soon as you have an address. You'll get the addresses of local doctors in the nearest library or from your nearest chemist. You then have to go to the doctor's surgery and ask to be placed on his/her list of NHS patients.

You will have to pay some charges towards the cost of medicines, dental costs, glasses and other appliances. At the time of writing it costs stg£3.05 for prescriptions, approx stg£11 for an eye test, stg£3.15 for having your teeth checked (this doesn't include cost of treatment), and getting glasses costs much more. (In certain circumstances, some people are exempt from these charges: ask your doctor about these exceptions when you visit the surgery.)

If you need hospital treatment, or if you need to consult a specialist, this will usually be arranged at no extra charge through your doctor. In an emergency, you may be admitted directly to the hospital. As well as the NHS there are various private health schemes in Britain, such as BUPA or PPP which provide private medical insurance cover.

EDUCATION

There are many universities, polytechnics and colleges of further education if you'd like to extend your education or improve your career prospects. But you do need to plan ahead for these courses.

For a university place, you have to have applied by 15 December of the previous year for courses starting in autumn. Apply through *UCCA* (Universities Central Council on Admissions), PO Box 28, Cheltenham, Gloucestershire GL5 O1HY. UCCA will forward your application to the relevant universities. (Exceptions to this are Oxford and Cambridge. You apply direct to these universities, and your application must be in by 15 October.)

For a degree at a polytechnic or college of higher education, apply through *PCAS* (Polytechnic Central Admissions System), PO Box 67, Cheltenham, Gloucestershire GL50 3AP. (Apply by 15 December for courses starting the following year.)

For art and design courses, apply through *ADAR* (The Art and Design Admissions Registry), Penn House, 9 Broad Street, Hereford HR4 9AP.

For a Bachelor of Education degree, apply through *CRCH* (Central Register and Clearing House), 3 Crawford Place, London WIH 2BN.

For details of A-level standard courses provided by further education colleges, apply to the local authority in the area you'll be moving to, or write to *The Education Information Office*, British Council, 10 Spring Gardens, London SW1 A2BN. Phone 071-930-8466.

Business courses are available at polytechnics and colleges starting each autumn. Apply early.

Nurse training, for advice and information write to *The ENB Careers Advisory Centre*, PO Box 356, Sheffield S8 0SJ. Phone 0742-555012.

For general information on degree and diploma courses in Britain, contact *The Education Information Office*, British Council, 10 Spring Gardens, London SW1 A2BN.

Scotland does not have polytechnics, but it does have colleges of higher education, which offer a range of degrees and HND courses on many topics including science, business and paramedical technology. You must apply individually to each college. However Alison Thaw at Paisley College operates a co-ordinating service for these colleges. For details of courses write to Alison Thaw, *Paisley College*, High Street, Paisley PA12 BE. Phone 034-8871241.

ADULT EDUCATION: CLASSES AND COURSES

For details on adult education in London see Ch 3 p.82 'Adult Education' and 'Adult Education' sections in other chapters).

STUDENT GRANTS

Students from EC countries are entitled to assistance from the UK government with some third-level education costs. This applies mainly to reimbursement of tuition fees. Most maintenance costs have to be met by students themselves. You can apply to the local education authority for a discretionary grant, but generally such grants are *very* hard to get. The Department of Education and Science issue a brief guide on the reimbursement of tuition fees. You can get a copy from The Department of Education and Science, Further and Higher Education 3 (EC Student Fees), Elizabeth House, York Road, London SE1 7PH. Phone 03071-934-9631.

FAMILY EDUCATION

If you are moving the entire family to Britain, then the matter of your children's schooling will be very much on your mind. In Britain, free education is provided for all children from the ages of five to eighteen, and it is compulsory from the ages of five to sixteen.

Nursery Education is provided for some three and four-year-olds and there are also informal playgroups in some areas. But childcare facilities are not necessarily available everywhere. Try to check this out before you decide to settle in a particular neighbourhood. For information, contact PPA (The Pre-School Playgroups Association), 61-63 Kings Cross Road, London WC1X 9LL. Phone 03071-833-0991.

Five-to-eleven-year-olds attend primary schools divided into infant and junior departments, or separate schools, or in some areas 'first' or 'middle' schools, catering for different age ranges.

*At *eleven years of age* secondary education begins, either at non-selective state-run comprehensives (catering for 90 per cent of state pupils) or at selective grammar schools. As well as a large number of independent fee-charging public and private schools educating pupils of all ages, there is a large number (about one-third of the total) of primary and secondary schools in England and Wales, supported by public funding, but run by religious denominations.

*At *sixteen years of age* pupils sit GCSE examinations (replaces GCE O levels). An Irish Pass Leaving Certificate is roughly equivalent to the GCSE exam.

*At *eighteen years of age* students sit A levels. An Irish Honours Leaving Certificate would be considered near to A Levels.

To help you decide on the right school for your children:

* *Schools and colleges run by local education authorities*: Write to the local education authority in the area you'll be moving to and ask them for information on what's available locally. Then write to the schools or colleges concerned and ask them to send you brochures and information on each. At that stage, you can arrange in advance to visit a number of schools in the area when you arrive in Britain.

* *Independent Public and Private schools*: Write to The Independent Schools Information Service, 56 Buckingham Gate, London SW1E 6AG. Phone 03071-630-8793/4.

You can also make general enquiries about children's education in Britain by writing to *The Department of Education and Science*, Elizabeth House, York Road, London SE1 7PH. Phone 03071-934-9000.

TRAVEL

Whoever coined the phrase 'It's better to travel hopefully than to arrive', might have added that it's even better to travel economically than to land in a new country with depleted funds to carry you through the first couple of weeks. Travel fares between Ireland and Britain can meet your budget if you book well in advance of the journey. There is a wide range of routes and prices to choose from whether you travel by sea or by air. So shop around. Remember that any price quoted to you will not include the extra IR£5.00 Government tax. And don't skimp on the travel insurance – it's well worth the extra money.

AIRLINES

AER LINGUS

Aer Lingus operates up to sixty-two flights a day between Ireland and London (Heathrow and Gatwick) from Dublin, Cork and Shannon. As well as London, they fly from Dublin to eight British regional airports: Edinburgh, Glasgow, Newcastle, Leeds/Bradford, Manchester, East Midlands, Birmingham and Bristol. All these routes have a minimum twice-daily service in summer. Commuter services from regional airports in Ireland connect through Dublin to an extensive route network of both cross-channel and European destinations. These services operate feeder flights to Dublin from Derry, Sligo, Knock, Galway and Kerry. Fares include Superapex, Apex, Shortstaypex, Excursion and Superbudget.
Reservations: Dublin 01-377777, Cork 021-274331, Limerick 061-45556, Belfast 084-245151.

RYANAIR

Flights from Dublin to London (Luton and Stansted), Cardiff, Liverpool and Coventry. Coach service from Liverpool on to Manchester and from Coventry on to Birmingham. Also flights from Knock to Coventry, Birmingham, Manchester, London; and from Galway, Shannon, Kerry, Cork, Donegal, Sligo and Waterford to London (Luton). Fares range from Superapex and Economy to Youth Fare.
Reservations: Dublin 01-774422. (3 Dawson Street, Dublin 2). Cork, Galway, Waterford, Shannon, Knock and Kerry: phone Freephone 1800-567890.

BRITISH MIDLANDS

Flights from Dublin to London (Heathrow) and from Belfast to London (Heathrow). Also Belfast to East Midlands. Fares include Apex, Pex and One-way fares at off-peak times.
Reservations: Phone 01-798733 (Dublin Airport) or call to a travel agent.

BRITISH AIRWAYS

Flights from Dublin to London (Heathrow), and Birmingham; also from Cork and Shannon to London. Fares include Apex (book well in advance), Youth and Excursion.
Reservations: Dublin 01-610666, Cork 021-317777, Shannon 061-61477.

STUDENT AIRFARES

Flights from Dublin, Galway and Cork to London. Check fares with USIT Office, 19-21 Aston Quay, O'Connell Bridge, Dublin 2. *Reservations*: Phone Dublin 01-6798833. Open Mon-Fri 9am-6pm, Sat 11am-4pm.

FERRIES

B&I LINE

Sailings from Dublin Ferryport to Holyhead; also from Rosslare to Pembroke Dock. Daily onward connections by ship/coach and ship/rail to many destinations in Britain. Fares include budget-priced single and return (add on fares from provincial points around Ireland). *Reservations*: B&I Line, 16 Westmoreland Street, Dublin 2. Phone 01-797977. Cork, 42 Grand Parade. Phone 021-273024.

SEALINK

Sailings from Dun Laoghaire to Holyhead, from Rosslare to Fishguard; also from Larne to Stranraer. Sealink operates through-services by ship/coach, also onward rail connections to many destinations in Britain. Fares incude single and return (add on fares from provincial points.)
Reservations: 15 Westmoreland Street, or Clery's, O'Connell Street, Dublin. Phone Dublin 01-807777 (same number for car-ferry terminal at Dun Laoghaire) Cork 021-272965, Limerick 061-316259, Rosslare Harbour 053-33115.

STUDENT SEA-FARES

Check with USIT offices. Even if you are not a student, you can avail of most USIT fares if you have a YIEE card (Youth International Education Exchange). It costs IR£5.00. USIT also has twenty-two offices around Britain.
Reservations and information: USIT, Aston Quay, O'Connell Bridge, Dublin 2. Phone 01-6798833. Cork, 10-11 Market Parade. Phone Cork 021-270900.

TIMING YOUR JOURNEY

One last word about travelling to Britain … It's better not to arrive there at the weekend. The employment agencies, advice centres and business organisations will be closed. Aim to travel on a weekday instead. In most cities, Mondays and Tuesdays are good business days and good days for your arrival.

MIND HOW YOU GO

Take great care with your baggage and your money on the journey; airports, sea-ports and train-stations are absolute havens for the pick-pocket brigade. And the last thing you need is to be relieved of your hard-earned cash and possessions en route. Keep travellers cheques, cash and all your travel documents stashed away.

If you've done all the basic preparations we've talked about then you've already given yourself a good head-start in Britain. Make the most of your move there –The best of Irish Luck to you – and don't forget to write home!

INFORMATION AND ADVICE CENTRES IN IRELAND

Dublin

BLANCHARDSTOWN YOUTH INFORMATION CENTRE
Main Street, Blanchardstown, Dublin 15. Phone 01-212077/012.

COMMUNITY AND YOUTH INFORMATION CENTRE
Sackville House, Sackville Place, Dublin 1. Phone 01-786844.

EMIGRANT ADVICE CENTRE
1A Cathedral Street, Dublin 1. Phone 01-732844.

TALLAGHT YOUTH INFORMATION CENTRE
Co Dublin VEC, Main Road, Tallaght, Dublin 24. Phone 01-516322/538.

YOUTH INFORMATION CENTRE
Bell Tower, Marine Road, Dun Laoghaire, Co Dublin. Phone 01-809363.

Cork

CORK YOUTH ENQUIRY SERVICE
YMCA 11-12 Marlborough Street, Cork. Phone 021-273056.

EMIGRATION INFORMATION OFFICE
34 Paul Street, Cork. Phone 021-273213.

YOUTH INFORMATION SERVICE
Ivy Cottage, Ashe Quay, Fermoy, Co Cork. Phone 025-32455.

Cavan

YOUTH INFORMATION AND RESOURCE CENTRE.
19 Farnham Street, Cavan. Phone 049-61188.

Clare

YOUTH INFORMATION BUREAU
Youth Centre, Carmody Street, Ennis, Co Clare. Phone 065-24137.

Derry

DERRY EMIGRANT BUREAU
22 Bridge Street, Derry BT 48 6JZ. Phone 080504-266266.

Donegal

LETTERKENNY EMIGRANT ADVICE CENTRE
Day Centre, Oliver Plunkett Road, Letterkenny, Co Donegal.

Galway

GALWAY EMIGRATION ADVICE SERVICE
Ozanam House, St Augustine Street, Galway. Phone 091-62434.

Kerry

YOUTH INFORMATION OFFICE
St Brendan's College, Killarney, Co Kerry. Phone 064-31748

YOUTH INFORMATION CENTRE
Ozanam House, Day Place, Tralee, Co Kerry. Phone 064-21674

Kilkenny

OSSARY YOUTH SERVICES
Desart Hall, New Street, Kilkenny. Phone 056-61200

Limerick

YOUTH INFORMATION BUREAU
5 Lower Glentworth Street, Limerick. Phone 061-42444

Louth

CENTRE FOR THE UNEMPLOYED
7 North Quay, Drogheda, Co Louth.

Mayo

CENTRE FOR THE UNEMPLOYED, EMIGRATION INFORMATION SECTION
Main Street, Castlebar, Co Mayo. Phone 094-22814

Offaly

BIRR YOUTH INFORMATION AND RESOURCE CENTRE
(Pastoral Centre, Nazareth House), Wilmer Road, Birr, Co Offaly. Phone
0509-21243

YOUTH INFORMATION AND ADVICE CENTRE,
St Mary's Youth Centre, Harbour Street, Tullamore, Co Offaly. Phone 056-
21869.

Sligo

YOUTH INFORMATION SERVICE
Market Street, Sligo. Phone 071-44150

Tipperary

EMIGRATION ADVISORY SERVICES (YOUTH IN NEED GROUP)
2 Ard Mhuire, Thurles, Co Tipperary. Phone 0504-23857

YOUTH INFORMATION SERVICE
Youth Office O'Brien Street, Tipperary. Phone 062-52604

Waterford

YOUTH INFORMATION AND ADVICE CENTRE
130 The Quay, Waterford. Phone 051-77328

Westmeath

YOUTH RESOURCE CENTRE
North Gate Street, Athlone, Co Westmeath. Phone 0902-78747

Wexford

ENNISCORTHY COMMUNITY INFORMATION OFFICE
The Atheneum, Castle Street, Enniscorthy, Co Wexford. Phone 054-33746.

YOUTH INFORMATION CENTRE
Ferns Diocesan Youth Service, Clifford Street, Co Wexford. Phone 053-23262

The above centres have different opening hours, so check before calling in for information. Many offices have information packs – a selection of reference material on London and other cities around Britain, including directories, guides, newspapers etc. Above all, they can advise you on the practical realities of emigration.

Philip Chevron: From a Radiator to a Pogue – And Other Notes from the Music Industry

Music producer, song-writer and Pogues guitarist Philip Chevron had just turned twenty when he went to London with The Radiators From Space band. By that time, he had already created something of a work-experience record at home in Dublin with jobs in an architect's office, a tomato farm, a record company and in the theatre; film extra work, music PR as well as TV appearances, concerts and gigs with early bands he formed such as The Jangles and Aisling. And then came The Radiators from Space band, the TV

Tube Heart *album and tour dates in London, tilting at fame and chart-hits on the British music scene.*

We arrived in London on a very sunny day in '77 and for most of us – certainly for me – it was our first time in an aeroplane. I'd been to London before, I used to go over with my mate Kieron for a few days – until the money ran out, basically. But this was going to London in style. The fancy car taking us to a luxury flat in Victoria. The only thing about the luxury flat was that all of The Radiators and the road crew had to live in it and it was actually designed for about three people! However, initially we were supposed to be there for three months, to do promotion and touring for the new album. And we thought we were going to be back in Dublin by Christmas. But we'd had a lot of resistance from the promoters in Ireland and effectively we couldn't get gigs, so we thought: well feck them, we'll stay in London, and I just ended up staying there for twelve years, for one reason or another. It was always just getting prolonged: it was never like 'I've emigrated to London' or anything.

I think my family probably knew that they weren't going to see much of me for a long time, in the way that mothers and fathers are kind of intuitive about these things, but in all honesty I thought that I was going over for three months and that we'd be back by Christmas.

The point was, The Radiators had always thought it was possible to be based in Ireland. It was a kind of an idealistic thing we had about staying here and we used to say it in interviews and all that – because there was no reason why not. U2, of course, subsequently proved that it could be done. But the reason that we couldn't do it was because we were being discriminated against after July '77, when a kid was stabbed to death at a gig we did in Belfield. It was nothing to do with us, we weren't even on stage at the time, but in terms of tabloid headlines, we kind of took the rap for it. Promoters got very scared. So that incident and punk linked together made it impossible for us to get gigs. A priest down in Kilcullen, God bless him, gave us a gig there, and apart from our farewell gig, that was the only gig we got after Belfield.

So we went to London but it didn't really happen for us. We went touring with Thin Lizzy, which wasn't our audience and we lost the audience we'd built up, to a large extent. And then we ran into all sorts of business problems. The record company perhaps under-estimated our ambitions at first and at that time we had no manager.

Ghostown, our second album, effectively sank without trace. First of all because it was delayed for a year, because the record company couldn't afford to release it. They couldn't afford to pay the producer,

Tony Visonti, who therefore hung on to the tape. And they were having cash flow problems, clinging on by their fingernails. And when the album eventually came out – about thirteen months after delivering the tapes to the record company – by that time we'd lost an awful lot of ground.

As a band, we'd had a year of inactivity while waiting for the album to come out and when it did, it was to an audience who were hardly holding their breath for it. And the subject matter – about a dreamer growing up in a repressed and anachronistic society in Ireland of the sixties and seventies – got largely misunderstood by huge sections of the British music press. And although in certain quarters *Ghostown* was regarded as 'The most important Irish album ever made', that didn't mean it sold and we never had a major hit single off it, which would have made a big difference. And at that stage, there weren't sufficient young Irish emigrants in Britain to latch on to it.

You know, I would get lump-in-the-throat letters from individuals, saying how much *Ghostown* had affected them, but in a wider sense it didn't capture people's imaginations at all. Interestingly enough, the record got re-issued last year and the music press reviewed it as if they'd always regarded it as a classic record. And it *still* doesn't sell!

So when it looked like we weren't going to immediately make our mark, Chiswick Records said, 'The lease on your flat is up. Please can you go and find yourselves bedsits or something.' And so all the depressing times started from that.

Initially we were getting a retainer from the record company. It wasn't very much but it was enough to keep us going. They were also paying the rent on our flats for a while, but then as Chiswick started to run out of money themselves, we were kind of left to our own devices.

I had a flat in Brixton and then, over a couple of years, in places like Maida Vale, Cricklewood and Camden Town. For about a year we were doing OK, but then as the record company ran into financial trouble they genuinely, and I think much to their sadness, couldn't afford to support us and we weren't really in a position to go out on the road. So everything was dependent on the success, or not, of *Ghostown*. And then we did the obvious thing – we signed on the dole.

So we did that until we got caught, basically. At that stage, the band had completely hit rock bottom. The record company, in a last-ditch attempt to get us on the radio, spent £16,000 on two songs, which is more than the whole *Ghostown* album cost. Unfortunately, the radio stations didn't like either of them. So that was it. We did one final tour of Ireland, and ironically enough, it was a really triumphant tour. We'd never had a reaction like that in all the years we'd been playing and we finally realised that at last we'd become a really good live band. But it was too late, because we'd no credibility with the record companies or publishers and we needed an injection of capital to keep us going for long enough to be able to prove ourselves. But we basically just lost heart.

The last year of The Radiators, we were all undergoing such depression. Our big plan, all this carefully laid groundwork and the fact that we'd really believed passionately in the music we were making: and to see it all come to nothing, to have left just a legacy of something we were all quite proud of ... it was shattering.

You do go through a period of grief after an experience like this, there's no doubt about it. I remember, I just used to lie in bed for most of the day. I couldn't even get up to write a song, just listened to LBC Radio all day. And if I could scrape together the money, I'd go down to the pub for a few pints and that would be my day.

At one stage we literally lived on cornflakes. I can tell you about six different ways to cook cornflakes! Because myself and Jimmy 'Crashe' Wynne, the drummer who was my flatmate, we had no money for some weeks. But in private flatland in London, the landlord supplies breakfast – not out of the goodness of his heart, but because it gives him technical recognition as a 'Bed and Breakfast' ... thus denying the tenant any rights.

So we would get a supply of cornflakes outside the door at the beginning of the week and a bottle of milk every day and a few slices of bread. And we got so bored eating cornflakes that we found ways to fry them, grill them and toast them!

One can laugh at it now, but we had to ration everything. The only thing to do, when the band wasn't working, was to watch television (a wonky one Jimmy found on a skip and repaired). We had to ration out TV programmes because our last fifty pence had just gone into the electricity meter. Ah, it was a real fumbling-down-the-back-of-the-sofa-for-the-ha'pennies job! And we were all getting on each others' nerves. Mark left and then there were three. Jimmy and I moved to Maida Vale and our depression eventually became mutually destructive. We just sort of took it out on each other. We were completely out of communication with Pete Holidai, who lived across the river in Woolwich. And really there wasn't a band anymore. It took that year and the triumphant tour of Ireland to realise it.

For a while, myself and Pete and Jimmy did some quiet gigs as the

Tic Tac Men, but we weren't really cut out for London pub gigs, because we were still doing mainly Radiators songs and they just weren't going down with the pints at all.

At that point, Pete made up his mind that he was leaving. Being a family man, he was under a lot of pressure to get regular work. So he went back to Kildare and that settled that, because there wasn't much point in myself and Jimmy carrying on, although we tried for a while. But the chemistry, the balance was upset. And I couldn't see how we could possibly do it without Pete. So that was the end of the Radiators.

The Murphia, Rock-On Records and Producing

The Murphia in London at that time was centred around Ted Carroll's Rock-On stall in Soho market. And it attracted all the Irish, like Frank Murray, who is now the Pogues' manager; Stan Brennan (who was); Roger Armstrong who had connections with Horslips and The Chieftains before that and ran Chiswick Record Company. And everybody was involved with everybody else's enterprises.

Then Ted opened the Rock-On shop in Camden, and when The Radiators came to an end I phoned up Ted and said 'Give us a job', and as it happened, they needed somebody part-time. And as the weeks rolled into months, I became more or less full-time. But I could still take off whatever time I wanted in order to produce records. That's what I decided to do at that point, although I needed the cushion of the reasonably secure job.

Rock-On was brilliant, because it introduced me to lots of music that I only had a vague sort of notion of before. I mean, I knew all the classic R&B ... and soul and country and jazz, but this was a specialist second-hand record shop and Bob Dunham, who still works there occasionally, taught me practically everything about music that I didn't know, the more obscure, but no less outstanding R&B stuff and soul and country and all that ... all of which has since influenced the music I do myself.

So this went on for four years and in that space of time I also produced seven albums and a jukebox-full of singles. And I made my own records. I produced bands like The Tall Boys, The Prisoners, The Men They Couldn't Hang, as well as people like Agnes Bernelle. I did my own single *The Captains and The Kings*, produced by Elvis Costello and a twelve-inch EP of Brecht and Weill songs. [Full title: 'Philip Chevron sings songs from Bertolt Brecht and Kurt Weill's *Happy End* (1929): *Songs from Bill's Dancehall'* Mosa Records MOEP 4-12]

And I started a record company for a while – which I don't recommend to anybody. Basically you have to run it all yourself.

After *The Captains and the Kings* came out, I asked Frank Murray to manage my production work and I was also doing a lot of work for IMP Records, Elvis Costello's independent label.

Then Frank Murray decided to take on managing The Pogues. And as a consequence of that, I ended up producing The Pogues, which was the first time I actually met all of them, although I'd been going to their gigs right from the beginning.

Poguetry in Motion

The very first Pogues gig I ever saw was at Dingwalls, at the end of '82. I could hardly believe the assault on my one good ear! But you could tell straight away that if they stuck at it they were going to be very good, very quickly. I went to see them at least once a week in The Hope and Anchor, or The 100 Club, places like that. And every time I saw them they just got better and better. It was at The Bull and Gate, Kentish Town Road, where it all clicked for me. They'd got their style together. They looked like characters out of a Flann O'Brien novel and I realised the charm of the band, as well as their burgeoning musical talent.

That was the night I felt really envious that I wasn't in the band.

I'd actually known some of The Pogues for years. Shane was in The Nips [a band called The Nipple Erectors] when The Radiators were starting to play in London. But it never occurred to me that I would fit into a band ever again. Then one night in The Devonshire Arms, Kentish Town, Frank Murray was telling me that Jem (Finer) the banjo player wanted to take paternity leave. And they needed somebody to replace him. And I found myself saying: 'I'll play banjo if you like.'

This was for a German tour and I'd never played banjo in my life! But I heard myself saying this and I'm not sure to this day whether Frank subtly brought me into the band or whether he just guilelessly said that they needed a banjo player. Not that it matters anyway ... I played my heavy-metal banjo on this German tour. Talk about Clawhammer!

And then I did this Scandinavian tour as well with them and by this stage I couldn't bear to part from them ... and they were rather fond of me as well. So it coincided nicely with Shane's decision to stop playing guitar and concentrate on singing. So I became The Pogues' guitarist.

I remember going up to Ted Carroll in the shop and saying 'Look, I still want to work in Rock On – but here's my schedule for The Pogues for the next three months and here's when I can work in Rock On.' (I had it written out really neatly for him) – and Ted just looked at me, looked at the three pages, tore them up and said: 'You're fired!' And I said, 'Thanks Ted' – because that was actually what I wanted him to say, but I couldn't make the decision, you know. And that was the end of my career as a shop assistant in London!

I joined The Pogues in '85, just before the band's second album *Rum, Sodomy and The Lash* came out. This was at the tail-end of Dandy Rock music really and The Pogues' music had a spirit behind it that nobody else possessed.

The Pogues just came at the right time, because in the middle of all this sort of 'new romantic' glamour and excessive synthesiser music, here was something that was actually live again. And it might have been very rough, but its heart was in the right place.

To a degree The Pogues' music has a base in Irish emigrant experience. Somebody like Shane McGowan grew up with The Dubliners, The Clancy Brothers, that kind of stuff, but at one remove, because he was hearing them in London, where his parents moved from Tipperary when he was six. You always get a slightly different perspective on it from one remove.

For the London-Irish, there was a gap of cultures, between their native culture and the indigenous one. And while you're struggling to fit into a society that is not your native one, then you're going to close ranks to a certain extent. And I think that's what happened to the forties and fifties wave of emigrants.

Lots of things that mightn't have been given the time of day at home suddenly become very important. The dance halls, the Saturday night lounges, the Irish clubs, the London/Irish festivals, the Irish dancing, the local GAA teams. All these things are badges that identify the Irish as a culture that has integrated into London society, but has retained a separate identity. That's the sort of milieu that Shane would have grown up in.

But that's only a part of The Pogues' music: it's also about all the other cultures in London. You could walk into a bar or little Greek restaurant in Camden, for instance and on the jukebox, you'd have a reggae record, followed by Big Tom, an old R&B record, followed by *Rembetiko* (native Greek blues music), or Dermot O'Brien on the accordion. And it's the same in Brixton: there's a mutual tolerance and respect everybody else's culture.

And The Pogues are like the jukebox-gone-human. You know, a cross-fertilisation of cultures in London and anybody who had any sense of their surroundings would be drawn to that. The way that various members of the band, who come from places like Manchester, Devon, Eastbourne, and myself from Dublin – were drawn. And we were all sort of lost when we got to London first.

And with The Pogues now, people get drawn to this culture of a dispossessed people in London, which is also inextricably bound up with Irish culture.

It's reflected in the kind of audiences The Pogues get. A mix of young, middle-aged and slightly older, even; from (in the mid-eighties) Rockabillies to anybody who was fed up with the charts' stuff. And we don't have to explain to the audience what we're doing. There's an understanding of what we're about and there's a kind of community about it. We're now on a world stage of course, but it's the same kind of audience – only bigger!

Back to Base

Now I'm based back in Dublin again. For a couple of reasons: first of all, after The Radiators' experience here, I had made up my mind that I was never going to set foot in the country again. But I softened over the years as I kept coming back at Christmas to see my parents. And after that, I was coming back more often to produce a band, or do radio or TV appearances. And the more I came back, the more I liked the place. But also, palpably it was changing. And as the population got younger, it was becoming clear that Dublin was a nice place to live in, for all its faults.

Secondly, I found that it was getting to the point where, every time we touched down at Heathrow at the end of a tour, I would get this sinking feeling ... 'Oh, no – back in London.' And I discovered that I liked the idea of touching down in Dublin instead. Because when you're on the road as much as we are, the pace of life here really appeals to me after the madness and incessant flying and travelling and hotels that constitute touring. So I'd find I could relax in Dublin in a way I couldn't do in London. I just felt I wanted to go somewhere I could determine my own pace of life. And I can do that here, which I really like.

Another reason for leaving London was the fact that it had gotten to the point where I was sick of paying extortionate rent there and the property boom had happened at the time I started thinking about leaving.

If you can't get council housing – and unless you have a family, or you are a single parent, you won't even get onto the council waiting list – then you're stuck with private landlords, who are greedy bastards, there's no two ways about it. You pay up to stg£80 a week for the most basic living facilities and you've got no security of tenure whatsoever. I thought of buying something, I got so sick of landlords, but it became impossible to buy anything in London with the property boom. That's why there are so many homeless people in London now. I mean, when I was living in places like Camden and Brixton ten years ago, they were easier days. You could basically use the black economy to your advantage – go on the dole and then also do odd jobs. And you'd find a squat to live in maybe or a reasonably cheap place to stay.

But that was then, and now when I go there, people are sleeping on the streets, round the West End and down the Embankment. It's dreadful and the alarming fact is that an identifiable number are Irish and just sixteen or seventeen years old.

What are they gonna do when they can't find anywhere to live and they can't sign on the dole? They're going to choose one of the few options left to survive – sell their ass. That's what's happening. They go there thinking: 'It's going to be different for me. I've got five honours in the Leaving. I'm qualified!' But it just isn't like that in London. It takes an incredibly short space of time to get broken down. The fact that you got five honours in the Leaving Cert, or that you're a graduate, doesn't qualify you to live in London, unless you've thought it out very, very carefully.

I'm now in a position where I've had a certain amount of success as a musician and songwriter. But if The Pogues finished tomorrow you know, I wouldn't go back there to live.

Forward Notes

For the foreseeable future, I'll be contributing my ha'pworth to The Pogues. And now that I'm back in Dublin, I'll be doing more gigs, guesting at various shows for people, they're the sort of things that I like. I really enjoy doing things separate to the band, and, as time allows, I'll do more of that.

In terms of the more distant-flung future … Well, I still desperately want to write musicals for Broadway and I'd like to get going on that.

CHAPTER 2

London Town

*London – it's a struggle of a town. But you can make
a go of it. A lot falls to yourself.*
Broadcaster Seán Bán Breathnach

Knowing the Underground system is essential to survival in London.

Raidió na Gaeltachta broadcaster Seán Bán Breathnach left his native
Galway for London at the age of sixteen. 'My brother Pádraic, who
was eight years older than me and a qualified mechanic, was going
to take up work there and, of course, nothing else would do me but
to go with him.'

Seán and Pádraic stayed with their uncle in North London and Seán
was working on a building site within the week. 'The first job was on
a site. I was up at six-thirty in the morning to meet the van at Enfield.
Twenty of us were packed into it for the thirty-mile drive to the site.

I was tea-boy and odd-job fellow there and I suppose I wasn't much use to start out with, for the foreman said to me, "Why didn't you stay at school?"'

Seán admits that he was unprepared for life in London: 'I had never been further than Galway before.' And if it hadn't been for his uncle looking after him, he couldn't have coped with the tough working day and the strange city environment. Seán was working on the sites for two-and-a-half years and after that he got work with a plasterer and floor-layer. But right from the beginning he had been doing some part-time work as a disc-jockey in the local youth club, and this turned out to be Seán's first step towards a career in broadcasting.

Seán heard that a cousin of Alan Freeman, the well-known London DJ, was on the look out for young disc-jockey talent for his agency. Someone told him about Seán Bán, and one night he went along to the club to watch Seán Bán spinning the discs. He liked SBB's style and this resulted in a steady round of club-work in London, followed by a broadcasting course in Hertfordshire. 'I came home after three years,' says SBB, 'and hard as it was, I know that London made me.'

Surviving big city life, he says, means sticking to a few basic guidelines: 'Keep asking for information. Talk to people who have been there before you. They will help, if you ask them. Remember that you are vulnerable when you're new to a place, so stick to your pals there … and to start off with, anyway, don't wait for the "right job" to come along. Do anything at all at the beginning just to keep the pounds coming in.'

London Town

Some two hundred years ago, Dr Samuel Johnson unwittingly gave London tourism its most enduring copy-line by declaring: 'When a man is tired of London, he is tired of life; for there is in London all that life can afford.'

And certainly if you are visiting London with a fair bit of money on you for entertainment and sight-seeing – or you've been living and working there for some time – Johnson's claim still holds true. As capital cities go, London is hard to beat, from the music clubs and cinemas to West End theatre and dance, the art exhibitions, the concerts, places of historic and architectural interest, the parks and the river walks, the museums, the street markets, the silver vaults, the auctions, Covent Garden, the carnivals, the festivals, the restaurants, window-shopping in the West End … the variety of entertainment is endless.

But if you are going to London to work for the first time, or to look for work, it's a very different experience. Anyone who tells you that getting used to London life is an easy process is either side-stepping the truth, or they've forgotten just what it felt like to be a raw recruit in Britain's capital city.

The fact is, from the moment you arrive in a big station like Kings Cross or Euston and get swept into the tide of commuters, you have started a new way of life, and there is a lot to get used to: the noise level, the packed underground and the busy streets, the unfamiliar customs, different accents, the mix of languages, and the fact that *your* accent isn't always understood there. The sheer scale and size of the city itself takes time to get used to.

So don't worry if you feel a bit disoriented during your first couple of months in London. It's a human characteristic to feel uneasy in new territory, a strange city with no familiar landmarks, where the people aren't given to passing the time of day with you, let alone 'having the crack'.

London is as different from Dublin or Cork as Munich or New York – and a good way of dealing with that feeling of strangeness is to simply accept that it will take time to get your bearings. It helps if you get in contact with any friends or relatives you may have in London and meet up with them as soon as possible. And then get going on the practical matters in hand, like finding yourself somewhere long-term to stay and looking for regular work.

First things first: You should book into the temporary accommodation you've organised. You will be asked to pay for this in advance and once you've done this, it's wise to place the rest of your money in a nearby bank or post office account, holding onto a basic sum for daily living expenses. Never keep a lot of money on you, or in your accommodation. Banking hours in Britain are 9.30am-3.30pm on weekdays, and some have a late evening and a Saturday morning facility as well. (For local branches of Allied Irish or Bank of Ireland in London, check phone book.)

ACCOMMODATION PROBLEMS: WHAT TO DO

IRISH CENTRES

Sorry to seem pessimistic about this, but if your accommodation plans have somehow fallen through and you have nowhere to stay, then the first port of call should be the nearest Irish Advice Centre. The staff at these centres will do their best to find you somewhere to lay your head and this will mean either hostel accommodation or lodgings with a local landlord or landlady. These centres can also give you advice on employment, social security problems, entitlements etc.

Centre	Phone	Times
HARINGEY IRISH COMMUNITY CARE CENTRE 72 Stroud Green Road N4	071-272-7594 or 071-272-9230	Open Mon-Thurs 10am-5pm and Fri 10am-4pm (Closed from 1pm-2pm)
IRISH ADVICE CENTRE 55 Fulham Palace Road Hammersmith W6	081-741-0466	Open Mon-Fri 9.30am-12.45pm and 2.15pm-5pm (Wed opening 11am)
THE LONDON IRISH CENTRE 52 Camden Square NW1	071-485-0051	Open Mon, Tues, Thurs, Fri from 9.30am-4.30pm (closed for lunch, 1am-2pm), Wed 2pm-4.30pm, Sat 9.30am-12.30pm (emergencies only Sat
SOUTH LONDON IRISH WELFARE ASSOCIATION 138-140 Hartfield Road Wimbledon SW19	081-543-0608 (Centre) 081-540-0759 (Welfare)	Open Mon-Fri 10am-5pm

These centres are all part of the Irish chaplaincy scheme in Britain, which provides specialised services for Irish people, ranging from outreach work to running hostels. For list of hostel accommodation, see p.55.

OTHER ADVICE AGENCIES

BRENT IRISH ADVISORY SERVICE
Electric House, 296 Willesden Lane NW2. Phone 081-459-6286
Open Mon 2pm-5pm and Wed 3pm-7pm or call for appointment
Provides information/advice on housing, jobs, welfare, education, legal matters etc. Publishes *Irish in Britain* directory

HOUSING ADVICE SWITCHBOARD. Phone 071-434-2522
Has a 24 hour all-year-round phone line service for single homeless
General housing advice 10am-6pm
Emergency service, 24 hours.

THE LONDON IRISH WOMEN'S CENTRE
59 Stoke Newington Church Street N16. Phone 071-249-7318
Information/advice on housing/welfare/legal problems etc
Drop-in times: Tues, Wed, Thurs, 11am-1pm and 2pm-5pm
Women's counselling: Thurs 2pm-4pm
Welfare Advice sessions: Tues 10.30am-12.30pm
Call for appointment if possible.

NEW HORIZON YOUTH CENTRE
1 Macklin Street WC2. Phone 071-242-0010 or 071-242-2238
Open Mon-Fri 10.30am-1pm
Helps young unemployed (16-21) with accommodation problems
and runs workshops and a wide range of activities at the centre.

PICCADILLY ADVICE CENTRE
100 Shaftesbury Avenue W1V 7DH. Phone 071-434-3773
Open Mon-Thurs 10am-9pm, Fri, Sat, Sun 2pm-9pm
Provides a wide range of practical advice and information to young homeless
or new to London.

THE ROGER CASEMENT IRISH CENTRE (ISLINGTON)
131 St John's Way, N19 (Archway tube). Phone 071-281-3225;
Advice Service 071-281-4973.
Information/advice on housing problems/social welfare etc
Also, wide range of social activities, training courses and classes.
Call advice line for appointment.

SOHO PROJECT
142 Charing Cross Road WC2. Phone 071-836-8121
Open Mon-Fri 11.30am-1pm
Advice and drop-in centre, housing referrals, short-term counselling.

ADVICE AND HELP FOR TRAVELLERS IN LONDON

If you are a traveller and you or your family need help and advice
with social security, housing or other problems, then the Irish Centres
listed on p.220 should be able to help. Some centres have travellers'
support groups as well.

Brent Irish Advisory Services also has a travellers' support group,
and can help with housing, welfare, legal problems etc. Electric
House, 296 Willesden Lane NW2. Open 2pm-5pm Mon, 3pm-
7pm Wed, or call 081-459-6286 for appointment.

Councils: Camden, Haringey and Southwark Councils have workers dealing specifically with travellers issues. Call main council
switchlines for more information.

The Haringey Irish Community Care Centre has a travellers'
support group. The centre is open from 10am-5pm Mon-Thurs and
from 10am-4pm Fridays, and you can get advice on education,
housing, social security and other problems. Staff there can send
to Dublin for your birth certificate if you've forgotten to bring it
with you. They can put you in touch with other travelling families
in the borough. You'll find them at 72 Stroud Green Road, N4.
Phone 071-272-9230 or 071-272-7594.

London Gypsy & Traveller Unit run by Save the Children Society.
You'll find them at Jadwin House, 205-211 Kentish Town Road,
London NW5. Phone 071-267-6723.

The Roger Casement Irish Centre, Islington (advice and information), 131 St Johns Way, London N19 3RQ. Phone 071-281-
3225/281-4973

Traveller Education Team, c/o Ilderton School, Varcoe Rd, London SE16 3LA. Phone 071-237-1174.

TRANSPORT: GETTING AROUND LONDON

THE UNDERGROUND

The tube is the cheapest and fastest way of getting around London. Collect a free underground map at the nearest station and invest in a one-week or monthly travel card, which covers all your bus, underground and train journeys at a cheap rate. Transport fares are worked out in zones. The cost depends on how many zones are crossed in a journey, rather than the actual length of the journey.

BUS

London's extensive bus network is a good way to travel when you are getting to know the city. Buses halt automatically at stops with white signs and the red London transport symbol, but halt at stops with red signs only if you actually raise your arm and hail them.

Running Times:
Buses and tubes start about 6am and run until midnight. Check timetables at bus stops or at travel information centres. Night buses run through Central London from 11pm to 6am. They have the letter 'N' before the bus number and their stops have blue and yellow route numbers. Timetables and route maps are available from travel information centres, at many underground stations and also at airports. Ask for the 'buses for nightowls' leaflet.

Green-Line buses serve the London suburbs. Check with the *Green-Line Travel Information Centre*, Eccleston Bridge SW1, Victoria Underground/British Rail. Phone 081-668-7261.

Intercity Buses: The main inter-city bus operator National Express Coaches run from Victoria Coach Station, Buckingham Place Road SW1. Phone 071-730-0202. Open 8am-10pm daily.

BRITISH RAIL

Network South-East covers London and suburbs. Travel enquiries 071-928-5100. Maps and timetables from the British Rail Travel Centre, 12 Regent Street SW1.

TAXIS AND MINICABS

The official black cabs are considered the best form of taxi transport. Usual tip is 10 per cent to 15 per cent. A driver can refuse a fare that takes him or her more than six miles outside city centre. A taxi with the 'for hire' sign on is under no obligation to stop for you. If you phone for a cab, expect an additional 'pick up' charge.

Minicabs don't always have meters and it's wiser to stick to black cabs until you get to know the reputable minicab services.

CAR HIRE

You need at least one year's driving experience, plus a full driving licence (current) to hire a car. Ask for weekly/holiday rates as well as daily rates.

ACCOMMODATION: RENTING A FLAT, A BEDSIT, A HOUSE

If you've been staying with friends, or in a short-term hostel for your first few weeks in London, and you need somewhere you can call your own, then you should start searching for a more permanent place as soon as you can. Otherwise you'll find that the money you've set aside for rent and a deposit will disappear on daily living expenses.

You'll need a fair amount of determination and all your wits about you to find somewhere to live at a reasonable rent. There is a critical shortage of private rented accommodation in London. The standard and condition of what's available isn't particularly good and on top of this, the January 1989 Housing Act has brought about many changes for private tenants. These include an end to protected tenancies for those whose tenancies started since January 1989, the introduction of a market rent replacing the fair rent system, and less security of tenure.

In other words, eviction of tenants is easier than before and with rent control for new tenancies now ended, the result will be a rise in rents. Increasing inflation and interest rates won't help the situation. There are now new categories of tenancy: assured, assured shorthold, landlord/landlady resident type tenancies, and unprotected tenancies. To protect your rights as a tenant, talk to *Housing Advice Switchboard* (071-434-2525) or call *SHAC* (The London Housing Aid Centre) for advice, phone 071-373-7276. If you are a victim of harassment from your landlord, remember that your local council can also help.

COST

To give you some idea of the kind of rent you can expect to pay, here are some samples from *The Evening Standard* columns. These are January 1990 prices, so take them as an absolute base-line guide.

Single bedsit, Camden town – stg£70 per week
One-bedroomed flat, Victoria – stg£125 per week
Two-bedroomed flat, Brixton – stg£225 per week

Studio flat, Fulham area – stg£120 per week
House sharing, Brixton – stg£75 per week
House to rent, three-bedroomed semi – NW2 stg£180 per week.

Landlords usually look for one month's rent in advance, plus one month's rent as deposit. And since January '89 landlords are within their rights to charge a premium as well – an extra payment which will not be returned.

If you are 'signing on', you are not entitled to assistance from the DSS to pay returnable deposits on accommodation. If you are unemployed or on low wages and you do find somewhere to live, you can claim housing benefit to help with the rent. Housing benefit is now administered by the local authorities, so call to your local council to apply, or ask at your local DSS office about this.

WHERE TO LOOK

*Check *The Evening Standard* for accommodation vacancies.

*Get the weekly local borough papers: *The Fulham Times, The Kensington News, The Harrow Observer* etc. *The Irish Post, The London-Irish News* and *Time Out* magazines also carry accommodation ads.

**Housing Advice Switchboard* (071-434-2525) have up-to-date news of private lettings for single people each week.

*The Irish Centres usually have a good network of local landlords/landladies.

**Capital Radio Flatshare* produces a free list of flatshares. This can be collected at *Capital Radio,* Euston Tower, Euston Road NW1 (opposite Warren Street tube station) on Tuesdays from 11am. But be there early – it's a very popular service. Phone 071-388-1288.

*Accommodation Agencies usually charge a fee of one, or two weeks' rent, plus VAT. These agencies are bound by the Accommodation Agencies Act 1954, which makes it an offence for them to charge a fee for registration or for giving you addresses. If you are asked to pay a fee or deposit *before* taking a flat or room, you are advised not to pay. The fee is payable only when you have accepted the accommodation. Some estate agencies do not charge fees, but some will charge a set administration fee.

ACCOMMODATION AGENCIES IN CENTRAL LONDON

Agency	Fees Charged	Phone
DEREK COLLINS Panton House, Panton Street W1	No fee charged	071-930-7986
FLATLAND 69 Buckingham Palace Road SW1	1 week+	071-828-9302 071-828-9303 071-828-9304
JENNY JONES 40 South Molton Street W1	No fee charged	071-493-4801
LONDON ACCOMMODATION BUREAU 102 Queensway W2	1 week+	071-727-5062

NORTH LONDON ACCOMMODATION AGENCIES

Agency	Fees Charged	Phone
BUSY BEE LTD 22 Baron Street N1	2 weeks+	071-278-8184 071-278-8185 071-278-8186
CALEDONIAN ACCOMMODATION 61 Caledonian Road N1	2 weeks+	071-278-9178 071-278-9179
NORTH LONDON SERVICE 108 Fortis Green Rd N10	1 week+	081-883-9878

SOUTH LONDON ACCOMMODATION AGENCIES

Agency	Fees Charged	Phone
FLATMATES UNLIMITED 313 Brompton Road SW3	1½ weeks+	071-589-5491
SOUTHSIDE ACCOMMODATION	1 week+	071-622-8383 071-622-6792

WEST LONDON ACCOMMODATION AGENCIES

Agency	Fees Charged	Phone
PEACH BUREAU 142 Shepherd's Bush Road W6	2 weeks+	071-602-4596
WEST LONDON AGENCY 7 Station Bldgs, Ealing W5	2 weeks+	081-992-7052 081-992-7773

EAST LONDON ACCOMMODATION AGENCIES

Agency	Fees Charged	Phone
AUSTIN RICHARD 206 High Road, Woodford Green, Essex	2 weeks+	081-505-2040 081-505-4434
PERAL & CLOUTTS LTD 116 Clarence Road E5	No fees charged	081-985-5359

PLANNING YOUR FLAT/HOUSE-HUNTING

Looking for a flat or house in London is a highly competitive business. It's a concrete jungle out there! So stack the odds in your favour by bringing references (from your bank, employer etc.) with you. Dress business-style and polish up your 'perfect-tenant' manner. It all counts! Arrange appointments to see places in geographic order, so that you aren't travelling from one end of London to the other in the course of an afternoon. Keep an eye out for local launderettes, late-night shops and a tube station or bus service nearby.

WHAT TO LOOK FOR WHEN RENTING ACCOMMODATION

These are the kind of things your mother would remind you about if you were flat-hunting in Dublin, Galway or Cork. And if we'd only remembered this checklist ourselves when first renting flats, we'd have avoided some overpriced shoe-box sized places, with built-in mice and mould! So when you're looking at a flat or bedsit, don't forget the following points:

* Check the walls and ceilings for signs of damp patches.

* Check for faulty wiring/electrical fitments.

* Look in the press under the kitchen sink for signs of damp patches.

* Check bed-base and mattress condition (once you've paid your

50

rent, you are going to have to lie on it!)

* Check windows and doors for security ... and gale-force draughts!

* Make sure the shower or bath works and that the cooker is safe and working.

* Check the skirting boards and behind furniture for signs of mouse-holes etc.

* Rap on the connecting walls to ensure they are solid. If they are just thin partitions, you'll be able to hear your neighbour breathing down the back of your neck and sooner or later this will cause unneighbourly rows!

* Finally, ask yourself if you honestly feel you'll have enough room. Even if it *is* a bedsit you're renting, you'll still need a minimum amount of space to exist in. If you feel unsure about this, or if the place doesn't pass most points on the checklist, then don't take it. You will find somewhere more suitable if you keep looking. Remember, it has to serve as home and refuge for you, so don't hand over any money unless you are happy with the place.

RENTING ACCOMMODATION

Before handing over rent and deposit for a flat, bedsit, or house, make a list of everything in it, including any existing damage such as scorch marks on surfaces, broken furniture etc. Then get the landlord/land-lady to sign it. This is to protect your deposit. Otherwise the landlord could refuse to return your deposit when you move out by claiming that you had damaged some of the property.

Get a receipt for the advance rent and deposit you've paid. And keep a rent book, recording all payments signed by the landlord. You may be asked to sign an agreement or contract with the landlord. This will affect your right to remain in the place, so, as we mentioned at the beginning of this section, talk to *Housing Advice Switchboard*, an Irish advice centre, or your local *Citizens' Advice Bureau* (phone number and address of main office listed p.63 – they'll tell you where the nearest CAB to you is). Bring a copy of the contract if you can.

POLL TAX

In 1990, the government introduced a poll tax, or community charge. Poll tax replaces household rates and everyone over the age of eighteen has to pay it, whether their income is stg£90 or stg£900 a week, unless they are entitled to exemption or a rebate. There are three kinds of poll tax/community charge:

**Personal community charge*: Everyone over eighteen must pay the personal community charge, unless you're entitled to an exemption. If you are homeless and sleeping rough, or a long-term patient in hospital, for example, you don't have to pay. Some people may be entitled to a rebate of up to 80 per cent. Anyone on a low income can apply for a community charge rebate. Some people may have to pay just 20 per cent of the full community charge, for example, those on income support, students in full-time education, and residents of hostels.

**Standard community charge*: Owners and tenants of second homes or empty properties have to pay standard community charge, which can be up to twice the personal charge.

**Collective community charge*: Owners of communal accommodation such as hostels pay a collective community charge. They then collect this charge from their tenants.

How much poll tax will you have to pay?

The charge varies from area to area, but the average rate for England and Wales is stg£363 per person

What happens if you evade paying poll tax?

Penalties for not complying with poll tax regulations, or failure to pay can be tough. An initial fine of stg£50 can be imposed on anyone who fails to supply relevant information, or gives false information deliberately. Failure to pay can result in more severe financial penalties.

To find out more about poll tax and how much you must pay, contact *Housing Advice Switchboard* (071-434-2522), or go to your local *Citizens' Advice Bureau*.

A useful guide to the community charge is available from *The Institute of Housing*, 14–16 Torwood Close, Mercia Business Village, Coventry CV4 8HX.

COUNCIL HOUSING

Getting a council flat can take ages. Under the Housing (Homeless Persons) Act, local authorities are supposed to provide accommodation for people with children, for pregnant women and their partners, for those who are over retirement age, for people with disabilities, for people made homeless by an emergency (such as a fire) and for those who think they're vulnerable for other reasons. But the local council can refuse to help you if they think you have made yourself 'intentionally homeless'. For example, if they think you have left adequate housing in Ireland of your own free will, then they are not obliged to house you in Britain.

The council will also want to establish whether you have a 'local connection' and if you are in 'priority need' when considering your application for housing. You have a local connection if you, or someone in your family, has lived in the area for some time (usually for at least six months in the last year, or for three of the last five years); or you have a job in the area; or you have family who have been living in the area for five years; or you need to be living in the area for some special reason (to be near a particular hospital etc); or if you are fleeing domestic violence. Single people, or a couple without children, wouldn't be considered to be in priority need, but some London councils do have special schemes for single people. Contact CHAR (Housing Campaign for Single People) for more details. *CHAR,* 5-15 Cromer Street, London WC1. Phone 071-833-2071.

Even if the council decides you are not in priority need, you should still get housing advice from them and you should be allowed to sign on the council waiting list and be considered for housing. This is important because some housing associations make signing-on the council waitinglist a condition before they will consider your application to the association for a home.

If you are homeless and you feel you are in one of the priority groups listed above, then you should go to the nearest homeless persons section of the council (address in phone book). Bring along any helpful documents to the interview with you. If you are pregnant bring a GP's cert or letter confirming pregnancy. If you have children, bring the children and their birth certs. If you face eviction bring the eviction notice from the landlord. If you are a victim of violence, bring legal letters/injunctions/GP records or hospital records with you.

Once a local authority has accepted responsibility for rehousing you temporary accommodation should be provided while you're waiting for a permanent place. This can mean, however, a lengthy stay in bed-and-breakfast hotels. The B&B hotels are depressing. They lack family facilities and it's too easy to get forgotten about unless you keep the local authority aware of your need for permanent housing. So contact local advice agencies or support groups like Irish Women's Housing Action, c/o London Irish Women's Centre, 59 Stoke Newington Church Street N16. Phone 071-249-5771, or SHAC (The London Housing Aid Centre), 189a Old Brompton Road W5. Phone 071-373-7276.

HOUSING ASSOCIATIONS

These are non-profit-making organisations which let property at reasonable rates. Until January '89, housing association tenants were 'secure' tenants, but lettings are now assured or shorthold-type tenancies, and as subsidies are lower, it is expected that housing association rents will rise. The housing shortage in London means that it is extremely difficult to get housing association accommodation. But you can get advice from the following:

CARA IRISH HOMELESS PROJECT
424 Seven Sisters Road, Manor House N4. Phone 081-800-2744.

HOUSING CORPORATION
149 Tottenham Court Road W1. Phone 071-387-9466.

INISHFREE HOUSING ASSOCIATION
296 Willesden Lane NW2. Phone 081-451-5199.

NATIONAL FEDERATION OF HOUSING ASSOCIATIONS
175 Grays Inn Road WC1. Phone 071-278-2951.

HOUSING CO-OPERATIVES

Housing co-ops manage property or become owners of property and rent it to members. There are perhaps 8,000 accommodation units around London at the moment and the waiting list for these is huge. But you can write to *The National Federation of Housing Co-ops* (at 88 Old Street EC1) for a copy of their directory (cost stg£3). Then write to your local co-ops, asking to become a member.

Empty Property Unit advises people on setting up co-ops themselves. Their address is also 88 Old Street EC1. Phone 071-253-0202.

SHORT-LIFE HOUSING

Short-life housing is property awaiting development or demolition. It can be available for six months or up to a couple of years. You don't have security of tenure in short-life housing, and you may have to share. The conditions are usually pretty poor. It's really a stop-gap, not a solution to a housing problem. And it's getting tougher all the time to find short-life housing in London. You can get more information from *An Teach Housing Association*, phone 081-365-1751, or from *Inishfree Housing Association,* phone 081-451-5199.

HOUSE-BUYING

If you are considering house-buying in London, you should look very carefully before leaping into the market. House prices are very high and the British Building Societies Association recently reported that the number of people falling behind with their monthly mortgage repayments was increasing fast and that homebuyers, unable to keep pace with their repayments, were running up massive debts. So be wary of taking on a hefty mortgage you may not be able to cope with. You can get further information from the *SHAC Group*, who produce the leaflet 'Buying Your Own Home' (phone SHAC 071-373-7276).

HOSTELS IN LONDON

There are many different types of hostels in London. Some are for specific nationalities. Some take only women, or only men. A number of hostels offer short-term stays and others will let you stay for up to a year or longer. Some hostels will take you only if you are working. Demand for hostel space is very heavy and you have to write (or phone) well in advance. However, not *all* hostels require this (see below for details). The weekly rate for hostels varies from stg£40 to stg£90.

LONG-TERM HOSTELS

These take working people and those looking for work, and some take students.

Hostel	Age Group/Sex	Facilities
AUSTIN HOUSE 72 Hammersmith Grove Hammersmith W6 Phone 081-741-0466	Mixed:16-30 Irish Chaplaincy Hostel	Breakfast Evening meal Laundry

How to Apply: must be referred by Hammersmith Irish Support and Advice Centre. (This centre also has new mixed hostel. Phone 081-741-0466.)

ADA LEWIS TRUST 2 Palliser Road W14 Phone 071-385-8248	Female:18-55	Self-catering

How to Apply: contact the Ada Lewis Trust, Empire Way, Wembley for an application form. Phone 071-251-6091.

BEACON HOUSE 7-9 Dock Street E1 Phone 071-481-1326	Mixed: 18-65	Laundry Meals

How to Apply: call for details of vacancies.

BEACON HOUSE 30-31 Leinster Square W2 Phone 071-229-2220	17-63	Meals Laundry

How to Apply: call/write for details of vacancies.

BEACON HOUSE Castle Lane SW1 (off Victoria Street) Phone 071-828-9137	17-63	Meals provided Some self-catering Laundry

How to Apply: write in advance for details of vacancies.

CONWAY HOUSE 20/22 Quex Road Kilburn NW6 Phone 071-624-2918	Male:16-25 Irish hostel	Breakfast Evening meal Laundry

How to Apply: cannot be booked in advance; apply on arrival.

LONDON HOSTELS' **ASSOCIATION** 54 Eccleston Square SW1 Phone 071-828-3263	Working only Mixed: 16-50	Some meals provided

How to Apply: phone/write for application form. Two weeks' rent and deposit.

ST BRENDAN'S LODGE 4 Craven Park NW10 Phone 081-965-9089	Male: 18-26 Irish hostel	B & B

How to Apply: phone or write to check vacancies.

ST LOUISE'S 33 Medway Street SW1 Phone 071-222-6588	Female: 18-24 Irish hostel	Self-catering

How to Apply: phone or write in advance.

LONDON CITY YMCA Errol Street EC1 Phone 071-628-8832	For working people only Mixed: 18-30	Some meals Laundry

How to Apply: write/call several months in advance.

YMCA BARBICAN Fann Street EC2 Phone 071-628-0697	Married couples and single: working only	Some meals Laundry

How to Apply: write for details. References required.

YMCA (SOUTH LONDON) 40 Stockwell Road SW9 9ES Phone 071-274-7861	20-32	Meals Laundry Library

How to Apply: write for details of vacancies. One week's rent and deposit
Membership fee.

YMCA HORNSEY   Male mostly: 18-35   Meals
184 Tottenham Lane N8   Laundry
Phone 081-340-2345   Gym

How to Apply: write for application form. One week's rent plus deposit.

The long-term hostels mentioned above are just some of the range available in London. For a full list, ask your local Irish Centre or an advice agency like *Piccadilly Advice Centre*, 100 Shaftesbury Avenue, London W1V 7DH. Phone 071-434-3773.

EMERGENCY ACCOMMODATION

If you have no money and you need somewhere to stay tonight, the following hostels and night shelters offer free short-term, emergency accommodation.

Hostel	Age Group/Sex	Facilities	Length of Stay
BENBURB BASE 369-71 Camden Road N7 Phone 071-607-7968	Male: 16-25	Meals provided Showers	a few weeks
CENTREPOINT 25 Berwick Street, Soho Phone 071-287-9134	Mixed: up to 20 years	Meals provided Showers	a few days
CAMDEN SHELTER 9 St Pancras Way NW1 Phone 071-387-2926	Mixed: over 25s	Meals Showers	max 3 nights (Open from 10pm)
PROVIDENCE ROW NIGHT SHELTER 50 Crispin Street E1 Phone 071-247-2159	Mixed: 17-60	Breakfast	(Open from 6pm)
RIVERPOINT 229 King Street Hammersmith W6 Phone 081-741-2888	Mixed: 16 years and over	Some meals Showers	max 7 nights

DSS RESETTLEMENT UNITS

These are temporary board-and-lodgings units provided by the Department of Social Security for homeless people. They are institutional-type lodgings. You have to shower when you arrive. Accommodation is the dormitory sort, and you're expected to see a resettlement officer in the morning. The conditions are extremely basic and, to be honest, DSS units should be your last option. If you do decide to avail of them, however, keep in mind that, due to the shortage of accommodation in London even these resettlement units are likely to be full. So get there early.

DSS UNITS FOR MEN (open at 4pm)

BRIDGE HOUSE
50 Kingsdown Close W11. Phone 081-960-3268.

DEAN STREET
West End House, Dean St W1. Phone 071-437-2577.

DSS UNIT FOR WOMEN
(open from 4.30pm)
Camden Women's Reception Centre
2-5 Birkinhead Street WC1. Phone 071-278-6466.

LANCELOT ANDREWS HOUSE
Southwark Reception Centre, 96 Great Guildford Street SE1.
Phone 071-633-9655.

POUND LODGE
Pound Lane, Willesden NW10. Phone 081-451-0946/7.

SPUR HOUSE
12a Ennersdale Road SE13. Phone 081-318-5521.

DAY CENTRES

If you are staying in emergency accommodation, you'll probably find that the daytime hours stretch even longer than the nights and it can be lonely as well as expensive if you are on your own in London. But there are some day centres you can visit that offer a wide range of facilities and activities. Here are some of these centres:

Centre	Age Group	Times	Facilities/ Services
CRICKLEWOOD HOMELESS CONCERN 60 Ashford Road Cricklewood NW2 Phone 081-208-1608	16+	Tues and Fri 11am-4pm Mon, Wed, Thurs by appointment only	Advice/ Information Meals (small charge) Launderette/ Showers
LONDON CONNEC-TION CENTRE St James Cafe, 12 Adelaide Street WC2 Phone 071-321-0633 (Also runs Soho Project)	Under 25s	Mon-Fri 8am-4pm and 6pm-9pm	Café/cheap food Information Classes Music/sport Showers/ Launderette
NEW HORIZON 1 Macklin Street WC2 Phone 071-242-0010/ 242-2238	16-21	Mon, Tues, Wed, Fri 8am-5pm, Thurs 1pm-5pm	Advice/Infor-mation classes and workshops

NORTH LAMBETH DAY CENTRE (Over Waterloo Bridge beside church) Phone 071-261-9622	Any age	Mon-Fri 1pm-4pm Mornings by appointment	Welfare and housing Advice/information Medical help Classes
THE PLACE St Martin-In-The-Fields WC2 Phone 071-930-4137/930-1781 (Always very busy, so get there an hour before it opens.)	21+	Mon, Tues, Thurs, Fri 2pm-5pm also Fri 10.30am-1pm Sun 9.30am-1pm Evenings Mon-Thurs 6pm-9pm	Advice/Information Classes Cheap food Laundry
WEST LONDON DAY CENTRE 136 Seymour Place W1 Phone 071-402-5468	25+	Mon, Tues, Thurs, Fri 9.15am-4.15pm Wed 9.15am-2pm Sat, Sun 10am-3pm	Advice/Information Classes/ Cheap café Showers

HELP AND ADVICE: GENERAL

When you are living in an unfamiliar city with family and friends on the other side of the Irish Sea, there are times when problems can get on top of you because you don't really know who to talk to about them. The following agencies can help and advise you:

Agency	*Times*	*Services*
LESBIAN AND GAY SWITCHBOARD Phone 071-837-7324	24-hour telephone	Advice and support service
LONDON FRIEND 275 Upper Street N1 Phone 071-837-3337	Telephone service 7.30pm-10pm Every evening	Advice and counselling service for gay people
NEW GRAPEVINE 14 St John's Street WC2 Phone 071-278-9157/278-9147	Tues, Thurs 2.30pm-6.30pm Wed 2.30pm-8.30pm	Sex education and advice for young people
SALVATION ARMY ADVICE BUREAU (HQ) 101 Queen Victoria Street EC4 Phone 071-236-5222		Helps homeless, aged, people in crisis Drug, alcohol problems

SAMARITANS Phone 071-328-33400	24-hour telephone	Offers help to the despairing
ST-MARTIN-IN-THE- FIELDSSOCIAL SERVICE UNIT St Martin's Place WC2 Phone 071-930-4137	10am-8pm daily	Helps with personal problems

IRISH CHAPLAINCY SCHEME IN BRITAIN

Director: Rev Bobby Gilmore Ssc,
21 Hatchard Road,
Upper Holloway N19 4NG
Phone 071-263-1477

Assistant Director:
Rev Colm O'Gallchoir,
15 St John's Villas,
Upper Holloway N19 3EE
Phone 0 71-272-8195

PARISHES

Acton East
Rev Michael Dorgan (Cloyne),
Sr Christina Heskin,
St Aidan's,
Old Oak Commmon Lane,
Acton, W3 7DD
Phone 081-743-5732

Luton [1]
Rev Martin Noone (Dublin),
Rev Hugh Kavanagh (Dublin),
33 Westbourne Road,
Luton Beds LU4 8JD
Phone 0582-28849

St George's Cathedral [2]
Rev Mairtin Mac A' Bheatha,
Cathedral Clergy House,
Westminster Bridge Road SE1 7HY
Phone 071-928-5256/401-2532

Stonebridge Park
Rev Noel Naughton (Killaloe),
Five Precious Wounds Presbytery,
Brentfield Road, Stonebridge Park
NW10 8ER. Phone 081-965-3313

Tooting Bec
Rev John Mulligan (Tuam),
9 Tooting Bec Road SW17 8BS
Phone 081-672-2179

Dover [2]
Rev Dave Murphy (Cork),
St Paul's Presbytery,
103 Maison Dieu Road,
Dover CT16 1RU
Phone 0304-206766

Northampton South [1]
Rev Michael O'Donnell Cssp,
130 Towcester Road,
Far Cotton,
Northampton NN4 9LH
Phone 0604-768483

Shepherd's Bush
Rev Patrick J Flynn (Kilmore),
44 Ashchurch Grove,
Shepherd's Bush W12 9BU
Phone 081-743-5196

Tollington Park
Rev Jimmy Walsh (Galway),
St Mellitus Presbytery,
Tollington Park N4 3AG
Phone 071-263-6583

Tottenham
Rev Patrick McGinn (Clogher),
729 High Road,
Tottenham N17 8AG
Phone 081-808-3554

Upper Holloway
Rev Colm O'Gallchoir (Raphoe),
Rev Declan Foley (Kildare),
Rev Loughlin Brennan (Cashel),
Rev Mick Lally,
Sr Catherine McInerney,
15 St John's Villas,
Upper Holloway N19 3EE
Phone 03071-272-8195

Warwick Street
Rev Ivan Tonge (Dublin),
24 Golden Square, Warwick Street
W1R 3PA
Phone 071-437-1525

Wembley
Rev Kieron Blake (Killaloe),
The Presbytery, High Road,
Wembley, Middlesex, HA9 6AG
Phone 03081-902-0081

Willesden Green
Rev Anthony O'Brien (Cloyne),
Clergy House, Peter Avenue,
Willesden Green NW10 2DD
Phone 081-451-4677

All parishes are in the diocese of Westminster except where indicated: [1]*Northampton,* [2]*Southwark.*

MEDICAL MATTERS

If you are sick and in need of urgent medical attention, there are
24-hour walk-in casualty departments in London hospitals you can
go to.

Area	*Hospital*	*Phone*	*Underground*
CAMDEN AND EUSTON	University College Hospital Gower Street WC1	071-828-9811	Euston or Warren Street
CITY CENTRE/VICTORIA	The Westminster Hospital Dean Ryle Street Horseferry Road SW1	071-828-9811	Pimlico
NORTH-WEST	The Royal Free Hospital Pond Street NW3	071-794-0500	Belsize Park British Rail: Hampstead Heath

If you are not registered with a doctor, you can go to the *Walk-In Medical
Centre,* 13 Great Chapel Street W1 (off Dean Street). Hours: Mon-Fri
12.45pm-4pm.

CHEMISTS (open late)

Chemist	*Times*	*Underground*
BLISS 5 Marble Arch W1	9am-midnight daily	Marble Arch

BLISS 50 Willesden Lane NW6	9am-midnight	Kilburn
WARMAN FREED 45 Golders Green Road NW11	8.30am-midnight daily	Golders Green

DENTAL SERVICES

Hospital	*Times*	*Underground*
GUY'S HOSPITAL **DENTAL SCHOOL** St Thomas St SE1 Walk-in dental emergency service	Mon-Fri 9am-4pm Sat, Sun 9.30am- 9.30pm Treatment free on weekdays – not on Sat/Sun.	British Rail: London Bridge

ALCOHOL PROBLEMS

ALCOHOLICS ANONYMOUS
11 Redcliffe Gardens SW10. Helpline open 10am-10pm. Phone 071-352-3001. Phone (Office) 071-352-9779.
Help, discussion groups, meetings.

BRENT ALCOHOLIC COUNSELLING SERVICE
For appointment, phone 071-253-6221.

DRUG ABUSE PROBLEMS

BRENT COMMUNITY DRUG PROJECT
Helplines 081-965-9716/84.

CITY ROADS CRISIS INTERVENTION CENTRE
358 City Road EC1. Phone 071-278-8671.
Open 24 hours a day, 7 days a week.

COMMUNITY DRUG PROJECT
7 New Church Road SE5. Call for appointment, phone 071-703-0559

FAMILIES ANONYMOUS
88 Caledonian Road N1. Phone 071-278-8805.
For families/friends concerned about, or involved in, drug abuse.

TRANX
Phone 081-427-2065, 081-427-2827 (24 hours).
Helps ex-tranquilisers/sleeping pill addicts.

SEXUALLY TRANSMITTED DISEASES

AIDS

AIDS MINISTRY
Father Gerry Ennis, 73 St Charles Square W10 6EJ. Phone 081-969-9073.

AIDS TELEPHONE HELPLINE
Phone 0800-567123 (24 hours). Confidential, free help and information.

BODY POSITIVE
Phone 071-373-9124. Open 7pm-10pm daily. Support for HIV positive people.

LEGAL LINE
Phone 071-831-0330. Open Wed 7pm-10pm.
Advises on AIDS-related legal problems.

LONDON LIGHTHOUSE
178 Lancaster Road W11. Phone 071-792-1200.

TERRENCE HIGGINS TRUST
52-54 Grays Inn Road WC1. Phone 071-242-1010.
Open from 3pm-10pm daily. Support, help and advice.

If you are worried that you might have a sexually transmitted disease, the following are special clinics that offer a totally confidential and free service:

JAMES PRINGLE HOUSE
Middlesex Hospital, 73-75 Charlotte Street W1. Phone 071-636-8333.
Mon-Fri 9am-6pm.

PRAED STREET CLINIC
St Mary's Hospital, Praed St W2. Phone 071-927-1649.
Open Mon, Tues, Thurs, Fri 9am-5.30pm, Wed 10am-5.30pm.

UNIVERSITY COLLEGE HOSPITAL
Gower Street WC1. Phone 071-387-9300.

LEGAL HELP AND ADVICE

CITIZENS' ADVICE BUREAU
Greater London Office 136-144 City Road EC1. Phone 071-251-2000
Free advice on financial, legal and personal matters. This office can tell you where your nearest CAB is.

THE IRISH EMBASSY
17 Grosvenor Place, London SW1 7HR. Phone 071-235-2171
Emergencies: outside office hours, leave a message on the answering machine

LAW CENTRES FEDERATION
Phone 071-387-8570. Open Mon-Fri 10am-6pm. Free legal advice

THE LAW SOCIETY
The Law Society's Hall, 113 Chancery Lane WC2. Phone 071-242-1222
Mon-Fri 10am-6pm. Free advice on choosing a lawyer/solicitor

NATIONAL COUNCIL FOR CIVIL LIBERTIES (NCCL)
Phone 071-403-3888

RELEASE
169 Commercial Street E1. Phone 071-377-5905
24-hour emergency line 071-603-8654. Free legal advice for anyone who has been arrested. Confidential drugs counselling

THE PREVENTION OF TERRORISM ACT

The Prevention of Terrorism Act (PTA) contains a provision which allows the police to stop you and detain you at 'port of entry', that is, when you get off the plane or boat in Britain. You can be asked to produce identification and they have the right to ask you to state where you are going and why. You can also be detained for up to forty-eight hours initially and this can be extended to seven days without charging you for any offence. If you are worried that you may be stopped on entry to Britain, you should:

* Carry official identification with you, such as your birth cert/passport.

* Have telephone numbers of useful contacts on you, such as Release, The National Council for Civil Liberties (NCCL) and The Irish Embassy.

* Ask to phone a solicitor, or relative or friend if you are being taken to an interrogation room, or being questioned by police.

SERVICES FOR WOMEN IN LONDON

Centre	Times	Services
CATHOLIC CHILDREN'S SOCIETY 73 St Charles Square W10 Phone 081-969-5305		Pregnancy counselling, adoption, work with homeless families in B&B hotels
IRISH WOMEN IN ISLINGTON 12 Hornsey Road N7 (off Holloway Road) Phone 071-609-8916	Mon-Fri 10.30am-4pm	Information/advice on housing/social welfare problems Education classes
LIFE PREGNANCY CARE SERVICE 83 Margaret Street IN7HB Phone 071-637-1529	Mon-Fri 10.30am-4.30pm thurs 6pm-8pm	Free pregnancy testing. Confidential pregnancy counselling
LONDON IRISH WOMEN'S CENTRE 59 Stoke Newington Church Street N16 Phone 071-249-7318	Drop-in times: Tues-Thurs 11am-1pm Welfare advice sessions: Tues 10.30am-12.30pm	Information/advice on practical/legal/social welfare problems. Wide range of classes, courses, social activities. Organises annual women's conference. Acts as contact-base for women's groups.
SOUTH LONDON'S WOMEN'S CENTRE 302/304 Barrington road Brixton SW9 7AA Phone 071-274-7215	Drop-in times: Mon-Fri 10.30am-5pm	Advice on housing/welfare rights/health etc

FAMILY PLANNING ASSOCIATION
27-35 Mortimer Street W1
Phone 071-636-7866

Mon-Thurs 9am-5pm
Fri 9am-4.30pm

Advice/information

BROOK ADVISORY CENTRES
(Head Office, 153A East Street SE17)
Phone 071-708-1234

Help for under-25s with sexual problems

If you are pregnant and need accommodation go to the nearest homeless persons unit (check address in phone book.) Bring a doctor's letter confirming the pregnancy. After office hours, phone emergency social worker 071-278-4444.

LONDON RAPE CRISIS CENTRE
Phone 071-278-3956 (weekdays 10am-6pm) or 071-837-1600 (24 hours)

WOMEN'S REFUGE
If you are a victim of violence, phone 071-837-9316.

For details of a local refuge Women's Aid provides a 24-hour emergency service 071-251-6537.

CHAPTER 3

Jobs in London and the 'Loadsa Money' Myth

A good appearance is vital at interviews!

When you first decided to move to London the odds are that your decision was fuelled by friends already based there who seemed to be doing well on the workfront, and who told you that there were plenty of jobs and 'loadsa money' to be made. And of course there's more than an element of truth in this. Many Irish people have been very successful in finding highly paid interesting work in London and others have managed to get regular casual jobs, even if these jobs aren't particularly well-paid or secure in the long term.

What they *don't* tell you, however, is that there are 400,000 people in London without work at the moment and that thousands more are pouring into the city from all around Britain looking for jobs. The level of competition for employment is intense and even good pay-rates get eaten up by high accommodation and transport costs.

And if you ask your Irish friends in London who are on good salaries just how much is left in their wallets after they've paid the rent and transport costs, you'll see the 'loadsa money' myth bite the dust.

The fact is, even if you are qualified, experienced and determined, getting a job in London is a tough time-and-money-consuming business, and if you haven't much work experience, and you are unqualified or without a skill, then getting work is three times tougher.

So, as Brendan Behan once remarked (in an entirely different context), 'Brace yourself!' and be prepared for a fair amount of time spent knocking on doors and going through a lot of interviews before you are offered work. It does take some time to get a decent job in a city the size of London. However, dogged determination and a well-organised approach to the employment scene will almost certainly pay off.

Below, you'll find a basic guide to the routes you can take on the hunt for work. But also use any contacts you may have and ask everyone you know to keep a weather-eye out for jobs that might suit your skills in their own workplace.

On the presentation front, a bit of press-and-polish, appearance wise, can give you the edge at interviews. Small details, like having neat folders for your CVs and references to offer agencies or prospective employers, always help.

Olive Ahearn, an Irish manager of a busy employment agency in London says that the way someone presents themselves for an interview counts for everything: 'They have got to impress you and be confident and reliable.' So present a good, business-like, confident image and it will improve your employment chances considerably.

FINDING A JOB: WHERE TO LOOK

NEWSPAPER – VACANCIES COLUMNS

The Evening Standard (early edition out in the West End from midday). Check the daily newspapers, magazines like *Time Out*, *The Irish Post* and the *London-Irish News*.

*There are also local borough papers like *The South London Press*, *The Hackney Gazette*, *The Fulham Times*, *The Haringey Advertiser*, *The Kensington News*, *The Harrow Observer*, *The Wembley Observer*.

Local Councils: Hackney Council, for instance, issue regular job bulletins. Brent Borough also has a vacancy bulletin. You'll often see council job advertisements in *The Irish Post* or *The London-Irish News*.

*The Public Library: Libraries stock daily newspapers and other community publications. Many also stock The Irish Post and *The London-Irish News.*

*The Irish Centres: Check with staff in the centres for employment agency lists and news of local jobs.

**Capital Jobfinde*r: Run jointly by Capital Radio and the employment service, it is aimed at 16-20-year-olds. They have a self-service jobs display unit in the foyer of *Capital Radio*, Euston Tower, Euston Road NW1. Free service.

EMPLOYMENT PROCEDURES

Below, we list some employment agencies in various fields. While you are doing the rounds of these, get going on applying for your national insurance number. You can get this at the local tax office, while you are sorting out your tax. When you do start work, you'll be asked about your P45, the form that details your earnings, tax paid to date etc, if you have worked in Britain before. If you haven't worked in Britain then you'll have to go along to the tax office anyway to get yourself onto the correct tax code. And the earlier the better. You can also apply for your national insurance number at the Department of Social Security or unemployment benefit offices. Everyone who is working, or looking for work in Britain must have a national insurance number.

TAX

The income tax rates in Britain are
Incomes up to stg£20,700 – basic rate of 25 per cent
Incomes over stg£20,700 – higher rate of 40 per cent

Tax-Free Allowances for Britain

Single Person – stg£3,005
Married couples are taxed separately and their personal allowances are stg£3,005 each
The married couples allowance is stg£1,720. (Normally, this is allocated to the husband, but it can be transferred to the wife instead.)

As well as paying income tax, you must pay national insurance contributions. This is usually 9 per cent of your earnings.

EMPLOYMENT AGENCIES

If you are looking for full-time permanent work through a commercial employment agency, then their services should be free to you. They charge the employers. When you go along to an agency for the first time, a recruitment consultant will interview you and go through your CV to find out what work would suit you best.

Then they set up a number of job interviews for you to go to, and this is where Olive Ahearn's tip about presentation comes in. If you make a good impression on the agency and convince them that you are reliable and fairly capable, they will spend time and effort trying to find you decent work. On the other hand, if you seem a bit slapdash and disorganised, they may decide you are not worth the effort. The big agencies in particular, take this kind of tough-hearted approach, because they have their choice of thousands of job-hopefuls in London. So save the good suit for these agency interviews and dazzle the recruitment consultants with your capabilities! You can also increase your job-options by going to several agencies and getting on their books, rather than pinning your hopes on just one.

EMPLOYMENT AGENCIES:

SECRETARIAL (AND RELATED JOBS)

ALFRED MARKS
237 Euston Road NW1. Phone 071-387-0024.

ATLAS STAFF BUREAU
31-33 Chancery Lane, High Holborn WC1. Phone 071-831-0012.

ATLAS STAFF BUREAU
152-154 Bishopsgate EC2. Phone 071-247-7444.

BROOK STREET BUREAU PLC
172 Bishopsgate EC2. Phone 071-283-7935.

CARA PERSONNEL
32a St Anne's Road, Harrow, Middlesex. Phone 081-427-7473.

CAREER CARE GROUP LTD
41/2 London Wall EC2. Phone 071-588-2567.

CLAYMAN AGENCY LTD
180 Bishopsgate EC2. Phone 071-247-6721.

EMERALD STAFF AGENCY
241-3 Pentonville Road, Kings Cross N1 9NG. Phone 071-278-6272.

SHOP WORK

ALFRED MARKS BUREAU
80 Cheapside EC2. Phone 071-236-6832.

ATLAS EMPLOYMENT
275 Regent Street W1. Phone 071-493-2021.

BROOK STREET BUREAU
108 Fenchurch Street EC3. Phone 071-481-8441.

SELECT APPOINTMENTS
118 Old Broad Street EC2. Phone 071-628-1625.

HOTEL AND CATERING WORK

ABACUS INDUSTRIAL-CATERING DIVISION
24 Notting Hill Gate W11. Phone 071-792-0146.

ALFRED MARKS CATERING
57 Shaftesbury Avenue W1. Phone 081-429-2543.

BLUE ARROW
23/4 Wormwood Street EC2. Phone 071-638-4961.

CONNECTION CATERING
198-204 Tower Bridge Road SE1. Phone 071-403-7660.

BAR WORK

CATHY COYNE AGENCY
National House, 60 Wardour Street W1. Phone 071-437-4773.

SHAMROCK AGENCY
21 Manor Gardens N7. Phone 071-272-7878.

NURSING AGENCIES

BRITISH NURSING ASSOCIATION
443 Oxford Street W1R. Phone 071-629-9030.

GROSVENOR NURSING AGENCY
8 Goldhawk Mews W12. Phone 081-746-0440.

HIBERNIAN NURSING AGENCY LTD
7 Caledonian Road N1. Phone 071-278-1664.

FASHION INDUSTRY

ATLAS EMPLOYMENT
53 Oxford Street W1. Phone 071-287-2288.

AU PAIR/NANNY JOBS

BELGRAVIA BUREAU
35 Brompton Road SW3. Phone 071-584-4343.

NANNY SERVICE
9 Paddington Street W1. Phone 071-935-3515.

REGENCY NANNIES
50 Hans Crescent SW1. Phone 071-584-7265.

SOCIAL WORK

REED CARE (part of the Reed Healthcare Group)
Phone 071-439-0657.

Also contact local borough councils for news of vacancies.

COMPUTER PERSONNEL

ALPHA NUMERIC
Walton House, Liberty House, 222 Regent Street. Phone 071-734-5431.

COMPUTERSTAFF
7 Dacre Street SW1. Phone 071-222-7070.

ELAN COMPUTING LTD
The Old Forge Business Centre, 7 Caldonian Road W1. Phone 071-833-3436.

CONSTRUCTION/ENGINEERING

EMANCO LTD (RECRUITMENT CONSULTANTS)
8 Great Russell Street WC1. Phone 071-323-0821.

MONTROSE CONSTRUCTION SERVICES
41/42 London Wall EC2. Phone 071-588-8694

ACCOUNTANCY

ALDERWICK, PEACHELL & PARTNERS
125 High Holborn WC1. Phone 071-404-3155.

REED ACCOUNTANCY
54 South Molten Street W1 (by Bond St Tube). Phone 071-491-4272.

REED ACCOUNTANCY
94 Baker Street W1. Phone 071-486-3227.

TEACHING

In April 1990, ILEA (the Inner London Education Authority) transferred its responsibility for education to each of the thirteen London boroughs. There is a shortage of teachers in London but the pay isn't all that attractive. The holidays are shorter than in Ireland, and, with big classes to manage, it can be tough going. You can get brochures on teaching jobs in London from your local education authority. *The Irish Post* also carries teaching vacancies.

National newspapers like *The Guardian* and *The Independent* carry advertisements for different job areas on different days: for instance, on Mondays *The Independent* advertises computer vacancies while creative and media jobs are advertised in *The Guardian*.

CASUAL WORK: TEMPING

Casual work or temping means taking work for a day, a couple of days, or for weeks at a time. You are paid in cash or by cheque, by the day or by the week. And you get work through an agency, a job centre, or directly through the employer. The employer does not deduct income tax and national insurance contributions. You or the agency are supposed to do this.

Casual work is legal, although it's illegal not to pay tax and national insurance. If you are signing on and taking casual work, you are supposed to tell the Unemployment Benefit Office what hours you've worked and how much you've been earning and they reduce your benefit payment accordingly.

Temporary work may be a good way of earning money quickly, but you have little or no employee rights (for instance, no comeback against unfair dismissal) and most casual jobs are poorly paid, with long hours and often unsafe conditions, (see 'Your Rights at Work' p.74)

Some employers, most agencies and all job centres will ask for your NI (national insurance) number and your name and address and will often ask for references.

If you do decide to take temping or casual work you should check the following with your employer or agency:

* When will they pay you? Daily, weekly, a week in arrears?
* Is the job based in London, within reasonable travelling distance?
* If the job is outside London, do they pay your fares?
* Do they deduct tax and insurance?

A great deal of casual work is given out through the agencies, who charge the employer or company for their services. Most agencies interview you first in their office and put your name on their books. You then call to the office each morning, or phone in to see if there is work for you. The agencies should find you work fairly quickly and once they get to know that you are reliable, you should get the better jobs that are going.

RATES FOR TEMPING OR CASUAL WORK

Catering assistants – stg£3.00 per hour
Kitchen porters – from stg£3.00 per hour
Chefs – stg£6.00 per hour
Chamber maids – stg£3.00 per hour
Waiting staff – stg£4.00-stg£5.00 per hour
Cook – from stg£4.00 per hour
Fast-Food Restaurants – stg£3-stg£4.00 per hour
Secretarial (copy typist) – stg£6.00 per hour
Top Secretarial skills – up to stg£9.00 per hour

These are not good pay rates, especially when you consider that your national insurance contributions and tax have to be paid out of this and that the cost of living in London is high. So try to hold out for a rate that at least leaves you something to live on after you've paid your rent, transport costs etc.

CASUAL WORK/TEMPING

Hotel/Catering Work
CITY CATERING SERVICES
205 Victoria Street SW1 (near Victoria tube). Phone 071-834-6665.
Long-term and short-term jobs.

INDUSTRIAL OVERLOAD
8 Little Turnstile, Holborn WC1. Phone 071-242-5374.

JOYCE GROVE STAFF AGENCY
8 Bloomsbury Way WC1. Phone 071-831-3066.
Open 8.30am-5.30pm. Chefs/kitchen portering (mainly live-in work).

MANPOWER
98 New Bond Street W1. Phone 071-491-3970.
Open 8.30am-6pm. Portering/post-room work/messengers.

CASUAL WORK: CONSTRUCTION

The construction industry in Britain has a strong tradition of Irish
input, and many Irish men who started out digging trenches back in
the forties are now major employers.

If you have a friend or relative in the industry it's not hard to 'get
a start', but, if you are inexperienced, the money isn't great and it can
be very dangerous work. The building trade has claimed the lives of
many Irish workers in recent years and there have been scores of
on-site accidents.

A great deal of the British building industry operates on the black,
i.e. no social security or tax contributions are paid, so you have no
legal standing or insurance if you have an accident or fall ill. Nor do
you qualify either for unemployment benefit if you are laid off. The
practice of signing on without informing your DSS office that you
are taking casual work is illegal and it also leaves you wide open to
pay-rates as low as stg£20 a day. So you'll be better off all round if
you work 'on the books' in construction. To get more advice and
information and to find out about jobs going in the business, contact
UCATT (The Union of Construction, Allied Trades and Technicians),
924 London Road, Crayford, Kent. The national number is 071-622-
2442. You can also contact *The Construction Safety Campaign*, 72
Copeland Road SE15, phone 071-732-3711 for information on health
and safety at work.

CASUAL WORK: JOB CENTRES

Job centres are government-run agencies, similar to Irish FÁS Centres. They are 'self-service', i.e. they have job cards on display and if
you spot any that might suit you, one of the centre workers will give
you more details and help arrange an interview for you with the
employer. The job centre staff can also tell you about training

schemes, and give careers advice. The job centre services are free.

CHISWICK JOB CENTRE
319 Chiswick High Road W4. Phone 081-995-4071.

EDGEWARE ROAD JOB CENTRE
182 Edgeware Road W2. Phone 071-724-1351.

HAMMERSMITH JOB CENTRE
73 King St W6. Phone 081-741-1525.

HOTEL AND CATERING JOB CENTRE
1/3 Denmark Street WC2. Phone 081-497-2047.

For a full list of Job Centres, check the telephone book under Manpower Services Commission. The centres listed below are ones that specialise in certain work areas. *The Hotel and Catering Job Centre*, 35 Mortimer Street W1 is the major job centre for casual work in London.

Centre	Times	Type of work
FULHAM JOB CENTRE 376 North End Road SW6	From 7am	Labouring jobs
KILBURN JOB CENTRE 292/294 Kilburn High Road NW6		Building Labouring jobs
MARYLEBONE JOB CENTRE 46 Lisson Grove NW1	Be there by 7am	Mainly kitchen porter work
VICTORIA JOB CENTRE 119 Victoria Street W1	Be there by 5am	Mainly kitchen porter work
WARDOUR STREET JOB CENTRE 195 Wardour Street W1	Be there by 6.30am	Furniture removal jobs, some labouring

YOUR RIGHTS AT WORK

Employment protection laws safeguard your rights as an employee. These rights include the terms and conditions of your employment, notice of dismissal and unfair dismissal, redundancy payments, health and safety rules, maternity pay, equal pay and regulations regarding sex and race discrimination. For some employees, there are also regulations concerning the hours they work and minimum wage levels. To protect these rights, you should join the appropriate trade union.

TRADE UNIONS

Trade unions offer protection and support of your rights at work. The TUC (Trades Union Congress) is the national centre of the trade union movement in Britain. Its affiliated membership comprises seventy-eight trade unions, representing almost nine million people – nearly 90 per cent of all trade unionists in Britain. For a full list of trade unions, contact the *TUC* at 23-28 Great Russell Street WC1. Phone 071-636-4030.

CASUAL WORK: TEMPING

You are regarded as self-employed for tax and national insurance purposes if you are contracted to work for a company, rather than employed by them. As a self-employed worker you don't have the same level of protected rights as an employee, because you don't have a contract of employment. However, even if your rights are limited as a casual worker you should still join a trade union. You can follow up cases of discrimination or non-equality, for example, through the union, so contact the TUC for more information.

RIGHTS AND ENTITLEMENTS: SIGNING ON

In Britain, you are entitled to social security benefits if you are out of work, if the DSS decides that your income isn't enough to live on, or if you lose your job. You are also entitled to some benefits if you are sick, injured or disabled.

Even if you hope to get work immediately, it is still worth signing on as unemployed and applying for income support because it is rare to find work straight away. It can take weeks, or even months, to get a job depending on your circumstances and you need to have some money to keep you going. You may also be able to claim housing benefit and poll tax rebates, to help with your housing costs.

The British social security system is, however, extremely complicated and it takes time to get to know how it works. Below you will find a guide to the main areas that will concern you, together with a list of agencies and advice centres that can help you with any specific problems you might have. If you are unsure about completing claim forms, or your entitlements, you should get advice before filling them out. Otherwise you could be causing yourself unnecessary hardship – filling out forms incorrectly will hold up your first benefit payments, and it already takes a minimum of two weeks to receive your first benefit even *without* delays. When you are new to the workings of the British social security system, it is confusing, so if you are in any doubt check it out!

RIGHTS AND ENTITLEMENTS: INCOME SUPPORT

Income support is a payment for those who do not have enough money to live on. (Usually you are signing on and available for work, or categorised as someone who, through sickness or disability, is not available for work.) Income support is means tested, so your right to it depends on the amount of money you have coming in each week. It is paid two weeks in arrears and the rates of pay are based on age (see Ch 1 p.22 for Income Support rates). You can get income support if you have savings of less than stg£8,000 and your income support may be taxed.

If you are under 18 years of age, you will not get income support while looking for work unless you register for a place on a Youth Training Scheme. (YTSs are similar to FÁS training courses.) It is very hard to get a YTS place, but if you do you *may* also be able to get income support in certain circumstances (if, for example you have a partner and child living with you). You may also qualify for income support if you can show that you would otherwise suffer severe hardship. This will be decided by staff at your social security office.

Part-time work: If you work less than twenty-four hours a week you can still claim income support. However, your earnings will be taken into account when the amount of income support you will receive is being calculated. You must also state that you are prepared to take a suitable full-time job if offered one.

INCOME SUPPORT AND HOUSING BENEFIT

BENEFITS WHILE WORKING

If you are not able to get income support because your earnings are too high, or you work more than twenty-four hours a week, you may still be able to receive housing benefit to help with your housing costs. Your local citizens' advice bureau will help you work out how much you would receive.

It is likely to be several weeks before you get housing benefit but it will be backdated to the date you first filled in your application form. You will be expected to provide proof of your earnings, either by producing wage slips, or by getting your employer to fill in a form stating how much you earn and bringing that along with you.

HOUSING BENEFIT

Housing benefit is a government scheme paid for by local councils to help people meet the cost of their rent and poll tax (formerly rates).

It can be claimed by anyone on a low income whose savings are less than stg£16,000. It meets only what the local authorities decide are 'reasonable' rent costs. If you are on income support and living in a hostel, you are entitled to maximum housing benefit. Maximum housing benefit should cover the 'rent' part of your hostel charge and some other services, but it won't cover all hostel costs, such as meals provided, heating and lighting in your room and water rates. These costs can come to an extra stg£10-£15 per week.

If you are not on income support, then you can claim housing benefit at your local council. If you are claiming income support, you will get a housing benefit claim form at your unemployment benefit office. Send it, or bring it, to the council. Housing benefit is paid by cheque to you, or directly to your landlord.

UNEMPLOYMENT BENEFIT

Unemployment benefit (UB) is a national insurance benefit. To get it, you must have worked in Britain and have paid enough national insurance contributions. So this will apply to you only if you have been living in Britain for some time. If it does, then you may qualify for both unemployment benefit and income support, or just one of these, depending on your circumstances. You should check this out at an advice agency, or a citizens' advice bureau.

You must be both capable of work and available for work to qualify for unemployment benefit. UB is taxable. According to the April 1990 rates you receive stg£37.35 UB weekly for yourself and stg£23.05 for your spouse, or a person caring for your child or children.

TRANSFERRING UNEMPLOYMENT BENEFIT

As stated in Ch 1, you may be able to transfer unemployment benefit from Ireland *if* you had been getting UB at home for at least four weeks before going to England. It can be claimed for a total of thirteen weeks only.

THE SOCIAL FUND

If you are faced with an exceptional expense that you find hard to pay for out of your regular income, you *may* be able to get a payment from the social fund. There are several types of payment: a community care grant, maternity expenses payment, funeral payment, and cold weather payment. You must be on income support or getting housing benefit or family credit to qualify for any of these.

None of these grant payments has to be repaid. However, the social fund is cash-limited and even families and individuals in severe crisis have not necessarily been successful when applying for these payments. It is highly unlikely that young Irish people would get this payment.

Budgeting loans and crisis loans are other forms of Social Fund assistance for urgent needs. These loans have to be paid back. You are not automatically entitled to a crisis loan, however great your need might be. The decision on whether you get a crisis loan or not is down to your local DSS office. You can apply for it (you don't have to be on income support to claim a crisis loan) but again, it is unlikely that young Irish people would be granted this kind of emergency-need loan.

FAMILY CREDIT

Family credit is a tax-free benefit for families supporting at least one child under sixteen (or under nineteen if in full-time education up to A-level standard). To qualify, you or your partner must be working for twenty-four hours a week or more, and hold not more than stg£8,000 in savings.

SICKNESS BENEFIT

If you can't work because of sickness or disablement and you cannot get statutory sick pay, then you may be entitled to sickness benefit if you have paid enough national insurance contributions in the UK or Ireland. If you had an accident at work, or contracted an industrial disease, you may still get sickness benefit, even if you haven't paid enough national insurance contributions.

CHILD BENEFIT

You can claim a child-benefit payment if you are responsible for a child under sixteen (or nineteen if in full-time education) regardless of your income or national insurance contributions. Claims can be made as soon as the child is born. It is paid in arrears each month into a bank or building society, or by a book of orders which you can cash at the post office.

ONE PARENT BENEFIT

This (as well as child benefit) is available for single parents, regardless of their income or national insurance contributions.

SIGNING ON

To claim for social security benefits, you must go to your nearest unemployment benefit office (UBO) to sign on. Check the address of the nearest UBO in the phone book and ring them to make sure they deal with your area. (Remember that you need to bring at least two forms of identification with you: birth certificate and passport etc.)

At the UBO, go to the 'Fresh claims' counter for a signing-on card. If you're claiming income support, you'll get a B1 form to take away and complete. If you're unsure about how to fill out the form, bring it to an advice centre for help. The completed form should then be sent to the DSS office. To save time, you can bring it in yourself and wait to be seen by a DSS official. This may mean waiting several hours. It will be at least two weeks before your first payment comes through, and there can be further delays. But stay in touch with the DSS office. You'll get the best results by remaining persistent but polite.

If you have no address, you can still claim DSS benefits in the way we've described. Usually you will be sent to a DSS unit – a large shelter, with strict rules, no privacy and very basic facilities.

DSS OFFICES

In London, your postal address determines which DSS office you will use. (Check with your unemployment benefit office.)

Remember to check the opening hours of your local unemployment benefit office. Generally the times are 9am to 3.30pm Monday to Friday. But they vary from office to office. Camden Town office, for instance, opens from 9am to 1pm and 2pm to 4pm Monday to Friday. But Hackney UBO hours are 9am to 3.30pm Monday to Thursday, 10am to 3.30pm Fridays and there is no signing between 12.30pm and 2pm.

EMERGENCY SOCIAL SECURITY OFFICE

If you are stranded without money and have nowhere to stay, outside usual office hours, then go along to the *Emergency Office*, Keyworth House, Keyworth Street SE1 (near Elephant & Castle tube). Phone 071-407-2315. Open Mon-Fri 6pm-10pm, Sat 9am-10pm, Sun and Bank Holidays 2pm-10pm. Outside the Emergency Office hours listed above, go to the nearest Irish centre for advice and help.

If you are unsure about the benefits you should receive, or you need more information, call Freephone Social Security 0800-666555.

YOUTH TRAINING SCHEME

If you are under eighteen (unless you are in full-time education or you have a job) then you must register for a place on a Youth Training Scheme (YTS) otherwise, except in very limited circumstances, you will not be able to claim income support.

Youth Training Schemes provide on-the-job training and further education opportunities in a wide range of fields from office work to carpentry, painting and decorating etc. Courses last one or two years and you are paid a training allowance. On the two-year course you receive stg£28.50 a week in the first year, rising to stg£35 in the second year. On the one-year course, you get stg£35 a week from the fourteenth week. Register for a place at your local careers office.

YOUR RIGHTS AS A TRAINEE

When you start a YTS, you should be given a training agreement, setting out your rights and responsibilities as a trainee. You should not have to work more than forty hours a week and you are entitled to some paid holidays. If you are sick while on a YTS, you may get up to three weeks' leave, providing you inform your employer and follow the firm's usual sick-leave procedure.

If you don't get paid, or you are taken off the scheme, you may be entitled to other benefits. You should get advice on this.

Remember that the Race Relations Act, the Sex Discrimination Act and health and safety regulations are there to protect you. If you are unhappy with your work conditions, go to your trade union or careers office.

You may be able to get income support on top of your training allowance if you are in board-and-lodgings accommodation or in a hostel. If you are a tenant, you may be able to get housing benefit from your local authority.

TRAINING OPPORTUNITIES IN LONDON

If you haven't been able to find regular work in London – or if the job you're in pays very low wages, involves long hours and offers no real prospects, then you should look at the training opportunities that are available.

THE MIGRANT TRAINING SCHEME

The Migrant Training Scheme was set up to provide vocational training and employment opportunities for young people in the 16-25 age group. MTS is particularly concerned about meeting the needs of young Irish people and the six-months-long programme has about 200 places on it. The scheme covers areas like new technology, office and business skills, community care, construction, tourism and leisure. Trainees are paid a living and travelling allowance and may be helped with accommodation problems. Some of the courses are based in London Irish centres and others in colleges and information technology centres. For more information, contact *The Migrant*

Training Scheme, Great Northern House, 79-81 Euston Road NW1 2RU. Phone 071-860-5507.

KILBURN SKILLS

Kilburn Skills is a training project aimed mainly at 16-19-year-olds. Their programmes include bricklaying, carpentry, catering, computing and electronics, office skills, painting and decorating and plumbing. Courses last for two years. To register, go along to Kilburn Skills on Wednesdays between 2.30pm and 5pm. There is a waiting list for some courses (such as bricklaying), but 15 to 20 trainees are interviewed each month. Trainees on courses get a living allowance, plus a travel card. Contact *Kilburn Skills* at 10 Wellington Road NW10. Phone 081-969-7865.

SAFE START

Safe Start is an Irish community-funded group recently set up to provide services for young Irish immigrants. It aims to provide accommodation, information and advice, and practical assistanc with job-seeking and training opportunities. Safe Start works with MTS and has a network of employers around London who offer suitable employment and training. For more information contact *Safe Start*, 71 Cricklewood Broadway NW2 3JR. Phone 081-452-0182.

GOVERNMENT TRAINING AND EMPLOYMENT SCHEMES

If you are over eighteen and have been signing on at an unemployment benefit office and available for work for six months or more, then Employment Training offers up to a year's training to help you get back to work. The range on offer includes off-the-job training and practical placement with local employers or on projects.

There is also training for people who want to set up their own business – as well as Special Enterprise training for unemployed managers and graduates. While training, you get an allowance and some travel costs and some child-care costs are paid for. Training bonuses are also offered. For more information contact your local job centre and ask them about Employment Training programmes.

CAREERS OFFICES

Careers offices are run by the local education authorities for 16-20-year-olds who have recently left education, or who are out of work and need information and advice. Careers office staff can also tell you about training schemes that might suit you.

CAREERS OFFICE
Second Floor, Mappin House, 4 Winsley Street W1. Phone 071-631-0077. Open Mon-Fri 9am-5pm.

CAREERS OFFICE
55 North Wharf Road W2. Phone 071-723-0177. -Open Mon-Fri 9am-
4.30pm. Appointment necessary for first visit.

Both offices have a daily vacancies board.

You can get information on other careers offices from *Piccadilly
Advice Centre*. Phone 071-434-3773.

GET SMART! COURSES AND CLASSES IN LONDON

One of the great advantages of settling in a city like London is the
wide range of education opportunities on offer. And if the notion of
dusting down the brain-cells and getting back into education seems
like a grim action-replay of your schooldays, then think again!

There is such a broad choice of courses and classes available at
London's universities, colleges, polytechnics and local schools that
you can pick the kind of subjects you'll really enjoy, whether it's film
studies or foreign languages, a video production course or drama
classes, business studies or botany. You can take a course that's
work-related to boost your job prospects or help you change careers;
you can catch up on areas of education you feel you missed out on at
school; or simply take up studies in an area that interests you in order
to broaden your horizons. The options are endless.

Generally speaking, the cost of further education shouldn't break
the bank and although competition for places in universities and some
polytechnics is very heavy (as we stressed in Ch 1), there are also
many other course and classes that you can join fairly quickly, with
minimum qualification requirements. It all depends on what your
education needs are and where your interests lie.

If you want to enter third-level education, but you don't have the
basic qualifications, an 'Access' course of general education is available at a number of colleges and community schools.

If you have been unemployed for some time and want to get back
to work, there are some 'Second Chance' courses available, part-time
and full-time. These include courses like NOW (New Opportunities
for Women) and WOW (Wider Opportunities for Women), as well
as a number of other local authority-run courses.

If you are working, but want to increase your training and qualifications on a part-time or day-release basis, then bodies like The City
and Guilds of London Institute offer courses in all sectors of industry
and public service. The London Chamber of Commerce and Industry
also offers qualifications in areas like languages, business and secretarial studies.

BTEC (The Business and Technical Council) runs the full range
of certificate and diploma courses, from business studies to leisure,

agriculture, construction etc.

Adult education: If you yearn to learn car mechanics, or potter about with pottery, get into geology, or perhaps conquer the computer world, then Adult Education classes give you scope. There are daytime and evening classes held in local institutes or schools, and the cost is usually very reasonable.

WHERE TO GET INFORMATION AND ADVICE ON WHAT'S AVAILABLE

In April 1990 ILEA (The Inner London Education Authority) transferred its responsibility for education to the individual borough authorities – so your local education authority now handles information on all education opportunities in your area.

The Education Guidance Services for Adults are borough-funded groups, offering free education guidance to people over twenty years of age. They carry leaflets and information on all available courses, and give you counselling and advice on education options. They can also tell you how to go about applying for the various courses, and supply phone numbers, addresses etc. You'll find your local education guidance service at:

Brent
BRENT ADULT EDUCATION ADVICE SERVICE
38 Craven Park Road NW10. Phone 081-961-3703.

Camden
CALA (CAMDEN ADULT LEARNING ADVICE)
58 Phoenix Road NW1 1EU. Phone 071-388-4666.

Greenwich
GRETA (GREENWICH EDUCATION AND TRAINING ADVICE CENTRE)
12-14 Wellington Street SE18 6PF.Phone 081-854-2993.

Hackney
HACKNEY EDUCATION ADVICE SERVICE
Urban Studies Centre, 6-8 Lower Clapton Road E5 0PD. Phone 081-968-2272.

Hammersmith and Fulham
EDUCATION AND TRAINING ADVICE FOR ADULTS
241 King Street W6 9LP. Phone 081-741-8441.

Islington
EDUCATION ADVICE SERVICE FOR ISLINGTON ADULTS
12 Barnsbury Road N10HB. Phone 071-278-3761.

Kensington and Chelsea
KENSINGTON AND CHELSEA LEARNING ADVICE FOR ADULTS
51 Golborne Road W10 5NR. Phone 081-968-8532.

Lambeth
LEO (LAMBETH EDUCATIONAL OPPORTUNITIES)
166a Stockwell Road SW9. Phone 071-733-3155.

Southwark

INSET (INFORMATION & ADVICE NETWORK
on Southwark Education and Training)
175 Rye Lane SE15 4TL. Phone 071-635-9111.

Tower Hamlets

THE EDUCATION SHOP (TOWER HAMLETS EDUCATION ADVICE)
75 Roman Road, Bethnal Green E2. Phone 081-981-3164.

Wandsworth
WANDSWORTH EDUCATION SHOP
86 Battersea Rise SW11 1EJ. Phone 071-350-1790.

Westminster
WESTMINSTER EDUCATION ADVICE
36 Church Street NW8. Phone 071-724-5051.

For details of Outer London borough services contact one of the above.

IRISH STUDIES

There are many opportunities to pursue Irish Studies in London. The
Polytechnic of North London, for example, offers qualifications in
Irish Studies. Entry for mature students is flexible. You can do a short
foundation course as a course in its own right or as an introduction to
the degree course. Information from *The Irish Studies Centre,* Polytechnic of North London, 1 Prince of Wales Road NW5. Phone
071-607-2789 (ext 4092).

St Mary's College of Higher Education (Strawberry Hill, Twic-
kenham, Middlesex TW14SX) now offers a full-time undergraduate Irish Studies degree course. Entry requirements are high but
mature students are welcome. Applications through the UCCA
system. Information from Jim O'Hara, Senior Lecturer, St Mary's.
Phone 081-892-0051.

Classes at Irish Centres: Many of London's Irish Centres offer
Irish language classes and related studies, ranging from literature
to lace-making.

BAIS (British Association for Irish Studies) can give further information on available courses. BAIS, 9 Poland Street, London W1V
3DG. Phone 071-439-3043.

The London-Irish Women's Centre also run radio-production,
video and photography classes. Details from 59 Stoke Newington
Church Street N16. Phone 071-249-7318.

THE OPEN UNIVERSITY

The Open University operates nationwide, by sending its educational material to students in their own homes or workplaces. On many of the longer courses, students have their own tutor and counsellor and can meet up with them and fellow students at local study centres. Degree and other courses run from February to October each year. Short courses are usually presented twice a year. For advice and more information, contact the enquiry service at your local *Open University Regional Centre*. For London, *Parsifal College*, 527 Finchley Road NW3 7BG. Phone 071-794-0575.

General enquiries should be addressed to *Central Enquiry Service,* The Open University, PO Box 625, Milton Keynes MK7 6DN.

In most institutions, the minimum age for a mature student would be twenty-three or twenty-four, but this varies. St Mary's College, for instance, accepts mature students from twenty-one years. So check with each college or university individually.

COURSES AND CLASSES: USEFUL PUBLICATIONS

The Polytechnics: Free annual leaflet listing full-time and sandwich degree, HND, degree equivalent and D.HE courses at all thirty polytechnics. From *CDP*, Kirkman House, 12-14 Whitfield Street W1P 6AX. Phone 071-637-9939.

Polytechnic Courses Handbook: Lists syllabuses for all full-time courses and a profile of each polytechnic. Available from *CDP* (Committee of Directors of Polytechnics) Kirkman House, 12-14 Whitfield Street W1P 6AX. Phone 071-637-9939.

Grants to Students: A Brief Guide: Free from local education authorities, or from the Department of Education and Science, Publications Despatch Centre, Honeypot Lane, Canon's Park, Stanmore, Middlesex HA7 1AZ.

A Survey of Access Courses in England: From *The School of Education*, University of Lancaster LA1 4YW. Phone 0524-65201.

Mature Students: University Degree Courses: Booklet free from *UCCA*, PO Box 28 Cheltenham, Glos. GL5 01HY.

Opportunities in Higher Education for Mature Students: CNAA, 334 Gray's Inn Road WC1X 8BP

GERALDINE HICKEY: LONDON CALLING

Geraldine Hickey from Ballymun, Dublin, is a member of the women's radio group, Transisters [sic] and also works part-time at the London Irish Women's Centre, Stoke Newington. Geraldine first arrived in the city at the age of eighteen.

I came to London with a pal Lisa. Lisa had just finished her Leaving Certificate and I had been working in a supermarket for a couple of years. I was restless. I felt so restrained in the supermarket job. I knew I could do something better than that sort of work. One night, Lisa and myself just started talking about getting out of Dublin and we decided to come to London. There was no great plan. London was simply the nearest place to go to.

Lisa had an uncle who was living in Surrey. She contacted him before we left and he agreed to put us up and keep an eye on us, which was just as well because we knew nothing about the city. I remember the two of us arriving in Euston Station and having to ask if we were in London. We just didn't know.

Lisa's uncle collected us at the station and brought us down to Surrey. We had a small amount of money with us, but we had to find work and somewhere permanent to stay in London. We bought *The*

Evening Standard every day to check the rented accommodation and the job columns and after about a month, we found a place to stay in Haringey with a Greek family.

We rented two rooms in their house and paid a month's rent in advance for a bedroom and a kitchen. The woman of the house was very decent to us. Soon after we moved in I got work as a cashier in London Zoo, in the staff canteen. It seemed really exciting at first: there was a good social life among the staff there and it was quite a novelty working in a zoo! The hours were eight in the morning to four in the afternoon, five days a week, working every other weekend and the money wasn't too bad. Lisa also found work, selling advertising space for a company in the West End.

The early months were good in some ways, but I do have painful memories of that time as well. I was very shy and for a long time I was quite depressed, missing home and my friends. Lisa was with me, of course, but we were totally isolated in London. We used to go down to trendy places like Camden town at night, to try to break into social circles, get to know the interesting places to go. It was very hard going.

In Dublin we had loads of friends, but the city here is so big it can be lonely. And in trying to meet people to socialise with, we did run into some fairly dodgy types.

After nine months working at the Zoo I hated the job. The excitement had gone and the monotony of the job was grinding on my brain. So I left it, moved to Kilburn and went on the dole. At that time it wasn't a problem to get social security. It took just a couple of weeks. Now, of course, it's a great deal harder to get and takes ages to come through.

I didn't want to commit myself to another dead-end full-time job, so I did catering work after that, temping with agencies in the city. The money you were paid was basic minimum wage level and the conditions were pretty terrible.

One agency I worked for was particularly tough. The jobs they sent me on were horrendous. People were horrible to me, they just treated me like a slave. I worked so hard, I was exhausted all the time. Some of the women who temped with me did five days a week but all I could manage was three.

Some of the worst jobs were in the big banks or insurance companies in the city. You'd be serving up food to them, working in incredible heat behind the counter and your legs would be killing you and you'd be dying for a drink of water. But you had to smile and say 'Enjoy your meal' and they didn't even see you.

I also worked in a coffee factory and a department store coffee shop in Oxford Street. The pay was so bad that at one point I was living in a one-bedroomed flat with six others, just to survive.

The turning point came when I moved to Hackney about two years after coming to London. Most neighbourhoods in the city are quite depressing to live in, because people are moving in and out of them all the time and there's a feeling of transience, which is very unsettling. But Hackney was completely different.

People do actually live there permanently, so it's a much more settled environment and at the time it was very cheap. I signed on the dole again and I wasn't doing very much in the way of work. One day, when I was in the local library, I saw this notice on the wall that read: 'You can still go to college, even if you don't have qualifications.' It was advertising mature-student entry to college courses. I had left school early and I was so thrilled at the idea of going to college that I phoned up the local polytechnic at once, asking for information to be sent on to me.

When this arrived in the post, I was taken aback by all the academic jargon in the prospectus. So I went to the local Educational Guidance Service and they advised me to do an Access Course first – an introductory course to further studies. This course was in Hackney College.

It was a great step. The course tutor was very supportive and there was a mixed bunch of students. We studied subjects like social science, politics, feminism and English. I started reading a lot and exploring different ideas. The course really increased my self-esteem.

This led to a place on the Diploma in Higher Education course in Northeast London Poly. And I got a grant as a full-time student. Later on I did a woodwork course, a print-making course, then an art course. After the first taste of study on that Access Course I had become a total convert to developing my skills! I went on to do a 'New Horizons' course at City and East London College. This was in administration and it was specifically for women and geared towards helping you find a full-time job.

The London Irish Women's Centre in Stoke Newington is quite close to where I live. I had often meant to call in when I was passing by and one day I got the courage up to call them and offer to do some voluntary work. I found the atmosphere there was lovely, very supportive and welcoming. As well as doing voluntary work, I did many of the classes they run at the Centre, and after I did the administration course, I was offered a part-time job there.

Up to the time I started calling into the Centre, I had never really thought that much about being Irish in London. I did have to face the Irish jokes, of course, and at times you were made to feel very conscious of your Irish accent. And the image portrayed here of the Irish being 'thick' is very hurtful. The effect of all this at first, I suppose, is to play down the fact that you're Irish. Yet, hiding your Irish identity here means you are only hiding from other people's prejudices.

It took me a long time to feel proud of being Irish in London. And make no mistake about it, anti-Irish racism hasn't gone away, but I do feel that it's easier than it used to be here.

There are more Irish agencies now in the city and there is a much more positive image of the Irish here. There's the feeling that it's ok to be Irish and I have a lot of English friends now too.

Recently, watching the Irish/Italian World Cup match on television in a pub in Stoke Newington there were English and Irish people all around me and the atmosphere there was great. I felt really proud to be Irish and happy to be in London. It was such a contrast to the way I started out here, lonely and knowing nobody, eight years ago.

The turning point for me was taking on all those courses and then getting to know about the London Irish Women's Centre. That's where I did the Community Radio Course, which led to the forming of our radio group, Transisters. We are a women's radio collective and we produce features on various issues, such as women and homelessness and women and the poll tax.

We supply material to news-gathering services like Wings in the USA which takes stories on women's issues from all over the world. We're hoping to expand and set up links with other radio stations around Britain and also in Ireland. Working in radio has been a fantastic experience. The fact that you have an outlet, access to a medium where you can cover features and news stories of concern to women, it's very good for the confidence. It gives you the feeling of having some say in today's issues.

I do go back home to Dublin about once a year to see my mum. But I feel that London is my home now and I'm happy here. I suppose I really became an adult here. Things have worked out well for me although it's been a hard slog for much of the time.

That's why I'd like to do some work with young people within the Irish community on a part-time basis. I have a lot of empathy with young people who come to London and find it very hard to get on their feet at first. Our welfare worker at the Centre is inundated with calls from young Irish people who have just arrived in the city and are looking for work and somewhere to stay.

They could do with some help from people like myself who know the job agencies and accommodation agencies that are dodgy from the ones that are upfront. London is a very tough city, very big and frightening at first. New arrivals need all the help they can get.

CHAPTER 4

Time Off in London and Things To Do

London street entertainment is interesting and varied.

Your first couple of months in London are naturally enough taken up with looking for work and somewhere to stay and settling into city life. But all work and no leisure makes daily life a terrible grind – so it's worth taking time out to get to know the social side of London.

Even if you are on a tight budget, you'll find that London offers a wealth of social activities at reasonable cost and many events are absolutely free. It's a case of arming yourself with a 'What's On' guide and setting out to explore the city. The listings below will give you some idea of the range of activities on offer.

MUSIC VENUES

(REGULARLY FEATURING IRISH ACTS)

Venue	Telephone	Travel	Type
THE ARCHWAY TAVERN Archway Roundabout N19	071-272-2840	Archway	Showbands/Irish folk/contemporary
DICEY REILLY'S Neasdon Shopping Centre NW10	081-208-3539		Irish contemporary/trad music sessions
DINGWALLS Camden Lock NW1	071-267-4967	Camden Town	Rock and contemporary music
THE FIDDLER'S ELBOW Malden Road Kentish Town NW5	071-485-3269	Kentish Town/Chalk Farm	Traditional Irish sessions: weekends
HOPE AND ANCHOR 207 Upper Street N1		Highbury & Islington	Old Pogues' haunt. Varied contemporary/trad Irish music
THE MARQUEE 105 Charing Cross Road WC2	071-437-6601	Tottenham Court/Leicester Square	Progressive and pop/rock sounds
THE MEAN FIDDLER 28a High Street Harlesden NW10	081-961-5490	Willesden Junction (British Rail)	Rock, acoustic, blues, contemporary
MINOGUES BAR 80 Liverpool Road Islington N1	071-354-4440 071-359-4554		Sunday morning brunch and band (popular)
NELLEY'S NITESPOT Grosvenor Rooms 92 Walm Lane Willesden Green	081-451-0066	Willesden Green	Irish showbands/pop music
THE PLOUGH AND HARROW 419 High Road Leytonstone E11	081-539-1683	Leytonstone	Irish/Varied music. Disco Wed night

THE POWERHAUS 1 Liverpool Road Islington N1	071-837-3218	Angel tube	Varied: everything from Flaco Jiminez to Stocktons Wing!
SIR GEORGE ROBEY 240 Seven Sisters Road N4	071-263-4581	Finsbury Park	Irish and other con- temporary music
THE STAG'S HEAD 35 Hawley Road Camden Town NW1	071-485-1522		Traditional Irish music: weekends
THE SWAN STOCKWELL 215 Clapham Road SW9	071-274-1526	Stockwell	Celtic/con- temporary music. Disco upstairs
TOWN AND COUNTRY CLUB 9-17 Highgate Road Kentish Town NW5	071-284-1221	Kentish Town (British Rail)	Rock venue and R & B, current sounds
THE VENUE 2 Clifton Rise New Cross SE14	081-692-4077	New Cross (British Rail)	Irish and other con- temporary acts, Indie rock/disco
VICTORIA HOLLOWAY 203 Holloway Road N7	071-607-1952	Holloway Road	Irish Trad/folk music
THE WEAVER'S ARMS 98 Newington Green Road N1	071-226-6911	Highbury & Islington	Irish/ country/folk music

SPECIALIST MUSIC VENUES

AFRICA CENTRE 38 King Street WC2	071-836-1973	Covent Garden	Live music: Friday nights
BASS CLEF 35 Coronet Street Hoxton Square N1	071-729-2476	Old Street	Jazz, African and Latin music
BATTERSEA FOLK CLUB The Plough St John's Hill SW11	081-874-6637	Clapham Junction (British Rail)	

BRITISH MUSIC IN-FORMATION CENTRE 10 Stratford Place W1	071-499-8567	Bond Street
CAPITAL FOLKSONG CLUB Royal Oak, York Street W1		Baker Street
100 CLUB 100 Oxford Street W1	071-636-0933	Jazz/swing
RONNIE SCOTT'S 47 Frith Street W1	071-439-0747	Leicester Sq/Piccadilly Circus

IRISH DANCE CLUBS IN LONDON

Contemporary Irish music: popular singers/bands

THE GALTYMORE
194 Cricklewood, Broadway NW2. Phone 081-452-8652.

THE GRESHAM
643 Holloway Road N19. Phone 071-272-6725.

THE HIBERNIAN
Fulham Broadway SW6. Phone 071-385-0834.

THE NATIONAL
234 Kilburn High Road NW6. Phone 071-328-3141.

THE TOP HAT
268 Northfields Avenue, Ealing W5 (opposite Northfields tube).
Phone 081-840-5611.

THE IRISH CENTRES

The Irish Centres in London have a broad range of regular activities, from Céili music sessions and classes, to popular music nights, language classes etc. Camden Irish Centre, for instance, has social events on most nights of the week and Áras na nGael (Brent Irish cultural and community centre) has a wide range of activities including music, Irish studies, Irish dancing, training courses, and women's group meetings. Facilities include handball, racquetball courts, library, workshop-space etc.

The London Irish Women's Centre co-ordinates a network of groups, courses and classes including radio, photography, Irish dance, creative writing and video, women's conferences. Check with your nearest centre for details of their activities or see the listings in *The London-Irish News* and *The Irish Post*.

MORE IRISH ACTIVITIES!

THE ACTION GROUP FOR IRISH YOUTH
Organises the London-Irish Youth Forum which brings together groups and organisations concerned with the needs of young Irish people in London. AGIY also distributes a regular newsletter focusing on youth concerns, publishes an information guide and leaflets, hosts workshops and seminars on Irish youth issues. Contact Joan O'Flynn or Dave Murphy 071-278-1665.

COMHALTAS CEOLTÓIRÍ ÉIREANN
Organises regular Irish music, song and dance sessions in London (and right around Britain.) You don't have to be a genius fiddle-player or step-dancer to join them – Comhaltas welcomes anyone who enjoys their activities. For details of London-based groups contact Mrs Joan Burke (London Regional Sec), 304 Empire Road, Perivale, Greenford, Middlesex or phone 081-997-1784.

THE COUNCIL OF IRISH COUNTIES ASSOCIATIOn
This is the umbrella organisation for a network of groups all around Britain representing the various Irish counties. So if you hail from Kerry, Mayo, Leitrim, Donegal etc, then there's a group in London where you can meet up with people from your own locality and enjoy a wide variety of social events. The council, with Camden Irish Centre, runs the annual Roundwood Park Festival each year as well as St Patrick's Day activities and other events. For details of your county group call *Camden Irish Centre* 071-485-0052/1 or Sec John Connolly, 9 Melrose Avenue NW2. Phone 081-452-3124.

THE FEDERATION OF IRISH SOCIETIES
This is the umbrella group for Irish societies based in Britain. Some are very large groups, with their own premises (such as Camden Irish Centre and Manchester Irish Centre) and others meet in local halls and clubs. The societies are concerned with all aspects of the Irish community's welfare, educational, cultural and social. You'll find news of Irish society activities in *The Irish Post* and *The London-Irish News*. You can contact the federation direct at *Camden Irish Centre,* Mrs Cathy Conroy, Secretary, Federation of Irish Societies, London Irish Centre, Murray St, Camden NW1. Phone 071-267-5514.

GREENWICH IRISH TRADITIONAL MUSIC AND DANCE CLASSES
Wednesdays 7.30pm at West Greenwich House, 141 Greenwich High Road. Contact Fran Whelan, 37 Rathmore Road, Charlton SE7.

THE IRISH CLUB
82 Eaton Square SW1. Social and cultural activities. Music evenings, Irish Literary Society, Archaeology Society. Membership open to all Irish people. Contact Sec Owen Murphy 071-235-4164.

THE IRISH IN GREENWICH PROJECT
Organises the annual Féile an Earraigh festival in London and holds regular music nights in Woolwich town hall and other social functions. The Irish Women in Greenwich Group can also be contacted through the project for news of social outings, conferences and other activities. Details from 115-123 Powis Street, Woolwich SE18. Phone 081-317-1435.

THE IRISH IN ISLINGTON PROJECT
Runs *The Roger Casement Irish Centre* at 131 St John's Way, Archway, Islington N19. They organise Céili dancing classes, Irish music and Irish language classes and a range of other activities including office skills and computer training

courses. Contact 071-281-3225.

KILBURN IRISH YOUTH ACTION GROUP
Organises the Lá Féile na nÓg, Irish youth festival, every summer in Kilburn. Details c/o *Abbey Community Centre*, 222c Belsize Road NW6. Phone 071-624-8378.

THE LONDON-IRISH COMMISSION FOR CULTURE AND EDUCATION
Promotes and runs the annual Irish Arts Festival, Síol Phádraig. Also organises many other cultural events and educational programmes.
Details from Brendan Mulkere, *Brent Irish Cultural and Community Association*. Phone 071-624-3158.

ST GABRIEL'S COMMUNITY CENTRE
21 Hatchard Road N19 (Archway tube). Organises dances Saturday and Sunday evenings. Welcomes new members. Details from M. Mahon 071-272-1881.

THE TRADITIONAL IRISH MUSIC ASSOCIATION
Regular sessions at The Hibernian Club (behind Fulham Broadway tube station). Usually no admission charge, but a small collection is taken up during the evening. For dates and times call *The Hibernian* 071-385-0834.

THEATRE/ARTS GROUPS AND ACTIVITIES

BAIS (BRITISH ASSOCIATION FOR IRISH STUDIES)
Phone 071-439-3043. Supports those already involved in Irish studies and aims to promote and expand such studies throughout UK. Organises conferences and public lectures, publishes surveys and newsletters etc. Details on membership from Seán Hutton, executive director, BAIS, Poland Street W1V 5DG.

BRIDGE THEATRE COMPANY
Regular productions at Irish festivals and other venues. Informal casting service for Irish actors/actresses. For details contact G McDermottroe, 11 Merivale Road SW15. Phone 081-788-4944/450-2481.

THE FOUR PROVINCES BOOKSHOP
244-246 Gray's Inn Road WC1. Phone 071-833-3022.
Stocks a broad range of Irish books, cards etc. Connolly Association base.

GREEN INK WRITERS CO-OP
Fosters creative writing in the Irish community. Based at The Green Ink Bookshop, 8 Archway Mall N19. Phone 071-263-4748.
The shop stocks a broad range of Irish material, from fiction to politics.

IRISH DRAMA AND FOLK DANCING COMPANY (AND THE LONDON-IRISH YOUTH THEATRE)
A multi-media touring company with a youth theatre and training facilities. There are adult and youth drama classes, ballet, Irish and contemporary dance tuition. For details write to Rosemary Kennedy, 1 Victor House, Marlborough Gardens N20. Phone 081-361-0678.

IRISH PERFORMING ARTS SOCIETY
Mobile theatre company. Stages shows in public halls, play-readings and poetry. Also commissions new work from writers. For details contact D Daly, 66 Thornhill Road, Barnsbury Square N1 1JU. Phone 071-607-8250.

IRISH WOMEN'S ARTISTS GROUP
Can be contacted through Irish Women in Islington, 12 Hornsey Road N7. (Ask

for Anne Tallentine.) Phone 071-609-8916 (Mon-Fri 10.30am-4pm.

LIVIA
A London based group of Irish artists. Holds regular exhibitions.
For details contact Áras na nGael, 76-82 Salisbury Road NW6. Phone 071-625-9585.)

THE LONDON IRISH THEATRE COMPANY
Performs plays, poetry readings and music in theatre venues, Irish Centres, festivals etc. For details contact Liam de Staic, 50 Abdale Road, Shepherd's Bush W12. Phone 081-743-6650.

PORTRAIT THEATRE COMPANy
Contact The London Irish Theatre Company for details.

THE WILLESDEN GREEN LIBRARY CENTRE
95 High Road, Willesden Green. Phone 081-451-0294.
Irish books, newspapers, music recordings, also theatre, dance, cinema facilities.

STEP DANCING

The two main organisationsr representing step-dancing groups are:
AN COMHDHÁIL MÚINTEOIRÍ NA RINCÍ GAELACHA
Contact David Hawkins, 33 The Height, Charlton SE7. Phone 081-858-3973.

AN COIMISIÚN LE RINCÍ GAELACHA
Contact Seán Hennigan, 10 Wyles Road, Chatham, Kent NE4, or Richard Griffin, 60 Winfield Park, Hartspring Lane, Aldenham, Watford, Herts.

The above organisations can give you details of dancing classes and teachers; An Coimisiún also publishes a quarterly magazine, *Céim*. It is obtainable from their base, 6 Harcourt Street, Dublin 2. Phone (Dublin) 752220.

CINEMA

If you're a film buff, then you'll like the wide choice in London, from the West End cinemas to the local repertory houses. The West End prices are high, but remember that many major cinemas have discount prices for showings on Mondays and early afternoons. (Check *Time Out* and newspapers for information.)

There are low-cost films at places like
THE FRENCH INSTITUTE
17 Queensbury Place SW7. (Must book in person.)

THE GOETHE INSTITUTE
Princess Gate, Exhibition Road SW7. Phone 071-581-3344. (Postal and personal bookings only.)

THE ICA CINEMATHEQUE
Nash House, The Mall SW1. Phone 071-930-3647.

FILM SOCIETIES

CHISWICK FS
Chiswick Library, Duke's Avenue W4. Phone 081-994-1008.

HOLBORN FILM SOCIETY
Holborn Library, 32 Theobald's Road WC1.

Some film centres have free film showings. Check magazine/news-paper listings.

THEATRE – FRINGE

West End theatre-going is a costly business. Ticket prices can range up to stg£25, although there are tickets for some shows at half-price. Check with *SWET Ticket Booth*, Leicester Square (Mon-Sat 2.30pm-6.30pm). For real value (and some would say real theatre), check out the fringe venues. Prices range from stg£2.50-£15 depending on your choice.

Some fringe venues

BATTERSEA ARTS CENTRE
Old Town Hall, Lavender Hill SW11. Phone 071-223-2223. (British Rail)

BUSH THEATRE
Shepherd's Bush Green W12. Phone 081-743-3388. (Shepherd's Bush tube)

HALF MOON THEATRE
213 Mile End Road E1. Phone 071-790-4000. (Stepney Green tube)

HAMPSTEAD THEATRE
Avenue Road, Swiss Cottage NW3. Phone 071-722-9301. (Swiss Cottage tube)

KING'S HEAD
115 Upper Street N1. Phone 071-226-1916. (Highbury/Islington tube)

LYRIC STUDIO
King's Street W6. Phone 081-741-2311. (Hammersmith tube)

RIVERSIDE STUDIOS
Crisp Road W6. Phone 081-748-3354. (Hammersmith tube)

SOHO POLY
16 Riding House Street W1. Phone 071-636-9050. (Oxford Circus tube)

TRICYCLE THEATRE
269 Kilburn High Road NW6. Phone 071-328-1000. (Kilburn tube)

WAREHOUSE THEATRE
Dingwall Road, Croydon. Phone 081-680-4060.

WATERMAN'S ARTS CENTRE
40 High Street, Brentford, Middlesex. Phone 081-568-1176.

YOUNG VIC
66 The Cut SE1. Phone 071-928-6363. (Waterloo tube)

NB Some fringe theatres are clubs, so call to check whether membership is necessary.

For backstage tours of London theatres, contact *Stage by Stage*, 156 Shaftesbury Avenue WC1. Phone 071-379-5822 (Tues-Thurs and Sat). Tours cost stg£7 per person.

MUSEUMS AND GALLERIES

Doing the rounds of museums and galleries is a great way to get to know London. Admission to many of the following is free (although some are considering imposing a small charge in 1990-91, so enquire beforehand).

THE BARBICAN CENTRE
Barbican EC2. Phone 071-638-4141. Exhibitions, lectures etc. Admission free.

BETHNAL GREEN MUSEUM OF CHILDHOOD
Cambridge Heath Road E2. Phone 081-880-2415. Children's heaven – Branch of the Victoria and Albert Museum. Mon-Thurs Sat 10am-6pm, Sun 2.30pm-6pm. (Bethnal Green tube) Admission free.

THE BRITISH MUSEUM
Great Russell Street WC1. Phone 071-636-1555. The works of man – from mummies to sculptures. Mon-Fri 10am-5pm, Sat 2.30pm-6pm (Tottenham Court Road tube). Admission free.

CRYSTAL PALACE MUSEUM
Cottage Yard, Anerly Hill SE19. Phone 081-676-0700.
Open Sundays 2-5pm. (Crystal Palace, British Rail) Admission free.

HORNIMAN MUSEUM
100 London Road, Forest Hill SE23. Phone 081-699-2339. Man and his Environment – plus soundalive audio guide. Mon-Sat 10.30am-6pm

MADAME TUSSAUDS
Marylebone Road NW1. Phone 071-935-6861. Waxworks of the famous and infamous. Open daily 10am-5.30pm. (Baker Street tube). Worth a visit but be warned – there is a hefty admission fee!

MUSEUM OF LONDON
150 London Wall EC2. Phone 071-600-3699. Varied exhibitions, from crafts to couture. Tues-Sat 10-6pm, Sun 2-6pm. (Barbican, St Paul's tube)

MUSEUM OF MANKIND
6 Burlington Gardens W1. Phone 071-437-2224. Non-Western societies and cultures featured. Mon-Sat 10am-5pm, Sun 2.30pm-6pm. (Piccadilly Circus, Green Park tube). Admission free.

NATIONAL GALLERY
Trafalgar Square WC2. Phone 071-839-3321. Western European paintings, 13th-20th century. Mon-Sat 10am-6pm. Sun 2-6pm (Charing Cross tube).

TATE GALLERY
Millbank SW1. Phone 071-821-1313. National collection of British painting (from 16 century-1900). Houses national collection of 20th-century painting and sculpture. Mon-Sat 10-5.30pm, Sun 2-5.30pm (Pimlico tube). Admission free.

VICTORIA AND ALBERT MUSEUM
Cromwell Road SW7. Phone 071-938-8500/8441. British collection of applied art and design, sculpture. Also houses wide variety of collections from all over the world (South Kensington tube).

MARKETS

Markets in London can be good sources of street-wise buys and general entertainment

BERWICK STREET MARKET
Berwick Street W1. Foodmarket, dating back to 18th century.
Open Mon-Sat 9am-5pm. (Piccadilly Circus tube)

CAMDEN PASSAGE
Upper Street, Islington. Antique market during the week, plus flea market weekends. (Angel tube)

COVENT GARDEN MARKET AND JUBILEE MARKET
Was the home of wholesale fruit & veg market. Now area has been converted into shops, boutiques, cafés and craft market etc.

GREENWICH MARKETS
Greenwich High Road SE10. Two markets: The High Road Market has antiques and bric-a-brac and The College Street Covered market has crafts, second-hand clothes, paintings. Open weekends.

LEATHER LANE
Plant stalls, leather goods, fashion bargains. Lunchtime market Mon-Fri. (Chancery Lane tube)

NEW CALEDONIAN MARKET
Bermondsey Square SE1. Huge outdoor market, antiques. Open Fri. (London Bridge tube)

PETTICOAT LANE
Middlesex Street E1. Vast market, running through a series of streets. Fashion in New Goulston Street. Jewellery in Cutler Street. Open Mon-Fri and Sun.

PORTOBELLO ROAD MARKET
Portobello Road W11. Everything from antiques to African crafts. Mon-Sat (but the hours can vary). (Ladbrooke Grove, Notting Hill Gate tubes)

TIME OFF: THE HEALTHY LIFE

London life – as you will have discovered by now is fast-paced and fairly stressful, particularly in your first months, when you're coping with job-seeking, flat-finding and generally familiarising yourself with the new lifestyle. A good social life is one way of relaxing but then nobody can afford to go out on the town seven nights a week. So taking up some kind of sport or regular exercise is a healthy and fairly cheap alternative. It's a great way of making friends – and getting fit into the bargain.

SPORT: IRISH

Irish sport is thriving in London and the GAA (Gaelic Athletic Association) London County Board can give you information on all hurling, football, handball and camogie teams around the city.

Contact *The London County Board*, GAA Sports and Social Club,

West End Road, South Ruislip, Middlesex. Phone 081-841-2468.

Athletics
LONDON IRISH ATHLETICS CLUB
Contact J Dorgan, 16 Haydon Road, Oxehy, Watford, Middlesex

Camogie
CONTACT C O'NEILL
Chairperson (London Board), 59 Locket Road, Wealdstone, Middlesex.
Phone 081-451-5511.

Football
LADIES GAELIC FOOTBALL BOARD
Contact L Ryan. Phone 081-902-8320.

Handball
LONDON IRISH HANDBALL CLUB
Contact Michael Collins, c/o AIB, 3/4 The Broadway, High Road, Wood
Green N22 6DS.

Rugby
LONDON IRISH RUGBY FOOTBALL CLUB
Contact C Byrne, The Avenue, Sunbury, Middlesex.

Soccer
REPUBLIC OF IRELAND SOCCER SUPPORTERS' CLUB
Contact T Booth, 33 Exeter Road, Harrow, Middlesex HA2 9PW. Phone 081-
422-7722.

SPORT: GENERAL

Football
FOOTBALL ASSOCIATION
16 Lancaster Gate W2. Phone 071-262-4542.

Hockey
HOCKEY ASSOCIATION1
6 Upper Woburn Place WC1. Phone 071-387-9315.

Squash
SQUASH RACQUETS ASSOCIATION
Francis House, Francis Street SW1. Phone 071-828-3064.
Open 9am-5pm Mon-Fri. Contact SRA for details of membership and lists of
affiliated clubs around London.

Swimming
AMATEUR SWIMMING ASSOCIATION
Harold Fern Hse, Derby Square, Loughborough, Leicester.

Tennis
LAWN TENNIS ASSOCIATION
Palliser Road, Barons Court W14. Phone 071-385-2366.

SPORTS CENTRES

There are 100+ sports centres in London, check phone book for local
facilities. Most of them cater for court sports, gym activities, (ranging
from martial arts to weight training and aerobics) and swimming. All

the centres listed below have swimming pools.

BRITANNIA LEISURE CENTRE
40 Hyde Road N1. Phone 071-729-4485. (Old Street tube)
Open 9am-10pm daily. Admission under stg£1 but classes can cost stg£1-£4.

BRIXTON RECREATION CENTRE
Brixton Station Road SW9. Phone 071-274-7774. (Brixton tube)
Open 9am-10pm daily. Admission under stg£1 approx.

CENTRAL YMCA
112 Great Russell Street WC1. Phone 071-637-8131. (Tottenham Court Road tube) Open daily. Check weekly membership rates.

CRYSTAL PALACE NATIONAL SPORTS CENTRE
Ledrington Road SE19. Phone 081-778-0131. Open Mon-Fri 9am-10pm, Sun 9am-5pm. Admission stg£1 approx.

JUBILEE SPORTS CENTRE
Caird Street W10. Phone 081-960-5512. (Queen's Park, Westbourne Park tubes). Open daily.

HEALTH CLUBS

London health clubs vary from the sweat 'n' stretch aerobics and weights gyms, to the downright lap-of-luxury clubs. Many clubs operate on an annual membership basis, which can be several hundred pounds (some have a six-monthly rate). Other clubs run a pay-per-visit system which can be anything from stg£3-stg£8+ Check by phone which clubs allow you take a free or low-cost trial session. Then go along to several before making up your mind.

Some central clubs:

CITY GYMNASIUM
New Union Street EC2 (different hours for men/women).
Phone 071-628-0786.

DAVE PROWSE FITNESS CENTRE
12 Marsalsea Road SE1. Phone 071-407-5650.
Open Mon-Sat 9.30am-9pm, Sun10am-noon.

WESTSIDE HEALTH CENTRE
201 Kensington High Street W8. Phone 071-937-5386.

DANCE STUDIOS/CLASSES AND COURSES

Strut your stuff in dance classes! There's plenty of choice and cost per class is usually reasonable. Some studios run an annual membership + class-fee system.

DANCE ATTIC
212-214 Putney Bridge Road SW15. Phone 081-785-2055.
Aerobics/body-conditioning/rebounding etc. Open Mon-Fri 9am-10pm

DANCEWORKS
16 Balderton Street W1 (opposite Selfridges). Phone 071-629-6183.

Aerobics/jazz dance etc. Open Mon-Fri 8.30am-10pm, Sat-Sun 10am-6pm.

LONDON CONTEMPORARY DANCE SCHOOL
Evening Courses at The Place WC1. Phone 071-388-8430.

PINEAPPLE
Covent Garden WC2. Phone 071-836-4004.
Wide choice of dance classes.

CHAPTER 5

Manchester

In AD 79, while journeying from Chester to York, Agricola's legions built a camp on the banks of the River Irwell and named it 'Mancunium'. From these fairly *ad hoc* Roman beginnings, Manchester has evolved into the commercial and industrial capital of the north.

Manchester fostered the industrial revolution, led the fight for free trade, split the atom and developed the first commercial computer. It is also the city where Mr Rolls met Mr Royce (and where the first Rolls Royce was produced), where flashlight photography was invented and where the first passenger railway station was constructed.

We can't tell you what it would have been like to go there then – but we can give you an idea of what it's like to live in Manchester today. It is one of the most densely populated areas of Britain, with over half a million people living within five miles of the city centre and more than two million within fifteen miles. Manchester City is the hub in a cluster of other towns: Salford, Oldham, Bolton, Bury, Rochdale, Stockport, Tameside, Trafford and Wigan.

Manchester is renowned for banking (it's the second largest financial centre in Britain), for industry, communications and information technology, as well as for learning and research. Manchester and its neighbour, Salford, have the highest student population in Europe. The city is also renowned for its large, long-established Irish community. In the census of 1891, there were over 32,000 Irish people based in the Greater Manchester area. In the years following World War II, many thousands more young Irish people made their way to Manchester in search of work. And the children and grandchildren of those who settled in the forties and fifties make up Manchester's Irish community today, now estimated at 90,000.

So, it's not surprising that Greater Manchester is heaving with Irish social, cultural and sporting activities. There are close to thirty Irish organisations, including the Irish Centres and parish social clubs, eighteen county associations, fifteen football teams, several Comhaltas branches, Irish history groups, an Irish theatre group and a vast, ever-increasing number of entertainment venues.

If you decide to make Manchester your destination, you certainly won't be able to complain of feeling homesick for Irish culture!

Social activities, however, are best enjoyed when you've got steady work and a bit of money to spend. So let's take a look at the kind of jobs that Manchester offers.

EMPLOYMENT

Once known as 'The Workshop of the World', Greater Manchester's industrial past has given way to the computer age and the job scene covers a broad range of areas.

Manchester's central location (just two-and-a-half hours by train from London, served by a network of major motorways and Britain's largest regional airport) has attracted more building societies, banks and insurance companies than any other city outside the capital. It is also Britain's biggest centre of computing facilities and an important media base. BBC Northwest, Granada TV and many national newspaper branch offices are based in the city.

The main sources of employment are financial services, tourism, hotel and catering, manufacturing and construction. Clerical and secretarial skills are in demand as well as computer staff, advertising, marketing and sales personnel.

Of course, the area isn't without its employment problems: Greater Manchester's unemployment level is currently 8.2 per cent, but recruitment agencies in the city say that there are job opportunities for people with the right skills and experience.

Dubliner Clare Wynn, a recruitment consultant with Manpower Agency in the city, says that Manchester's job scene is very competitive, but the work is there for those who have 'good skills, good CVs and good presentation'. In the commercial field, this means having typing and word processor skills and, if possible, shorthand. And not just the girls – Clare says that, increasingly, employers expect male applicants to have decent keyboard skills as well.

Proper training makes a lot of difference to pay rates. Someone with the right word processor skills can earn half as much again as an unskilled worker.

FINDING A JOB: WHERE TO LOOK

*Check the local newspapers and trade journals. *The Manchester Evening News* carries pages of employment notices.

* Talk to staff of Irish Centres (see P.220 for list of centres).

* Visit local job centres and employment agencies

EMPLOYMENT AGENCIES

You will find employment agencies listed in the local directory, but to get you started, here are some of them:

SECRETARIAL AND RELATED

CLAYMAN EMPLOYMENT AGENCY
6 St Ann's Square. Phone 061-834-0129. Temp and full-time work: sec, financial and accounting. Open Mon-Fri 9.30am-5.30pm

CONNECTIONS AGENCY
182-184 Mosley Street, M2. Phone 061-962-9711. Temp and full-time work. Open Mon, Tues, Thurs, Fri 9am-6pm, Wed 9am-8pm

HMS STAFF BUREAU
75 Mosley Street, M2. Phone 061-228-6888. Temp work: clerical, office. Full time: sec, clerical, sales. Open Mon-Fri 8.30am-6pm

MANPOWER PLC
Heron House, 48 Brazennose Street, M2. Phone 061-834-0301. Full time and temp: sec. Open Mon-Fri 8.30am-6pm

NUMBER ONE BUREAU
88 Deansgate, M3. Phone 061-833-0873. Temp and full time: sec, office. Open Mon-Fri 9am-5.30pm

SOLUTION AGENCY
100 The Piazza, Piccadilly Plaza, M1. Phone 061-228-7228
Sec, clerical, accountants, engineers. Open Mon-Fri 9am-6pm

HOTEL AND CATERING

BROOK STREET BUREAU
55 Spring Gardens, M2. Phone 061-832-8135. Open Mon-Fri 9am-5.30pm

NURSING

BRITISH NURSING ASSOCIATION
King's House, King Street West, M3. Phone 061-832-9188

HMS NURSING SERVICES
75 Mosley Street, M2. Phone 061-228-6888

INDUSTRIAL/CONSTRUCTION

BERTRAM PERSONNEL GROUP
2nd Floor, Royal Buildings, 2 Mosley Street, M2. Phone 061-236-4593
(Construction work.) Open Mon-Fri 9am-5.30pm

HMS INDUSTRIAL PLACEMENT DIVISION
559 Chester Road, Old Trafford. Phone 061-872-9293. Open Mon-Fri 8.30am-6pm

PROFESSIONAL AND EXECUTIVE RECRUITMENT

BERTRAM PERSONNEL GROUP
2nd Floor, Royal Buildings, 2 Mosley Street, M2. Phone 061-236-4593
Sales, marketing jobs. Open Mon-Fri 9am-5.30pm

PER RECRUITMENT CONSULTANCY
75 Sankey Street, Warrington, WA1 1SL, Cheshire. Phone 061-832-3266 or
0925-52153. (Covers Manchester and Warrington). Specialises in middle and
senior management-level jobs in areas like finance, hotels, sales and marketing, engineering, computing. *Information* Bruce Colvin

TEACHING JOBS

For details of employment possibilities in Greater Manchester
schools, contact *Manchester City Councils Education Department
Office*, Cumberland House, Crown Square M3. Phone 061-234-5000.

COUNCIL JOBS

For details of any possible vacancies in Manchester Councils Social
Services Department, Recreational Services Department, or other
areas, contact *Manchester City Council*, Administrative Head Office,
Town Hall, Albert Square M2. Phone 061-234-5000.

JOB CENTRES

Manchester City
AYTOUN STREET M1 (industrial work). Phone 061-236-4433

FOUNTAIN STREET M1 (clerical and retail). Phone 061-839-1222

MOSS SIDE 4 Southcombe Walk. Phone 061-226-8232

STRETFORD Arndale House, Chester Road. Phone 061-365-7031

Check out the local job centre for employment notices. Ask the staff about job possibilities. You can also talk to the Employment and Enterprise group about work schemes (based at Washington House, New Bailey Street M3.) Phone 061-833-0251

CAREERS OFFICES

For career information and advice about YTS and other work-training schemes for 16-20-year-olds contact Manchester's *Central Careers Service Office* at Crown Square M3. Phone 061-234-5000/234-7107/834-6524, for location of other branches.

BENEFITS

If you can't get work and you have no money to live on, or if your income is too low to survive on, then you should go to the nearest unemployment benefit office, and claim income support. (For details of signing-on, see 'London', Ch 3 p.78)

UNEMPLOYMENT BENEFIT OFFICES: GREATER MANCHESTER

MANCHESTER CITY UBO AytounStreet M1. Phone 061-236-4433

LEVENSHULME UBO 1 Matthews Lane M12. Phone 061-224-6374

NEWTON HEATH UBO Bower Street M10. Phone 061-205-2267

OPENSHAW UBO Cornwall Street, Higher Openshaw M11. Phone 061-223-1424/223-5225

SALFORD UBO Trafford Road, Salford M5. Phone 061-848-9000

STRETFORD UBO Brunswick Street, Stretford. Phone 061-865-8741/865-8743

The UBO staff can tell you the location of your nearest Social Security office, where you can apply for income support and other benefits. The city social security office is *Manchester Central*, 22 Great Ancoats Street M6. Phone 061-228-2200.

You may also be entitled to housing benefit. *Manchester Housing Benefit* office is based at Heron House, 47 Lloyd Street (opposite the Town Hall). It is open Monday to Friday 9am-4pm or phone 061-834-0444.

You may also be able to get a number of other benefits (see London Ch 3 p.76). Your nearest Irish Centre may be able to help you on this matter, but you can also go to the nearest Citizens' Advice Bureau for advice on benefits and a wide range of other areas. The main *Manchester CAB* is based at Gaddum Centre, 274 Deansgate M3. Phone 061-832-7028.

Other local CABs are:

Altrincham 061-928-1129

Bury 061-761-5355

Cheadle 061-428-3153

Oldham 061-624-4870

Sale 061-872-2101/3800

Salford 061-736-4983

For a full list of CABs in the Greater Manchester area, contact *Citzens' Advice Bureaux Training Centre*, 2nd Floor, Macintosh House, Shambles Square M4 3AF. Phone 061-832-3332.

ACCOMMODATION

If you are moving to Manchester, then it's much the same story as London. You'll need to organise, in advance, temporary accommodation of some kind to get you over the first couple of weeks there, while you search for your own flat, bedsit or house.

The cost of renting a house or flat in Manchester may be less expensive than London, but it's not cheap either (near enough to Dublin levels) and as a big business and university city, demand for living space is high. So it could take you a month or more to find a place of your own.

ADVANCE ACCOMMODATION: TEMPORARY

IRISH CENTRES

If you write to managers of the main Irish Centres in Manchester, they may be able to find you local lodgings within the Irish community, or other recommended B&B accommodation.

IRISH ASSOCIATION CLUB
17 High Lane, Chorlton M21 1DC. Chairman: Noel Fitzmaurice, Steward: Margaret Fox. Phone 061-881-2824

THE IRISH WORLD HERITAGE CENTRE
10 Queens Road, Cheetham Hill M8 8UQ. Chairman Michael Forde. Phone 061-205-4007

MANCHESTER IRISH COMMUNITY CARE
St Lawrence's Presbytery, 3 Malvern Street, City Road, Old Trafford. Contact Sister Elizabeth Cahill. Phone 061-872-3104. Open Mon-Fri 10.30am-2.30pm Community Care will shortly be moving to 289 Cheetham Hill Road M8. In the meantime, you can contact Sister Elizabeth at St Lawrence's.

ST BRENDAN'S IRISH CENTRE
City Road, Old Trafford, M15. Manager Liam Bradshaw. Phone 061-872-2783

HOSTELS

There are several hostels in the Manchester area offering accommodation at reasonable prices. But demand is heavy, so write in advance to check vacancies.

Hostel	Phone	Cost	Facilities
ST VINCENT'S HOSTEL 67 Heathersage Road, Salford M13 0EW	061-224-5324	Rooms: single (per week): stg£30, shared stg£27	Showers, B&B plus self-catering

YMCA HOSTEL (male and female) 56 Peter Street, M2	061-834-6035 061-834-5907	Per night: from stg£12. Single rooms stg£13	Showers, restaurant
YWCA HOSTEL (male and female) Alexandra House, 73 Carlton Road M16	061-226-2768	Shared: from stg£5 per night. Bedsit per week: stg£21.70	Self-catering
YWCA HOSTEL (male and female) St John's Road, Altrincham, Cheshire	061-928-2107	Per week: stg£30	Self-catering

UNIVERSITY ACCOMMODATION
(CHECK FOR VACANCIES IN VACATION TIMES)

UNIVERSITY OF MANCHESTER
Conference Office, Dept C128, Oxford Road M13 9PL. Phone 061-275-2000

UNIVERSITY OF SALFORD
Conference Office, Salford M5 4WT. Phone 061-736-5843

ACCOMMODATION: RENTING A FLAT, A BEDSIT, A HOUSE

According to one of the accommodation agencies in Manchester, the cost of renting a place in the city is 'less expensive than London, but more expensive than Liverpool', which puts prices pretty near to Dublin levels. Average costs (Jan 1990):

bedsit – stg£25-£35 per week

one-bedroomed flat – stg£60-£65 per week

two-bedroomed house – stg£70-£80 per week

three-bedroomed house – between stg£85-£90 per week

WHERE TO LOOK

*Check *The Manchester Evening News* accommodation notices

*Manchester's 'What's On' Guide, *City Life*, carries some ads

*Accommodation Agencies. One city centre agency is *The Letting Centre*, 11 Whitworth Street, West M1 5WG, phone 061-236-9137. This agency has over 1,000 properties on file. Their charge is one week's rent plus VAT, *if* they find you accommodation. You'll find more agencies listed in the telephone directory. Remember that it is an offence (under the Accommodation Act '53) for agencies simply to charge a fee for registration or for showing you lists of accommodation. In general, you should not pay a fee until the agency has actually found you a flat, bedsit, or house. If you are in any doubt about this, check with your local CAB.

WHAT TO LOOK FOR

See advice on p.50, Ch 3!

HOUSING ASSOCIATIONS

Housing Associations are non profit-making organisations which let property at reasonable rates. The following are two Manchester-based housing associations:

NORTH BRITISH HOUSING ASSOCIATION LTD
88-100 Quay Street M3. Phone 061-831-7952

NORTHERN COUNTIES HOUSING ASSOCIATION
Prince's Buildings, 15 Oxford Court, Oxford Street M23 W2. Phone 061-228-3388. Northern Counties Association has over 2,000 properties in the city and they have blocks of accommodation for single people from time to time.

To get a full list of housing associations in Greater Manchester, write to *The Housing Corporation*, Elizabeth House, St Peter's Square M2. Phone 061-228-2951.

COUNCIL HOUSING

The demand for council housing in Manchester is extremely heavy and there are strict regulations concerning eligibility. These are centred around a 'local connection'. You must be Manchester-born, or have Manchester-born parents, or have a permanent job in the city, or have been five years resident in Manchester.

At the very least, you must have lived in Manchester for six months out of the past twelve months, or three years out of the past five. To find out where you stand in relation to these regulations go along to your local *CAB*, or talk to *North West Housing Aid*, Room 278-280, Corn Exchange Buildings, Hanging Ditch M4 3BP. Phone 061-834-4809/834-8456.

The Council's Housing Department is in the *Town Hall*, Albert Square, Manchester 2. Phone 061-234-5000.

BUYING A HOUSE

Greater Manchester has just under one million homes, one of the largest housing stocks of any county in Britain. The cost can range from an average of stg£50,000 (three-bedroomed terrace) to stg£135,000 (3/4 bedroomed detached). Asking prices for some city centre flats are stg£65,000-stg£67,000 (1989 figures). But as we said in Ch 2, p.54, you should think very carefully before buying, because recent interest rate rises have made it very difficult for people to meet mortgage repayments. In 1989, close to 14,000 homes were repossessed in Britain and now more than 70,000 borrowers are over six months in arrears. If you are secure about the financial side of things, then you'll find lists of estate agents in the telephone directory. And newspapers like *The Manchester Evening News* carry property pages.

ACCOMMODATION PROBLEMS: WHO CAN HELP

If your accommodation arrangements have come to grief, and you have nowhere to stay in Manchester, then contact *Irish Community Care* (ICC), St Lawrence's Presbytery, Malvern Street, City Road, Old Trafford, phone 061-872-3104, or 289 Cheetham Hill Road, Cheetham Hill M8. ICC is open from 10.30am-2.30pm Monday to Friday, so if it's outside these hours, contact the *Irish World Heritage Centre*, Cheetham Hill or St Brendan's Irish Centre, or *The Irish Association Club*, Chorlton (addresses and phone numbers p. 109). These centres will advise you and do their best to find you somewhere to stay.

STOPOVER HOSTEL
For women from 16-25 years, is a medium-term hostel, catering for up to ten residents at a time. The weekly charge is from stg£59 a week, (shared bedrooms) and staff can advise on social security, housing etc. *Stopover* is based at 8 Scarsdale Road M14. Phone 061-224-8594.

SHADES CENTRE
52 Oldham Street, Manchester (close to Piccadilly bus station). Shades is an information, advice and social centre for young people. Contact them at 061-273-7306 or 834-7360 (mornings).

NORTH WEST HOUSING AID
Room 278-280, Corn Exchange Buildings, Hanging Ditch M4. Phone 061-834-4809. Offers advice and referral services on housing and other problems. Open Mon-Fri 10am-5pm.

If you are homeless and have no money to live on, contact any of the above listed groups for advice before going to the council. The council cannot refuse to help you, but they will want to check that you are in fact homeless, in priority need, and not 'intentionally homeless'. They will also want to know whether you have a 'local connection'. It's a complicated process, so get expert advice on how to present your case to the council.

If you are single and homeless the city council has two direct access hostels, one for males, one for females. The council will send you to either of these hostels to be interviewed. If you don't have a 'local connection', you will be referred to B&B accommodation.

If you and your family are homeless go to the Town Hall reception centre, where you will be interviewed. Even if you have no local connection, the council you first go to must provide some help.

If you are based in another town in Greater Manchester, such as Salford or Oldham, then go to the nearest council area office.

If you have left your home because of your partner's violence, or threatened violence, even if you have no local connection, the council cannot send you back to an area where you would be at risk.

INFORMATION AND ADVICE SERVICES

COMMISSION FOR RACIAL EQUALITY Phone 061-831-7782

COMMUNITY RELATIONS Phone 061-834-9153

LEGAL AID Phone 061-228-1200

SOCIAL SECURITY (freeline social security) Phone 0800-666-555

FAMILY

FAMILY CONTACT LINE (Altrincham) Phone 061-941-1155

MARRIAGE GUIDANCE Phone 061-872-0303

ONE-PARENT FAMILY CENTRE Levenshulme Community Centre, Chapel St, M19. Mon-Fri 10am-3pm

PICCADILLY FAMILY CARE LINE Phone 061-236-9873

WOMEN: ADVICE AND HELP

CATHOLIC CHILDREN'S RESCUE SOCIETY
390 Parrs Wood Road M20 NA. Phone 061-445-7741. Pregnancy counselling and adoption agency

EQUAL OPPORTUNITIES COMMISSION
Overseas House, Quay Street, M3. Phone 061-833-9244

RAPE CRISIS LINE
Phone 061-228-3602. Call Tues and Fri 2pm-5pm. Wed, Thurs, Sun 6pm-9pm (24-hour answerphone). Write to PO Box 336 M60 2BS

WELL-WOMAN RESOURCE CENTRE
1 Pilling Street, Newton Heath M10. (Main women's health centre). Phone 061-205-1257

ADVISORY SERVICES FOR WOMEN

HOMELESS FAMILIES SECTION OF THE COUNCIL
Phone 061-234-4744. Emergency service 4.30pm-8.00pm, phone 061-224-6452. Emergency accommodation for women and children who are homeless due to violence.

OLDHAM WOMEN'S GROUP
Oldham Resource & Information Centre, 7-8 Commercial Road, Oldham. Phone 061-626-4130

THE PANKHURST CENTRE
60-62 Nelson Street M13. Phone 061-273-5673. Information on most women's issues.

ST MARY'S CENTRE (sexual assault referral centre)
Phone 061-276-6516. Mon-Fri 9am-8pm. Staff on emergency call all other times.

WOMEN'S AID
Contact c/o Manchester Town Hall. Phone 061-236-6540. Support, advice and safe accommodation for women victims of violence and abuse. Advice on housing, money, legal rights etc.

GAY SERVICES

GAY SWITCHBOARD 061-274-3999

MANCHESTER GAY CENTRE Phone 061-274-3814

MANCHESTER LESBIAN LINK
Advice/information. Write to PO Box 207 M60 1GL. Or Phone 061-236-6205. Mon-Thur 6pm-9pm

NATIONAL CAMPAIGN FOR GAY AND LESBIAN EQUALITY
23 New Mount Street M4 4DE. Phone 061-833-2990

CRISIS HELPLINES

DRUGS

ALCOHOLICS ANONYMOUS Phone 061-236-6569

ALCOHOL INFORMATION CENTRE Phone 061-834-9777

DRUGS HOTLINE (Greater Manchester Police) Phone 061-228-3276

GAMBLERS ANONYMOUS Phone 061-273-3574

LIFELINE PROJECT Phone 061-832-6353 (Joddrell Street, Manchester)

SAMARITANS Phone 061-834-9000

SEXUALLY TRANSMITTED DISEASES

BODY POSITIVE NORTHWEST
(Tues & Thurs 7.30pm-10pm). Phone 061-228-2212. Body Positive is a Manchester Aidsline co-ordinated group. Gives emotional/practical support to all who are HIV positive. Also co-ordinates the Family Support Group (for partners, friends or relatives of people with AIDS or HIV).

MANCHESTER AIDSLINE
(Mon-Fri 7pm-10pm). Phone 061-228-1617

STD CLINIC
(Males) 061-276-5200, (Females) 061-276-5212

HEALTH MATTERS

DOCTORS

To avail of NHS free GP and hospital services you must register with a local doctor. You'll find GPs' addresses in the phone book, or ask your local chemist. Cost of medicines and hospital treatment: see p.23, Ch 1. There are seventy-five public hospitals and three major private hospitals in Greater Manchester. Some public hospitals are:

MANCHESTER NORTHERN HOSPITAL
Cheetham Hill Road M8. Phone 061-740-2241

MANCHESTER ROYAL INFIRMARY
Oxford Road M13. Phone 061-276-4999

ST MARY'S HOSPITAL
(Maternity/children) Heathersage Road M13. Phone 061-276-1234

SALFORD ROYAL HOSPITAL
Chapel Street M3. Phone 061-834-8656

STRETFORD MEMORIAL HOSPITAL
Seymour Grove M16. Phone 061-881-5353

WITHINGTON HOSPITAL
Nell Lane M20. Phone 061-445-8111

WYTHENSHAWE HOSPITAL
Southmoor Road M23. Phone 061-998-7070

LATE NIGHT CHEMISTS

A&A PHARMACY
54 Wilmslow Road, Rusholme, Manchester. Open daily 9am-10pm.

CAMEOLORD LTD
7 Oxford Street M1. Open daily 8am-midnight.

COPELAND
37 Stamford New Road, Altrincham. Open Mon-Sat 9am-10pm, Sun 10am-1pm.

EDUCATION

Greater Manchester offers almost 1,500 state and private schools. You can get information on schools in the area you'll be moving to, from *The Independent Schools Information Service*, 56 Buckingham Gate, London SW1E 6AG. Phone 071-630-8793.

You should also write to *Manchester City Council's Education Department Office*, Cumberland House, Crown Square M3. Phone 061-234-5000.

There is a wide range of pre-school education in Manchester as well as specialist schools, such as Cheetham's renowned School of Music.

HIGHER EDUCATION

Manchester houses the largest higher education campus in Europe, encompassing Manchester University, The University of Manchester Institute of Science and Technology (UMIST), Manchester Polytechnic and Manchester Business School. Nearby is The University of Salford.

MANCHESTER BUSINESS SCHOOL
Booth Street WST 15. Phone 061-275-6333

MANCHESTER POLYTECHNIC
All Saints M15 6BH. Phone 061-228-6171

THE UNIVERSITY OF MANCHESTER
(Eleven faculties and a wide range of courses). Oxford Road M13 9PL. Phone 061-275-2000

UNIVERSITY OF MANCHESTER INSTITUTE OF SCIENCE AND TECHNOLOGY
(One faculty of twenty departments, scientific and technological, but with an extensive management science course and European studies) PO Box 88, Sackville Street M60 1QD. Phone 061-236-3311

UNIVERSITY OF SALFORD
(Bias towards engineering and science) The Crescent M5 4WT. Phone 061-736-5843

ADULT EDUCATION: CLASSES AND COURSEs

There is a great range of classes and courses in evening centres, community colleges and adult education centres around Greater Manchester. You can do BTEC, or City and Guilds courses; arts & crafts, languages, office skills and other courses that will help improve your employment prospects. There are also several 'access' courses (general education courses) available.

To find out what's on offer, where the classes are and how much they cost, contact *Manchester Education Advice Service for Adults*. The education advice worker at each EAS centre can help you work out which course will suit your needs. If you are based in Manchester City, contact

THE BIRTLES CENTRE
Town Centre, Wythenshawe M22 5RF. Phone 061-499-1455

THE EDUCATION ADVICE SERVICE FOR ADULTS
Moseley Road Centre, Moseley Road, Fallowfield M14 6WQ. Phone 061-224-8242

Leigh

LAMP EDUCATION SHOP
Lamp Community Bookshop, 22 Church Street, Leigh WN7 1QH. Phone 0942-606667. Normal shop hours for bookshop. Education Counselling service Tues & Thurs 10am-noon

Salford

SALFORD ADULT GUIDANCE UNIT
Pendleton House, Broughton Road, Salford M6 6LS. Phone 061-745-7233

Stockport

STOCKPORT EDUCATION ADVICE SERVICE FOR ADULTS (SEASA)
Stockport Job Centre, 268-274 Merseyway, Stockport SK1 1QR. Phone 061-480-0351

Tameside

TAMESIDE EDUCATION ADVICE SERVICE FOR ADULTS
Tameside College of Technology, Warrington House, Church Street, Beaufort Road, Ashton Under Lyne OL6 6NX. Phone 061-330-6911

Wigan

CONTACT FOR LEARNING AND EDUCATIONAL OPPORTUNITIES (CLEO)
Gateway, Standishgate, Wigan WN1 1XL Phone 0942-827686

THE OPEN UNIVERSITY

The Open University currently offers over 200 courses. Details from your *Open University Regional Centre*, Chorlton House, 70 Manchester Road, Chorlton-Cum-Hardy M21 1PQ. Phone 061-861-9823

TIME OFF AND THINGS TO DO

Mancunians take justifiable pride in the huge range of cultural and heritage attractions in the city and surrounding towns. It's the home of the famous Hallé Orchestra, the Royal Exchange Theatre Company, the Opera House and the Royal Northern College of Music.

It has over forty art galleries and museums; there are heritage centres and parks, markets and shopping areas, architectural attractions, leisure centres and sporting amenities, libraries and arts centres.

Manchester's 'What's On' guide, *City Life*, is published every other Thursday and the *Manchester Evening News* also covers arts events. There is also *City Life*, published by City Life Publications, 164 Deansgate M20 2RD. Phone 061-839-1320 The list below will give you some idea of the range of events on offer.

MUSIC: POP, ROCK, TRAD AND ALL THAT JAZZ

London used to be the Mecca for the music business but now Manchester is a serious contender. Stretford-born Steven Morrissey and The Smiths and more recently, the Stone Roses put Manchester on the music map.

Some Popular Music Venues

THE APOLLO THEATRE
Ardwick Green M20. Varied: pop music, dance etc

BAND ON THE WALL
Swan Street M4. Everything from pop to cajun music

THE BOARDWALK
Little Peter Street M15. Pop, current sounds

THE BUZZ
Southern Hotel, Mauldeth Road, West Chorlton. Pop, current sounds

FREE TRADE HALL
Peter Street M20. Caters for every music taste, from Christy Moore to the Czechoslovakian Army Band

GRANVILLE'S CELLAR BAR
Lansdowne Hotel, 346 Wilmslow Road M14. R&B, pop, jazz

THE GROVE CABARET CLUB
250 Plymouth Grove, Longsight, Manchester. Phone 061-224-7624. Features big names from the 'sixties', plus Irish contemporary sounds

INTERNATIONAL
47 Anson Road, M14. Current sounds

INTERNATIONAL 2
210 Plymouth Grove M13 (off Upper Brook Street). Phone 061-224-2655. Everything from The Ramones to Joe Strummer!

IRISH ASSOCIATION CLUB
17 High Lane, Chorlton M21. Phone 061-881-2824. Country, Irish and contemporary music

IRISH WORLD HERITAGE CENTRE
10 Queen's Road, Cheetham Hill M8. Phone 061-205-4007. Folk, country and pop. Call into the centre and pick up a programme of events

MANCHESTER POLYTECHNIC
Oxford Road M13. Regular rock, pop gigs

THE NEW ÁRD RÍ BALLROOM
85 Coupland Street M15. Phone 061-226-4685. Irish club, folk and country, current Irish sounds

THE RED LION
Chorley Road, Swinton. Regular jazz sessions

ST BRENDAN'S IRISH CENTRE
City Road, Old Trafford M15. Phone 061-872-2783. Regular Irish music. Call for details.

IRISH SOCIAL CENTRES AND ACTIVITIES

THE 32 CLUB
Higher Ardwick, Ardwick Green, Manchester. Phone 061-273-8832

COMHALTAS
O'Carolan's Branch, c/o Kevin Molloy, 4 Thedford Drive,
Crumpsall, M8 7NW.
St Wilfrid's Branch, c/o Pascal Madden, 31 Russet Road M9 3DL

CONRADH NA GAEILGE
Contact Liam Mac Lochlainn, 764 Windmill Lane, Denton M34 2FR. Phone 061-223-5539. Regular Irish language classes in Manchester.

COUNCIL OF IRISH COUNTIES ASSOCIATION
Seventeen Irish County groups in Greater Manchester. Contact Chairman Pat McKnight, 195 Lightbowne Road, Moston M10. Phone 061-682-4977.

THE FIANNA PHÁDRAIG PIPE BAND
Contact Terry Dowling, 1 Brayford Road, Woodhouse Park M22 6NS. Phone 061-437-5972

IRISH EDUCATION GROUP
Contact Joe Flynn, 16 Cranmer Road M20 0AW. Meets regularly at Cheetham Hill Irish Centre

THE PALACE SOCIAL CLUB
Farm Side Place, Levenshulme M19. Phone 061-257-3538

ST ALPHONSUS CLUB
Ayres Rd, Old Trafford M16. Phone 061-226-1259

ST EDWARD'S PARISH CENTRE
Thurloe Street M14. Phone 061-224-2589

ST JOSEPH'S CLUB
Plymouth Grove M13. Phone 061-224-2720

ST MALACHY'S CÉILI BAND
Contact Seán Dempsey, 9 Rossendale Avenue, Newton Heath M9 1FQ.
Phone 061-205-4197.

THE WYTHENSHAWE SOCIAL CENTRE
Brownley Road, Wythenshawe, Manchester. Regular Irish traditional music and Irish language classes. The Wythenshawe Irish Society has a full programme of social events. For more information contact Terry Dowling, 061-437-5972.

DANCING SCHOOLS

There are many Irish dancing schools in Manchester. Here are two of them:

EILEEN LALLY SCHOOL OF DANCING
The Irish Association Club, 17 High Lane, Chorlton M21. Phone 061-881-2824

MARY WALSH SCHOOL OF DANCING
Contact St Bernadette's Parish Centre, Princess Road, Princess Parkway, Withington M20. Phone 061-445-7911

DRAMA

THE AISLING PLAYERS
Regularly put on productions in Manchester's Irish Centres. Contact them at the *Irish World Heritage Centre*, Cheetham Hill. Phone 061-205-4007

THE IRISH IN MANCHESTER HISTORY GROUP
Give regular public talks, courses and workshops. New members welcome. For more information, contact Michael Herbert, 218 Maine Road, Moss Side M14 7WQ

THE IRISH WORLD HERITAGE CENTRE
Cheetham Hill. Open seven nights a week and activities include Irish dancing classes, judo, keep fit, pipe bands, drama, pool, darts and GAA sporting activities. Open since 1986, the centre has further development plans: a museum, library, craft workshops and a lecture theatre. Phone 061-205-4007

SPORT

GAA ACTIVITIES

There is a great choice of GAA sporting activities in Greater Manchester. For details on all GAA clubs and fixtures contact Paddy Johnstone, Chairman, *Lancashire County Board*, 7 Arnesbury Avenue, Sale, Manchester. Phone 061-973-9063 or St Brendan's Centre, Old Trafford. Phone 061-872-2783

SPECTATOR SPORTS

Cricket
LANCASHIRE COUNTY CRICKET CLUB
Old Trafford, Manchester. Phone 061-872-0261/872-5533

Football Clubs

MANCHESTER CITY FC
Maine Road, Manchester. Phone 061-226-1191. Ticket office: phone 061-226-2224

MANCHESTER UNITED FC
Old Trafford, Manchester. Phone 061-872-0261. Match, ticket information: Phone 061-872-7771

OLDHAM ATHLETIC FC
Boundary Park, Oldham. Phone 061-624-4972

Rugby League
OLDHAM RLFC
Watersheddings, Oldham. Phone 061-624-0368

SALFORD RLFC
The Willows, Weaste, Salford. Phone 061-736-6564

SPORTS FACILITIES

Cycling
BRITISH CYCLING FEDERATION,
c/o K Braddock, 3 Fownhope Road, Sale, Cheshire. Phone 061-962-1612

Football (Amateur)
MANCHESTER COUNTY FOOTBALL ASSOCIATION
(Sec Fred Brocklehurst) Brantingham Road, Chorlton M21. Phone 061-881-0299

Sports Centres
ABRAHAM MOSS LEISURE CENTRE
Crescent Road, Crumpsall, Manchester. Phone 061-740-1491/795-7277

ARDWICK SPORTS CENTRE
Hyde Rd, Ardwick, Manchester. Phone 061-273-6920

CHORLTON SQUASH COURTS
Manchester Road, Chorlton, Manchester. Phone 061-881-2130

FORUM SPORTS CENTRE
Leningrad Square, Manchester. Phone 061-437-8211/437-8367

LEES STREET RECREATION CENTRE

Openshaw, Manchester. Phone 061-231-2546

MOSS SIDE LEISURE CENTRE
Moss Side District Centre, Moss Lane East, Manchester. Phone 061-226-5016

Squash/Tennis
The Northern Lawn Tennis Club is one of the biggest squash and tennis clubs in Manchester. For details of clubs and facilities write to the club at *Palatine Road* M20. Phone 061-445-3093.

Swimming Pools
BANK MEADOW NEIGHBOURHOOD POOL
Lime Bank Street, Bradford, Manchester. Phone 061-273-4675

BROADWAY BATHS
Broadway, New Moston, M10. Phone 061-681-1060

CHORLTON BATHS
Manchester Road, Manchester. Phone 061-881-2130

HARPURHEY BATHS AND WEIGHT TRAINING ROOM
Rochdale Road, Manchester. Phone 061-205-2013

LEVENSHULME BATHS
Barlow Road, Levenshulme, Manchester. Phone 061-224-4370

VICTORIA BATHS
Heathersage Road, Manchester. Phone 061-224-4241

WITHINGTON POOL AND FITNESS CENTRE
Burton Road, Manchester. Phone 061-445-1046

MUSEUMS AND ART GALLERIES

Place	*Phone*	*Open*	*Collections*
BOLTON MUSEUM AND ART GALLERY Le Mans Crescent, Bolton	0204-22311	Mon, Tues, Thurs, Fri 9.30am-5.30pm Sat 10am-5pm	Everything from quilt weaving collections to natural history, geology and art.
CHETHAM LIBRARY Long Millgate, Manchester	061-834-9644	Mon-Fri 9.30am-12.30pm, 1.30pm-4.30pm	Founded in 1653, first free public library in Europe. Holds over 100,000 books and manuscripts
CITY ART GALLERY Mosley Street, M2	061-236-9422/ 236-5284	Mon-Sat 10am-5pm. Sun 2pm-5.30pm	Features works from 16th century onwards. Flemish, Italian, Dutch, English painters, also ceramics, silver, enamel displays

CORNERHOUSE Oxford Street, Manchester 1	061-228-2463	Tues-Sun noon-8.00pm	Broad range of works and theme exhibitions
THE JOHN RYLANDS LIBRARY Deansgate, Manchester	061-834-5343	Mon-Fri 10.00am-5.30pm	Rare books and manuscripts; collection of medieval jewelled bindings; facilities for specialists in Egyptology, archaeology etc.
MANCHESTER MUSEUM The University, Oxford Road	061-275-2634	Mon-Sat 10.00am-5.00pm	Botany, Egyptology, geology, zoology sections; aquarium. Huge range of collections
MANCHESTER UNITED MUSEUM Warrick Road North, Old Trafford, Manchester	061-872-1661	Daily (except Sat) 10.00am-4.00pm	Football fans' haven
OLDHAM ART GALLERY Union Street, Oldham	061-678-4653	Mon, Wed, Fri 10am-5pm Tues 10am-1pm. Sat 10am-4pm	Features Constable, Turner, local painters and pre-Raphaelite works
PANKHURST CENTRE 60-62 Nelson Street, M13	061-273-5673	Mon-Fri 10.00am-3.00pm Sat 2.00pm-5.00pm	Georgian house where women's social and political union was formed in 1903. Displays and exhibitions
PORTICE GALLERY AND LIBRARY Mosley Street, M2	061-236-6785	Mon-Fri 9.30am-4pm	Regular book exhibitions, art
SALFORD ART GALLERY Peel Park, The Crescent, Salford 5	061-736-2649	Mon-Fri 10am-4.45pm Sun 2.00pm-5.00pm	Largest collection of works by L.S. Lowry, and other exhibitions

OUTINGS

LYME PARK – is a 1,300 acre country park. Gardens, nature trails, countryside centre.

STOCKPORT MARKET – dates back 700 years. Part of the market is housed in a Victorian glass market hall.

TAMESIDE LEISURE PARK – features pool, beach area and water attractions. Within the leisure park complex is Even Fields stadium, home of Hyde United

Football Club.

TOMMYFIELD MARKET – in Oldham is a traditional northwest market (over 300 traders).

TOURIST TRAIL – Take a Granada TV Studios tour (experience Coronation St) Bookings phone 061-833-0880

TRAFFORD WATER SPORTS CENTRE – overlooks forty-five acres of water in Sale Water Park. Watersport facilities. Restaurant.

TRAVEL

BUS AND TRAIN INFORMATION SERVICES

Greater Manchester Passenger Transport Executive provides information about bus routes, local train times, fares etc. Write to PO Box 429, 9 Portland Street, Piccadilly Gardens M60 1HX. Phone 061-273-3322. Their enquiry office is open 7 days a week from 8am-8pm. Phone 061-273-5341.

BRITISH RAIL NETWORK NORTHWEST – For train timetables phone 061-832-8353

CITY BUSES – Enquiries (open 7 days a week from 6am-midnight) 061-627-5660, ext 15

GREATER MANCHESTER BUSES – (open 24 hours, 7 days a week). Enquiries 061-273-5341

MANCHESTER AIRPORT – Phone 061-489-3000

MAYNES BUSES – (24-hours) 061-223-2035, also office 061-223-8111

TAXIS

Taxi ranks at entrance points to Manchester railway, bus stations, airport and key areas in city centre and surrounding towns. Two Manchester City Taxi services:

Mantax Taxis 061-236-5133

Taxiphone Services Ltd 061-236-2322

You'll find more taxi telephone numbers in the yellow pages.

TRAVEL HOME

THE IRISH WORLD HERITAGE CENTRE, 10 Queen's Road, Cheetham Hill M8 8UQ, has a travel shop. Phone 061-205-4007, ask for Catherine.

CURRY TRAVEL SERVICES, 139 Wilbraham Road, Fallowfield M14 7DS. Phone 061-225-1133, is another Irish travel centre

TOURIST INFORMATION CENTRE, Manchester: Phone 061-234-3157

Shaun McCarthy: Tales from The Hotel Trade

The Midland Crowne Plaza Hotel in Manchester is one of the finest hotels in the north-west of England. Its general manager Dubliner Shaun McCarthy trained in Cathal Brugha Street College here and served his time in hotels around Dublin. Then Shaun went to London in the early sixties to seek wider experience in the hotel industry. His ambition was to get into the management side of the business.

I was seventeen-and-a-half and I thought I was very organised because I had a job with accommodation lined up and a couple of friends already in London. So off I went, with £32 in my pocket, very optimistic about the whole prospect of working in London.

I arrived at the club on Pall Mall, where I was due to start work and nobody knew who the heck I was. The person who had set me up with the job wasn't there and everyone else denied any knowledge of the arrangement. And of course, I didn't have anything in writing to show that I was promised work. So I didn't have a job and I didn't have accommodation and the shock to me was considerable.

London seemed like bedlam to me, compared to Dublin, and I didn't know my way around anywhere. Eventually I was directed to some cheap bed-and-breakfast places in Victoria. I would stay a night or two in one and then if I didn't like it, I'd move on again to another. And I went around the city looking for work in hotels.

I got lots of half promises at various hotels: 'We've nothing for you now, but come back Friday if you haven't got fixed up by then,' … that kind of thing. This went on for about three weeks and the best hope of work I got was in a small hotel just off Leicester Square, where the chef was Irish and was sympathetic when he heard my story.

He hadn't a vacancy in the kitchens at the time, but he told me to come back again at the end of the week and to my relief, when I did return, he said 'Right. You start on Monday.' I went in as a grill chef and it was a very busy hotel with about fifteen chefs employed there.

Then I found some digs in Victoria, so at least I had a base and a job and I was getting paid – thirteen pounds a week. The first room I rented cost me thirty-two-and-six a week, shared with another guy and the kitchen was half the size of a telephone box. But all I cared about essentially was having somewhere to put my suitcase and to know that when I finished work at night, I had somewhere to go back to.

I was happy just to be working and I had a small circle of friends, which helps to get you over the first couple of months in the city. But after a while, I wanted to do something else in the catering business and perhaps try to get into management. So I applied to various big companies, asking to go on their hotel management schemes and eventually I was taken on by Grand Metropolitan Hotels, who owned places like The Mayfair, The Piccadilly and The Washington.

It was great to get work with a big group like this and I stayed with the chain for about seven years, working in different hotels, in every department from kitchens to reception. It was the old-style practical kind of training. They didn't go in much for management theory and customer-psychology; you simply worked and asked questions later. I was never told what hours I would be working per week. You were simply given to understand that the job is the job and you do it! It was good experience.

After this, I did a year's stint back in Dublin at The Clarence as assistant manager, which I enjoyed, but then I got a major offer from The Trusthouse Forte Group to work for them in Sheffield and it was too good an opportunity to turn down. I stayed with Trusthouse Forte through till the eighties and in that time I worked in places like Leeds, Stoke-On-Trent, Liverpool and Swansea. I was happy enough in England. I was having a good time and I was always treated very well.

I'd never come across any kind of personal discrimination.

But at the same time, I never saw myself actually settling in England. I'd always had this notion at the back of my mind that I was going to go back to live in Ireland. My wife Beth liked the idea as well, but although we were definite in our own minds that we would go back, we had four children by then. The youngest was one and the eldest boy was about twelve.

So it was a big decision in the sense that the children had already been through several different school systems in different parts of England. We had to consider the fact that coming back to Ireland would mean yet another move in schools for them. Over the years, I got a number of offers from hotels in Ireland, but as a Dubliner, I was only really interested in coming back if the job was in my home city.

In the early eighties, Shaun was offered the position of general manager of a major hotel in Dublin and he accepted the offer, returning with the family after more than twelve years in England.

We were definitely coming back for good. It was great to be home and I loved everything about Dublin and I loved getting back into the swing of things in the city again. I liked the hotel and I liked the people working in it, but the job itself was very difficult.

The hotel was going through a tough period of cost cutting, with consequent job losses and after two years of overseeing this programme, Shaun felt it was time to move on. At the same time, he wanted to remain in Dublin, rather than return to Britain.

Having made the decision two years earlier to come back to Ireland, I thought, well I can't really uproot all the family and go back again to Britain. So I tried to see if I could set up on my own in the hotel business in Dublin.

I talked to various people in the hotel business and looked at ways of raising the money. But the whole process took too long and, generally speaking, things were quite poor in the hotel business at the time. So I decided, well this is it, I owe it to myself and I owe it to my family to find another post. So I went back to Britain. I took the first job I was offered, in a Liverpool hotel.

It was probably the only time that I made a career move without taking everything into consideration and making sure I felt it was absolutely the right decision. I wasn't particularly concerned about status. I was fortunate to be offered a job with the old company I'd worked for but in a smaller hotel than I'd previously managed for them. This didn't worry me because I looked on it as a move that gave me a base within the business again and allowed me bring the family back.

Since coming back it's worked out very well. I got the different moves within the business that I wanted and now, as general manager of The Crowne Plaza, I've got the kind of job I always wanted.

I've been connected with this hotel now for five years and I get enormous satisfaction from the job because I have total autonomy in my work, which is a very happy situation. It's a Holiday Inn Hotel but it's run as an entirely separate unit. I have to handle everything, and I think that one of the reasons I've been so happy here is the fact you get a free hand, you are allowed to manage independently.

Good management is obviously to do with balancing budgets and efficient organisation but it's mostly about people. You are dealing with staff on one hand, and customers on the other, and if you can make both sides happy, then you will have good service, which is the basis of a well-run hotel. This sounds easy, but actually it's quite hard to achieve!

I'm very happy in my work and I'm happy to be in Manchester. People in the North of England are more basic, easier to relate to than those in the south, generally speaking. They have no airs and graces and they are straightforward in their dealings. I have a lot of English as well as Irish friends here now.

I think if I hadn't gone back to Ireland when I did, I would have always had that feeling of wanting to return. I think I would have had periods of indecision about where I was going and what I was doing. The fact that I did give it a go at least helped get the wondering out of the way. I don't have the same obsession to go back now. There have been other offers from Dublin since I returned to Britain and the possibility is still in my mind. But unless something very radical in the way of a work-offer came up, I don't think I would go back to Ireland now.

That said, I most certainly always have been and always will be Irish. I love Ireland and I hate to hear anyone run it down in any way. And even after all this time, I can still feel homesick. I go back for holidays and it can take weeks after returning to Britain to get over the homesickness. I feel this damn longing all the time. There is always the pull, the yearning for anything Irish.

CHAPTER 6

Leeds and Bradford

Buskers in Leeds.

When Charles Dickens visited Leeds, he decided that 'You must like it very much or not at all.' And on our programme trips to Leeds (and neighbouring Bradford), we've liked it very much indeed.

Set in the industrial heart of West Yorkshire, bound by Bradford, Halifax, Huddersfield and Wakefield, Leeds developed into an important commercial centre with the arrival of the Leeds and Liverpool Canal and the growth of the textile industry. Manufacturing made the city great, and fabrics, footwear and engineering are still the mainstays of local employment. But as in Bradford, the once-great wool town, an increasing number of jobs today are centred on the service industry.

Leeds has a population of over 700,000 (Bradford 450,000) and its strategic location, combined with good road and rail connections and the Leeds/Bradford airport, is bringing increasing business from the southeast. The Department of Social Security has decided to locate its headquarters in Leeds. Midland Bank's new phone-banking operation is based here. Natwest and Barclays have their electronic banking offices in the city, and stg£100 million pounds worth of development is underway in Leeds today – solid brass-tactics that are part of the city's ongoing battle with its neighbours for the title 'Capital of the North'.

But Leeds and Bradford aren't just commercial centres. The area also includes the Pennine countryside, the Brontë landscapes and the Yorkshire dales. Both cities are university bases. Leeds has the third largest university in Britain and Bradford university, chartered in 1966, is housed in modern buildings near the city centre.

The whole area has growing cultural attractions: Leeds is the home of Opera North and the new stg£13 million West Yorkshire Playhouse. Bradford has The National Museum of Film and Photography and The Alhambra Theatre for drama and dance.

Then there are the Yorkshire folk, forthright but friendly, with a solid underlay of Irish-style wit and warmth, which isn't really surprising because Irish people have been settling in West Yorkshire since the mid-1800s. The local Irish community in the 1850s was almost 19,000. Today, it's estimated that there are 31,000 Irish people in the Leeds/Bradford area, most of these hailing from the western counties of Donegal, Mayo, Sligo, Galway, Clare and Kerry.

The focus for the thriving Irish social scene in Leeds is the Irish Centre on York Road, which offers everything from music to sporting and cultural activities. Bradford also has a range of Irish cultural groups and is currently fundraising for its own Irish centre.

EMPLOYMENT

The employment scene in Leeds is broadbased, ranging from manufacturing to the rapidly growing service sector. There are jobs in financial and legal services, computers, engineering, hotels and restaurants, sales, construction, secretarial services and tourism.

Unemployment in the Leeds area has come down from 7.7 per cent at the end of 1988 to 6.5 per cent today (1990).

Bradford's unemployment rate has fallen substantially and now stands at 7.1 per cent of the workforce. Here the jobs are mainly in distribution and other services, the hotel industry, the financial and business areas and manufacturing. There has been a shift from fulltime to part-time jobs, but most of these jobs are poorly paid, particularly in the service sector industries, such as retail and tourism.

The job scene in both Leeds and Bradford is extremely competitive and according to Derry-born Steven Warke, of Blue Arrow Personnel Services in Leeds, companies are looking for personality as well as skills. It's also important to present a good image and show lots of enthusiasm for the job!

FINDING A JOB: WHERE TO LOOK

*Local newspapers are *The Yorkshire Post* (daily) and *The Evening Post*. Bradford's daily newspaper is *The Telegraph and Argus*. There is also a free weekly paper, *The Bradford Star*. The 'What's On' magazine *Leeds' Other Paper* carries a small vacancies section.

*Check with Leeds Irish Centre for local job possibilities.

*Check with job centres and employment agencies in Leeds and Bradford.

EMPLOYMENT AGENCIES

There are over 200 employment agencies in the Leeds/Bradford area and you'll find a full list in the *Thomson Local Directory*. Here are a number of agencies, to get you started.

SECRETARIAL AND RELATED

ALFRED MARKS
4 Albion Place, Leeds 1. Phone 0532-448771. Full-time and temp work. Sec, legal, clerical. Open Mon-Thurs 9am-5.30pm, Fri 9am-6pm.

BERTRAM PERSONNEL GROUP
104 Briggate, Leeds 1. Phone 0532-442201. Full-time and temp work. Sec, executive jobs in sales and computers. Open Mon-Fri 9am-5.30pm.

BLUE ARROW PERSONNEL SERVICES
18 Park Row, Leeds LS1 5JA. Phone 0532-420066. Full-time and part-time work. Sec, WP, clerical, VDU, accounts etc. Open Mon-Fri 8am-6pm.

BROOK STREET
18a Market Street, Bradford BD1 1LH. Phone 0274-733721/736664. Temporary and full-time work. Sec, accounts, clerical. Open Mon-Fri 8am-6pm.

JOBS GALORE
2nd Floor, Arndale House, Charles Street, Bradford BD1 1EJ. Phone 0274-307220. Sec, clerical, financial work. Full-time, temp work. Open Mon-Fri 9am-5.30pm. (Call first for appointment.)

MANPOWER
73 Albion Street, Leeds 1. Phone 0532-424330. Sec, VDU work, reception work etc. Open Mon-Fri 9am-5.30pm.

SALES, CONSTRUCTION, ENGINEERS, INDUSTRIAL

BROOK STREET INDUSTRIAL
3rd Floor, 17 Albion Place, Leeds 1. Phone 0532-445191. Engineering, ware-

house, catering work. Open Mon-Fri 8am-6pm.

HMS RECRUITMENT
Suite 103, County House, Vicar Lane, Leeds LS1 7JH. Phone 0532-459361.
Short-term contracts and full-time work. Sales, construction, engineers. Open
Mon-Fri 8.30am-6pm.

HMS RECRUITMENT
4th Floor, Arndale House, Charles Street, Bradford 1. Phone 0274-723703.
Engineering and sales (senior appointments). Open Mon-Sat 9am-5.30pm.

ACCOUNTANCY

ACCOUNTEMPS
Gresham House, 7 St Paul's Street, Leeds LS1 2JG. Phone 0532-428978.
Clerks, accountants, temp work. Open Mon-Fri 9am-5.30pm. (Call for appointment.)

ACCOUNTANCY, FINANCIAL

PER (PROFESSIONAL EXECUTIVE RECRUITMENT)
Oak House, Park Lane, Leeds LS3 1EL. Phone 0532-445131. Professional,
managerial, technical recruitment. Open Mon-Fri 9am-5pm.

REED ACCOUNTANCY
12 Park Place, Leeds LS1 2RU. Phone 0532-459181. Open Mon-Fri 9am-
5.30pm.

COMPUTER STAFF

SAMPSON STAFF
Munro House, Duke Street, Leeds LS9 BAG. Phone 0532-468376. Open Mon-
Fri 9am-5pm.

HOTEL AND CATERING

CHRISTIE CATERING AGENCY
131 Cardigan Road, Leeds 6. Phone 0532-782244. Temp, permanent, freel-
ance work. Open Mon-Fri 9am-5pm.

LEGAL

DANIEL BATES PARTNERSHIP
Joseph's Well, Hanover Park, Leeds LS3 1AB. Phone 0532-461671. Open
Mon-Fri 9am-5.30pm.

NURSING

BNA (BRITISH NURSING ASSOCIATION)
Vasalli House, 20 Central Road, Leeds LS1 6DE. Phone 0532-445962.

TEACHING JOBS

There are several hundred schools in the Leeds and Bradford areas.
To enquire about vacancies, write to

Leeds
THE DIRECTOR OF EDUCATION
Leeds City Council, Selectapost 17, Merrion House, 110 Merrion Centre,

Leeds LS2 8DR.

Bradford
EDUCATION PERSONNEL
Second Floor, Provincial House, Bradford, BD1 1NP.

COUNCIL JOBS: GENERAL

Leeds and Bradford councils are big local employers. To check vacancies, you can write to the above addresses, marking it 'Council Personnel'.

JOB CENTRES

For job vacancies, advice about training schemes etc

Leeds
COMMERCIAL AND INDUSTRIAL JOB CENTRE
Fairfax House, Merrion Street LSU 8JU. Phone 0532-446181.

Bradford
PROVINCIAL HOUSE
Bradford 1. Phone 0274-392831.

CAREERS OFFICES

Information and advice on careers and training schemes

Leeds
CAREERS OFFICE
Leeds City Council, Selectapost 18, 7th Floor East, Merrion House, 110 Merrion Centre LS2 8JN. Phone 0532-463876.

Bradford
BRADFORD CAREERS OFFICE
40 Piccadilly, Bradford 1. Phone 0274-752326.

BENEFITS

If you haven't been able to find work and you have no money to live on, or if your income is too low to survive on, then you should go to your local unemployment benefit office (UBO) and claim income support. See Ch 3, 'London', p.78 for details of signing on.

UNEMPLOYMENT BENEFIT OFFICES (UBO)

Leeds
For those with surnames in the A-RED category, go to UBO, 35 Eastgate LS2 7RE. Phone 0532-440171.

For those with surnames in the REE to Z category, go to UBO, New York Road LS2 7PL. Phone 0532-440171.

Bradford
For those with surnames in the A to K category, go to 63 Vicar Lane, Bradford 1. Phone 0274-729520.

For those with surnames in the L–Z category, go to UBO, Clifford Street.
Phone 0274-729520.

SOCIAL SECURITY OFFICES

To apply for income support and other benefits
Leeds
LEEDS EAST OFFICE
Southern House, 529 York Road LS9 6TF. Phone 0532-406611.

LEEDS NORTH OFFICE
Hume House, Tower House Street LS2 8NT. Phone 0532-434533.

LEEDS SOUTH OFFICE
72 Merrion Street LS2 8LR. Phone 0532-459121.

LEEDS WEST OFFICE
Century House, Church Lane, Pudsey LS28 7RQ. Phone Pudsey 562201.

LEEDS NORTHWEST
21-22 Park Place LS1 2SL. Phone 0532-431791.

Bradford

If your postal district is 5, 6, 7, 11, 12, 13 or 14, go to Law Russell House,
Vicar Lane, Bradford 1. Phone 0274-394533.

If you live in postal districts 1, 8, 9, 15, 17 or 18, go to Westfield House, Manningham Lane, Bradford. Phone 0274-733355.

If you live in districts 2, 3, 4, or 10, go to The Leeds Road Office, Leeds
Road, Bradford. Phone 0274-308666.

HOUSING BENEFIT

You may also be able to get housing benefit.

In Leeds, housing benefit is dealt with at *The Housing Benefit
Department,* Dudley House, Albion Street LS2 8PN.

In Bradford, housing benefit is dealt with at *Britannia House,* Hall
Ings BD1 1HX.

You may also be entitled to a number of other benefits (See Ch 3
'London' p.76 for details of these.) You can ask about this at *Leeds
Irish Centre,* York Road. Open 10am-10pm daily. Phone 0532-
480887/480613.

Or contact *Leeds Central CAB*, Westminster Buildings, 31 New
York Street, Leeds 2. Open Mon-Fri 9.30am-3.30pm, Thurs noon-
6.15pm. Phone 0532-457679. Also supply details of other
Citizens' Advice Bureau branches in the Leeds area.

Bradford CAB, Thorpe Chambers, 12a Ivegate, Bradford. Phone
0274-725325. Open Mon, Thurs, Fri 10am-3pm, Tues, Wed
10am-noon.

ACCOMMODATION

Like Manchester, Leeds is a big commercial centre and the demand for rented accommodation is high, so you'll need to allow yourself a month or so to find yourself long-term accommodation there. And although Bradford is a much smaller city, remember that it is also a university base and that students take up many of the low-cost flats and bedsits. So organise yourself some temporary accommodation in Leeds or Bradford to tide you over until you find your own flat or bedsit.

TEMPORARY ACCOMMODATION: ADVANCE

RELATIVES

If you've any relations in Leeds or Bradford, check if they'll put you up for a few weeks, until you find your own place.

THE IRISH CENTRE

Write in advance to Tom McLoughlin, manager of the *Irish Centre,* York Road, Leeds LS9 9NT, West Yorkshire. He may know of lodgings in the local Irish community.

UNIVERSITY ACCOMMODATION

During university vacation time, you may be able to get temporary accommodation in Leeds or Bradford universities. They cater mostly for family or group bookings, in self-contained flats, or in B&B type accommodation.

Leeds University B&B prices are stg£14.95 (plus VAT). Write to *Bodington Hall,* Otley Road, Leeds LS16 5PT. Phone 0532-672521

The self-contained units (3/4 rooms), are stg£155 per week (Spring 1990 prices). Write to *Leeds University Commercial Office,* LS2 9JT. Phone 0532-336100

Bradford University prices for a single study bedroom B&B are stg£13.50 per night. Write to The Conference Officer, *University of Bradford,* Bradford BD7 1DP, West Yorkshire. Phone 0274-733466

HOSTEL ACCOMMODATION

YWCA
22 Lovell Park Hill, Leeds LS7. Phone 0532-457840. Cost (single room) stg£5.36 per night, plus 50p membership.

YWCA
St Ann's Lodge, St Ann's Lane, Leeds LS4. Phone 0532-758864. Cost (single room) stg£5.36 per night (stg£25 per week). Self catering.

Both hostels take male and female guests. Very popular accommodation. There is a waiting list. Call to check vacancies.

ACCOMMODATION: RENTING A FLAT, A BEDSIT, A HOUSE

Bedsits can be stg£120 per month and higher.
A two-bedroomed modern flat – stg£330 per month
Three bedroomed semi-detached – stg£350 per month (average)

Prices in Bradford can be cheaper, but it depends on the location.

WHERE TO LOOK

In Leeds, two useful agencies that give housing advice and information are

FIRST STOP
23 New York Street, Market Buildings LS2 7DT. Advises young people (twenty-five years or under) on housing problems and gives information on finding a place to live. Phone 0532-425123. Open Mon, Wed, Fri 10am-3pm; Tues, Thurs 1pm-6pm; Sat 10am-1pm. (First Stop has lists of landlords, landladies.)

HOUSING INFORMATION CENTRE
7/8 Market Buildings, Vicar Lane LS2 7JE. Phone 0532-462236. Council-run, for people of all ages. Open Mon-Fri 9am-5pm. (Gives lists of estate agents, housing associations and societies and general advice.)

In Bradford, the council has a Housing Information Centre in City Hall. For more information call 0274-753965.

*Check the local papers for accommodation columns: *The Yorkshire Post* and *The Evening Post,* Bradford's *Telegraph and Argus*, *The Bradford Star* and the *Leeds' Other Paper*.

*If you are seeking accommodation through commercial agencies, remember that you shouldn't pay a fee until the agency has found you a place.

*Get advice before signing tenancy agreements (from First Stop or the Housing Information Centre).

*What to look for when flatseeking: see advice on p50, Ch 3

HOUSING ASSOCIATIONS

Housing associations are non-profit-making organisations which let property at reasonable rates. There are over twenty Housing Associations in the Leeds area.

LEEDS HOUSING INFORMATION CENTRE
7/8 Market Buildings, Vicar Lanes LS2 7JE. Phone 0532-462236. This centre has a directory of housing association schemes and can advise on which schemes would suit your needs.

BRADFORD AND NORTHERN HOUSING ASSOCIATION
Butterfield House, Otley Road, Baildon, Shipley, West Riding, Yorkshire BD17 7HF. Phone 0274-588840. This association can advise you about properties in the area. There is a waiting list in Bradford at present and any property that may be available is likely to be one and two-bedroomed flats, rather than larger family accommodation.

COUNCIL HOUSING

Council housing is very hard to get anywhere in Britain, and Leeds and Bradford are no exceptions. There are long waiting lists and the 'local connection' ruling applies. (See 'Manchester' Ch 5, p.111.) But apply to the council anyway, because if you are on the council waiting list, it could help you get a place from a housing association (application forms from the Housing Information Centre or your local housing office). You can get advice on your case from the *First Stop Centre* in Leeds (Phone 0532-425123) and from the *Catholic Housing Aid Centre* in Bradford, St Patrick's Centre, Sedgefield Terrace, Westgate, Bradford 1. Phone 0274-726790/731909. Open Mon-Fri 9.30am-1.30pm, Mon, Tues 1.30pm-3.30pm, Evenings Tues and Thurs 7pm-8.30pm.

ACCOMMODATION: BUYING A HOUSE OR FLAT

Leeds' house prices are reckoned to be less expensive than Manchester's but it depends where you buy. North Leeds is pricier than South Leeds. A three-bedroomed semi has an average asking price of stg£49,000. A two-bedroomed flat (city centre) can cost from stg£60,000.

In Bradford a three-bedroomed semi ranges up from stg£45,000 and a two-bedroomed flat can be stg£30,000+.

Keep in mind what we say (p.54) about making sure you can afford mortgage repayments and seek advice before you enter the buyers' market. The Leeds and Bradford newspapers carry property pages. You'll find lists of estate agents in the phone book. *Leeds City Council Housing Advice Centre* also has lists of estate agents. Phone 0532-462236.

ACCOMMODATION PROBLEMS: WHO CAN HELP

If you are having problems with your present accommodation (bad conditions, difficulties with the landlord) or your short-term let has come to an end and you have nowhere to stay, then contact one of these groups for help and advice:

LEEDS ADVICE CENTRES

FIRST STOP
23 New York Street, Market Buildings LS2 7DT. Phone 0532-425123.

HOUSING INFORMATION CENTRE
7/8 Market Buildings, Vicar Lane LS2 7JE. Phone 0532-426236.

THE IRISH CENTRE
York Road, Manager Tom McLoughlin. Phone 0532-480887, or 0532-480613.

LEEDS: HOSTEL ACCOMMODATION FOR HOMELESS

Leeds has a range of accommodation for people with different housing needs. Here are some of them:

LEEDS HOUSING CONCERN
Young Persons Project, 236 Dewsbury Road LS11 6ER. Phone 0532-778833. Housing is usually single rooms in group homes.
Leeds Housing Concern also has a hostel for homeless single women over twenty-one years. Ask for details from First Stop. Phone 0532-425123.

LEEDS HOUSING CONCERN
Garforth House, 118 Domestic Street, Holbeck LS11 9SG. Sixteen-bed hostel, caters for men over twenty-one only. Phone 0532-440910.

THE SALVATION ARMY
Hostel for single women and women with children. Referrals through housing welfare (details from advice centres).

WOMEN'S AID
(PO Box 89, Wellington Street Post Office, Leeds 1) has hostel accommodation for women escaping violence. Details from above address, First Stop or any advice centre.

EMERGENCY HOSTELS (MALE)

(For eighteen-year-olds and over)
The hostels listed below offer basic accommodation only. Young people are not encouraged to use them, except in emergency circumstances.

DSS RESETTLEMENT UNIT
181 Whitehall Road LS12 6JQ. Phone 0532-458091. Very basic facilities.

SALVATION ARMY HOSTEL
36 Lisbon Street, Leeds LS1 4NA. Phone 0532-453436. Dormitory-type hostel accommodation.

BRADFORD AREA: CENTRES AND HOSTELS

CATHOLIC HOUSING AID CENTRE
St Patrick's Centre, Sedgefield Terrace, Westgate, Bradford 1. Phone 0274-726790 or 731909.

CITY CENTRE PROJECT
First Floor, St Patrick's Centre, Sedgefield Terrace, Westgate, Bradford 1.

Phone 0274-736507. City Centre Project caters for young homeless (16-25 years). Advice and hostel accommodation (very limited space). Opening hours Mon 1.30pm-6pm, Wed 9.30am-12.30pm, 4pm-6pm; Fri 9.30am-12.30pm.

KEY HOUSE
Keighley (about 10 miles outside Bradford), 15 Devonshire Street, Keighley, West Yorkshire. Phone 0535-600890. Advice centre plus hostel accommodation (limited space), male and female 17-25 years. Open Mon, Tues, Wed, Fri 9.30am-4pm, Thurs 2pm-6pm.

If you are homeless and have no money at all, contact any of the above listed advice centres in Leeds or Bradford. They will be able to tell you what kind of council help or other assistance may be available. They will also try to find you some kind of emergency accommodation.

Leeds' and Bradford's Citizens' Advice Bureaux can also advise you about benefits you may be entitled to, legal problems, landlord/tenant difficulties, consumer complaints etc. The service is free and confidential. (Phone number and address of main CAB office on p.63 – they can tell you where your nearest CAB is located.)

ADVICE AND INFORMATION SERVICES: GENERAL

BRADFORD INFORMATION CENTRE
City Hall, Bradford. Phone 0274-754042. Deals with queries about council services, local organisations etc.

COMMUNITY HEALTH COUNCILS
Leeds Western CHC. Phone 0532-457461
Leeds Eastern CHC. Phone 0532-439998.

COMMUNITY RELATIONS COUNCIL
Leeds. Phone 0532-430696/0.

FAMILY CARELINE
Phone 0532-456456. Mon-Fri 9am-9.30pm (counselling).

GINGERBREAD (SINGLE PARENTS) LEEDS
Westminster Buildings, New York Street LS2. Phone 0532-459580. Open Mon, Tues, Thurs, Fri 10am-2pm.

GINGERBREAD (BRADFORD)
45 Darley Street. Phone 0274-720564.

LEEDS' TRAVELLERS' SUPPORT GROUP
c/o Community Relations Council, Centenary House, North Street, Leeds 2.

LEGAL ADVICE
Harehills & Chapeltown Law Centre, 128 Roundhay Road LS8 5NA. Phone 0532-491100. (Bradford and Leeds central CABs also give legal advice.)

THE LINK CENTRE
7 Southbrook Terrace, Bradford. Phone 0274-309909. Open Mon-Fri 1pm-5pm, Sat 10am-1pm. (Counselling, support service).

SOCIAL SECURITY FREELINE SOCIAL SECURITY
Phone 0800-666555.

WOMEN: ADVICE AND HELP SERVICES

BRADFORD WOMEN'S HEALTH GROUP
c/o The Centre Against Unemployment, 108 Sunbridge Road.
Phone 0274-723304, 24-hour Ansaphone 0274-480022.

CATHOLIC SOCIAL WELFARE SOCIETY
31 Moor Road, Headingley, Leeds LS6 4BG. Phone 0532-787500.
(Pregnancy counselling and adoption agency).

EO BRADFORD
Via Bradford Information Centre. Phone 0274-754042.

EQUAL OPPORTUNITIES
Civic Hall, Leeds. Phone 0532-463000.

LEEDS RAPE CRISIS
Phone 0532-440058 (Leeds); Phone 0274-308274 (Bradford).

LEEDS WOMEN'S AID
Phone 0532-460401. Provides emergency accommodation, help.

LEEDS WOMEN'S CENTRE
229 Woodhouse Lane LS2 9LF. Phone 0532-421232. Information on health,
benefits, housing etc. Mon-Fri 11am-3pm.

WELL-WOMEN CLINICS
Advice and information about women's health. A number of clinics in the
Leeds area. For details phone 0532-781341.

WOMEN'S COUNSELLING AND THERAPY SERVICE
Oxford Place, Leeds 1. Phone 0532-455725.

WOMEN'S HEALTH MATTERS DROP-IN ADVICE CENTRES
Three locations in Leeds. *Main office*: Voluntary Action Leeds. 229 Woodhouse Lane, Leeds 2. Phone 0532-421734. Open daily. Phone before calling
in.

WOMEN TOGETHER SUPPORT GROUP (BRADFORD)
Phone 0274-577571/651652. For women afraid of violence at home.

GAY SERVICES

BRADFORD GAY SWITCHBOARD
Phone 0274-722206. Tues, Thurs, Fri, Sat 7pm-9pm.

BRADFORD LESBIAN LINE
Phone 0274-305525. Thurs 7pm-9pm (24 hour Ansaphone).

GAY SWITCHBOARD
0532-453588 (Leeds). Call 7.30pm-9.30pm, all nights except Tues.

HUDDERSFIELD GAY SWITCHBOARD
Phone Huddersfield 538070. Sun 6pm-9pm.

LEEDS LESBIAN LINE
Phone 0532-453588. Tues 7.30pm-9.30pm.

YORK LESBIAN LINE
Phone 0904-646812. Fri 7pm-9pm (24 hour Ansaphone).

CRISIS HELPLINES

DRUGS

THE BRIDGE PROJECT
Bradford Independent Drug Guidance, Equity Chambers, 40 Piccadilly, Bradford BD1 3NN. Phone 0274-723863 (24 hours).
Free advice service: Open Mon-Thurs 10am-5pm, Fri 10am-4.30pm.

TURNING POINT, LEEDS DRUGLINE
229 Woodhouse Lane LS2 9LF. Phone 0532-423182.
Free confidential service: advice, information and help with drug problems.
Open Mon, Tues, Thurs, Fri 10am-6pm; Wed 10am-10pm.

WADDILOVES DRUG DEPENDENCY UNIT,
44 Queen's Road, Bradford BD8 7BT. Phone 0274-547272 (office hours)
0274-497121 (24 hour line). Advice, information and treatment facilities for a
range of substance misuse problems. Self-referrals accepted.

WORKS EXCHANGE
Phone 0532-456618. Confidential information on where to obtain clean needles/syringes.

ALCOHOL PROBLEMS

ALANON
Friends and relatives of problem drinkers. Phone 0532-672887.

ALCOHOLICS ANONYMOUS (AA)
Phone 0532-454567 7pm-10pm. Other times phone 0532-456789.

LEEDS ADDICTION UNIT
40 Clarendon Road L29PJ. Phone 0532-456617. Advice, information for
those with alcohol and drug problems.

SAMARITANS BRADFORD
Phone 0274-547547.

SAMARITANS LEEDS
Phone 0532-456789 (for lonely or suicidal).

SEXUALLY TRANSMITTED DISEASES

BODY POSITIVE
Phone 0532-444209. Tues evenings 7pm-9pm. Self-help support for people
who are HIV positive.

BRADFORD STD CLINIC
St Luke's Hospital, Little Horton Lane, Bradford. Phone 0274-734744.
Mon-Fri 10am-11.45am; evenings (except Wed) 4.30pm-6.15pm.

LEEDS AIDS ADVICE
PO Box No 172 LS6 1DT. Phone 0532-444209. Mon, Wed, Thurs, Fri 7pm-
9pm or 0532-423204 office hours.

NATIONAL AIDS HELPLINES
Phone 0800-567123 (to talk to an advisor). National AIDS Helpline is free
and confidential.

PENNINE AIDSLINK, BRADFORD
Phone 0274-732939 (Mon-Fri 7.30pm-9.30pm).

THE SPECIAL CLINIC
Leeds General Infirmary, Blundell Street L1. Phone 0532-432799. Women
ext 2446, Men ext 3279. *Confidential Clinic:* separate services for males and
females. Open Mon-Fri 9.30am-noon.

HEALTH MATTERS

DOCTORS

To register with a doctor, go to the surgery and ask to be placed on
the GPs list of NHS patients. You fill in a form at the surgery for your
medical card or you can get one from the *Family Practitioner Committee*.

Leeds

FAMILY PRACTITIONER COMMITTEE
Aeu House, Bridge Street LS2 7RB. Phone 0532-450271.

Bradford
FAMILY PRACTITIONER COMMITTEE
Joseph Brennan House, Sunbridge Road, Bradford BD1 2SY. Phone
0274-724575. The FPCs can give you a list of doctors in your area.

HOSPITALS

If you need emergency treatment

Leeds
LEEDS GENERAL INFIRMARY
Great George Street L1. Phone 0532-432799.

ST JAMES'S HOSPITAL
Beckett Street, L9. Phone 0532-433144.

24-hour accident and emergency.

Bradford
BRADFORD ROYAL INFIRMARY
Duckworth Lane, Bradford 9. Phone 0274-542200.

PRESCRIPTIONS

You may be able to get free prescriptions if:
* Your income is low
* You are between sixteen and nineteen years and in full-time
education
* You are pregnant (and for one month after the birth)
* You are on family credit or income support.

If you feel that you are in any of these categories, check with an advice
centre about applying for free prescriptions.

LATE NIGHT CHEMISTS

Leeds
BOOTS CHEMISTS
19 Albion Arcade, Bond Street Centre. Phone 0532-433551. Open Mon-Sat 9am-9pm, Sun 2pm-6pm.

Bradford
'THE CHEMIST'
Hall Ings, Bradford also Boots Chemist, Darley Street, Bradford 1.

DENTISTS

WOODSLEY ROAD HEALTH CENTRE
Woodsley Road, Leeds 6. Phone 0532-444526. (For emergency treatment on Sundays and Bank Holidays open 9am-noon).

BRADFORD EMERGENCY DENTAL CLINIC
Bradford Royal Infirmary. Sun am.

EDUCATION

There are several hundred schools in the Leeds/Bradford area. You can get up-to-date information on Leeds schools from: *Selectapost 17,* Merrion House, 110 Merrion Centre LS2 8DR.

For information on schools in Bradford write to *Bradford Metropolitan Council,* Provincial House, Education Department, Bradford BD1 HNP.

For pre-school information on Leeds, contact the *Pre-School Playgroups Association* (regional office). Phone 0532-522848.

For pre-school information on Bradford, contact *Bradford Parent and Toddlers Association,* 19-25 Sunbridge Road, Bradford BD1 2AY. Phone 0274-308725.

HIGHER EDUCATION

BRADFORD AND ILKLEY COLLEGE OF FURTHER AND HIGHER EDUCATION
Great Horton Road, Bradford BD7 1AY. Phone 0274-753026.

BRADFORD UNIVERSITY
Great Horton Road, Bradford, West Yorkshire BD7 1DP. Phone 0274-733466. Engineering, natural and applied sciences and social sciences.

CITY OF LEEDS COLLEGE OF MUSIC
Cookridge Street LS2 8BH. Phone 0532-452069.

JACOB KRAMER COLLEGE (ART, CRAFTS & DESIGN)
Vernon Street, Leeds. Phone 0532-439931.

KITSON COLLEGE OF TECHNOLOGY (scientific/engineering)
Cookridge Street, Leeds 2. Phone 0532-430381.

LEEDS COLLEGE OF BUILDING
North Street L2. Phone 0532-430765.

LEEDS POLYTECHNIC
Calverly Street LS1 3HE. Phone 0532-462903/4. Three sites. Architecture, computing, engineering etc.

LEEDS UNIVERSITY
University Road LS2 9JT. Phone 0532-431751. Large civic university, sited just north of city centre. Wide range of subjects (the largest number of arts combinations in any university). Very good libraries and computing facilities.

THOMAS DANBY COLLEGE
(catering/community Services), Roundhay Road, Leeds 7.
Phone 0532-494912.

ADULT EDUCATION:
CLASSES AND COURSES

There is a vast choice of courses and classes in the Leeds/Bradford area, based in colleges, community centres and schools. You can choose your own course, practical or academic, part-time or full-time. Short courses are run regularly throughout the year, so you don't have to wait until the autumn to enrol.

To find out what's on offer, where the classes and courses are and how much they cost, contact Leeds Education Advice Service for Adults at *Education Advice for Adults*, Bramley Community Centre, Waterloo Lane, Bramley LS13 2JB. Phone 0532-556231. Open Mon and Wed 9am-noon, Thurs 9am-2.45pm. At other times phone 0532-560664. (Also has information on other education advice centres in Leeds.)

Bradford: *EASA (Education Advice Service for Adults)* at Central Library, Prince's Way, Bradford BD1 1NN.
Phone 0274-753657/8.

THE OPEN UNIVERSITY

Contact *The Regional Enquiry Service*, Fairfax House, Merrion Street, Leeds LS2 8JU. Phone 0532-444431.

TIME OFF AND THINGS TO DO

West Yorkshire is currently undergoing the kind of cultural rebirth that proves that there's much more to the region than brass bands and the Brontës. Spring 1990 saw the opening of the £13 million West Yorkshire Playhouse in Leeds. Opera North is also based in the city at The Grand Theatre with The English Northern Philharmonia and Leeds also has The City Varieties and The Civic Theatre.

Bradford's National Museum of Film and Photography sponsors its own theatre company and The Alhambra Theatre caters for touring theatre and dance companies. The National Theatre is planning to site its regional base behind The Alhambra.

Both cities boast a range of museums, art galleries, classical, jazz and popular music venues, parks, shopping centres, over half a dozen local markets and a wide choice of sport and leisure facilities.

You can get information on most activities from the local tourist centres.

Leeds
MUNICIPAL BUILDINGS
Calverley Street. Phone 0532-462454.

Bradford
TOURIST CENTRE
City Hall, Channing Way. Phone 0274-753682.

The local newspapers also carry listings of arts events and the weekly magazine *Leeds' Other Paper* features a full 'What's On' section. If your newsagent doesn't stock it, you'll find it at 52 Call Lane, Leeds LS1 6DT. Phone 0532-440069.

MUSIC: POP, ROCK, TRAD AND ALL THAT JAZZ

Breeding ground for bands like The Mission, The Wedding Present and Red Lorry, Yellow Lorry – Leeds' and Bradford's popular music scene is barely a beat behind Manchester. A wide range of rock, jazz and folk bands play regular dates in the following venues:

THE ADELPHI
1 Hunslet Road (off Leeds Bridge), Leeds 10. Phone 0532-456377.
Regular modern jazz sessions.

THE ASTORIA
Roundhay Road, Leeds 8. Phone 0532-490362/490914.
Varied: From Alias Ron Kavana to The Astoria All-Star Jazz Band!

BRADFORD QUEEN'S HALL
Morley Street, Bradford 1. Phone 0274-392712. (Rock and pop).

BRADFORD UNIVERSITY UNION
Great Horton Road. Phone 0274-734135. (Varied sounds).

THE DUCHESS OF YORK
Vicar Lane, Leeds. Phone 0532-453929. Popular venue, featuring current hot rock bands, some alternative cabaret nights.

THE DUCK AND DRAKE
Kirkgate, Leeds. Phone 0532-465806. Rock/blues.

THE GLOBE
Meanwood Road, Leeds 7. Phone 0532-624173. Weekends: Irish music.

IRISH CENTRE
York Road. Big music venue. Irish country/showbands weekends, but also features broad range of music during the week, from jazz sounds to contemporary Irish bands. For details contact Chris at *The Irish Centre*, York Road,

Leeds 9. Phone 0532-480887.

LEEDS POLYTECHNIC
Calverley Street, Leeds 2. Phone 0532-430171. Up and coming acts, varied programme.

LEEDS UNIVERSITY UNION
Woodhouse Lane, Leeds 2. Phone 0532-439071. Music ranges from young rock acts to today's established bands.

NEW ROSCOE
New Bristol Street, Leeds 7. Phone 0532-460778. Run by Dubliner Noel Squire, there are regular Irish music sessions and the juke box plays sounds from back home. The last time we dropped in, Noel served up green beer!

THE ROYAL PARK
Queen's Road, Leeds 6. Phone 0532-757494. Right royal rock (and roll!). Very popular venue.

ST GEORGE'S HALL
Bradford. Phone 0274-752376. Rock and folk gigs.

THE WHITE STAG
North Street, Leeds 7. Phone 0532-451069. Irish traditional music sessions, Sun lunch, Mon and Tues nights.

IRISH MUSIC GROUPS AND OTHER ACTIVITIES

Leeds Comhaltas: The Leeds Comhaltas branch is booming, with over 200 members and a good programme of regular events. There is a Tuesday night session at the Irish Centre, York Road. A céili is held every second Sunday of the month and there are music classes at the centre on Saturday afternoons. For more details, contact Comhaltas Sec Mary Gallagher, phone 0532-650456 (6pm-9pm) or call Irish Centre 0532-480887.

Bradford Comhaltas: Regular céilis and sessions, plus weekly Irish classes. For details contact the branch PRO Betty Ring, 1 Clubhouse Croft, Horbury, Wakefield WF 5NB West Yorkshire.

Irish Music Association – Bradford : Meets every Saturday night in the Yorkshire Riders Social Club and holds sessions and céilis in various venues. For information on all activities contact (Sec) Beryl Cassidy, 5 Harewood Grove, Heckmondwicke, West Yorkshire. Phone 0924-408600.

Bradford Irish Education Group: The group promotes the Irish perspective in local schools, organises seminars, annual conferences and fosters Irish language courses and classes. For details of their activities, contact Press Officer Joe Sheeran, c/o Carlton Bolling College, Undercliffe Lane, Bradford BD3 0DU. Phone 0274-633111.

SPORT

GAA ACTIVITIES

There are six local GAA teams, two senior and four minor. For details on all fixtures and activities, contact (Sec) Eddie Hosty, GAA Yorkshire County Board. Phone 0532-700428.

Cricket

The County and International Test ground at Headingley has at least three major county matches and a test match each season. For details contact:

YORKSHIRE COUNTY CRICKET CLUB
Headingley Cricket Ground. Phone 0532-787394.

Football

LEEDS UNITED FOOTBALL CLUB
Elland Road. Phone 0532-716037.

Golf

IRISH GOLF SOCIETY
Contact The Irish Centre for full details, Phone 0532-480887.

Over twenty golf courses in the Leeds/Bradford Area. Details on 0532-827426.

Rugby

Yorkshire has three professional league clubs and four senior union teams.

LEEDS RUGBY LEAGUE
St Michael's Lane, Headingley. Phone 0532-786181.

RUGBY UNION (HEADINGLEY CLUB)
Bridge Road, Kirkstall. Phone 0532-755029.

SPORTS AND LEISURE CENTRES

ARMLEY LEISURE CENTRE
Carr Crofts, Armley, Leeds 12. Phone 0532-795858.

CARLTON BOLLING SPORTS CENTRE
Undercliffe Lane, Bradford 3. Phone 0274-634846.

FEARNVILLE SPORTS CENTRE
Oakwood Lane, Leeds 8. Phone 0532-402233.

GRANGE SPORTS CENTRE
Haycliffe Lane, Bradford 5. Phone 0274-572923.

HOLT PARK SPORTS CENTRE
Holt Road, Leeds 16. Phone 0532-679033.

KIRKSTALL LEISURE CENTRE
Kirkstall Lane, Leeds 5. Phone 0532-786878.

MANNINGHAM SPORTS CENTRE
Carlisle Road, Bradford 8. Phone 0274-494927.

RICHARD DUNNE SPORTS CENTRE
Rooley Avenue, Bradford 6. Phone 0274-307847.

SCOTT HALL SPORTS CENTRE
Scott Hall Road, Leeds 7. Phone 0532-624721.

SOUTH LEEDS SPORTS CENTRE
Beeston Road, Leeds 11. Phone 0532-457549.

Most of the above centres have swimming pools, squash, aerobics etc. For more information and a full list of all sporting and recreational activities, contact *Leeds Leisure Services Information*, phone 0532-443713.

Bradford Leisure Activities: Call *Bradford Information Centre*, phone 0274-754042 or contact *Bradford Tourist Office*, phone 0274-753678.

THE GREAT OUTDOORS

The Leeds Outdoor Pursuits Centre (about nine miles northwest of the city) offers tuition in a wide range of activities, including sailing, orienteering, climbing, walking. For full details phone 0532-503616 or visit *The Leeds Outdoor Pursuits Centre,* Yeadon, Leeds 19.

MUSEUMS AND ART GALLERIES

Place	*Phone*	*Times*	*Collections*
ABBEY HOUSE MUSEUM Abbey Road, Kirkstall	0532-755821	Mon-Sat 10am-6pm, Sun2pm-6pm	Major folk museum, with reconstructed Victorian streets and shops. Visit also 12th century Kirkstall Abbey
ARMLEY MILLS INDUSTRIAL MUSEUM Canal Road, Leeds	0532-637861	Daily except Mon	Traces Leeds' industrial history. Demonstrations of sewing, spinning and tailoring. 1920s Armley Palace Picture hall shows early movies
CARTRIGHT HALL Lister Park, Bradford	0274-493313	Daily except Mon 10am-6pm	Includes prints by Bradford-born artist David Hockney set in Lister Park which contains botanical gardens
INDUSTRIAL MUSEUM Moorside Road, Bradford	0274-631756	Tues-Sun 10am-5pm	Victorian mill displaying machinery and workings of woollen industry. Regular exhibitions
LEEDS CITY ART GALLERY The Headrow, Leeds	0532-462495	Mon-Fri 10am-6pm, Sat 10am-4pm, Sun 2pm- 5pm	Old masters and modern works. Adjoining Henry Moore sculpture gallery.

LEEDS CITY MUSEUM Calverley Street, Leeds	0532-462465	Tues-Sat	Man-made artifacts and natural history
NATIONAL MUSEUM OF PHOTOGRAPHY, FILM & TELEVISION Prince's View, Bradford	0274-727488	Tues-Sun 10.30am-6pm	A treasure trove for visual fans. Includes largest cinema screen projector in the country
THE UNIVERSITY GALLERY Parkinson Building, Woodhouse Lane, Leeds	0532-431751	Mon-Fri 10am-5pm Free admission	Modern European works, ceramics, photography

THEATRES

THE ALHAMBRA THEATRE
Morley Street, Bradford 7. Phone 0274-752000.
Touring companies, dance and theatre, as well as local shows.

BRADFORD PLAYHOUSE
Chapel Street, Bradford 1. Phone 0274-720329.
Film showings, plus regular local theatre productions.

THE CITY VARIETIES MUSIC HALL
The Headrow, Leeds 1. Phone 0532-430808.
Movie stars like Charlie Chaplin, Laurel and Hardy appeared here in the early days. It was also home to the 'Good Old Days' TV show.

THE CIVIC THEATRE
Cookridge Street, Leeds 2. Phone 0532-462453.
Amateur and professional productions, dance, concerts etc.

LEEDS GRAND THEATRE AND OPERA HOUSE
New Briggate, Leeds 1. Phone 0532-459351.
The home of Opera North, the Grand also stages plays, concerts, musicals etc.

THE NORTHERN SCHOOL OF CONTEMPORARY DANCE
Chapeltown Road, Leeds 7. Phone 0532-625359.
Excellent performance venue. Full-time courses and community dance programme.

THEATRE-IN-THE-MILL
Shearbridge Road, Bradford. Phone 0274-393801.
Local and touring theatre, workshops etc.

THEATRE-IN-THE-POLY
Calverly Street, Leeds 2. Phone 0532-430171.
Touring and local productions as well as students' drama.

THE WEST YORKSHIRE PLAYHOUSE
Quarry Hill Mount, Leeds LS9 8AW. For details of current productions phone 0532-442111. Contains a 750-seat auditorium, plus a 350-seat courtyard theatre, a 100-seat studio/rehearsal room and a cabaret space in the restaurant.

YORKSHIRE DANCE CENTRE
St Peter's Buildings, St Peter's Square, Leeds 9. Phone 0532-426066.

Courses and classes in every dance form. Home to the Phoenix Dance Co.
Open every day.

OUTINGS

The Brontë Parsonage, Haworth, Keighley, West Yorkshire BD22
8DR. Phone 0535-42323. Once the home of the Brontë family, this
small Georgian parsonage eight miles west of Bradford contains
drawings, letters, manuscripts of the Brontë sisters. The parsonage is
open almost all year round.

Lotherton Hall (near Aberford, northeast of Leeds). Elegant Edwardian country house, with displays of oriental pottery, modern ceramics,
furniture etc. The adjoining bird garden is one of the largest of its kind
in Britain. Open all year Tues-Sun 10.30am-6pm. Phone 0532-
813529.

Temple Newsam House, about six miles southeast of Leeds. This
Tudor/Jacobean house stands in 900 acres of parkland. Now a museum, the collections include Chippendale furniture, sculpture, paintings and silver. Open Tues to Sun 10.30am-6.15pm. The parkland
incorporates Home Farm, which has a rare breeds centre. For details
phone 0532-647321 (house) 0532-645535 (parkland).

Roundhay Park, a major events park, with attractions ranging from
woodland to cultivated gardens; paddle boats, golf, tennis, bowling
and more. Tropical house and aquarium. For more details call 0532-
661850.

MARKETS

For almost 600 years, since 1488, Leeds has been a market and
shopping centre, with the famous Monday Cloth Market on the
parapets of Leeds bridge. And Leeds is the city where Mr Marks set
up his original 'Penny Bazaar' which evolved into the High Street
Marks and Spencer stores.

KIRKGATE MARKET, Leeds, boasts numerous food stalls and fruit stalls, bargains in bric-a-brac and clothes, cafés and bakeries serving rib-sticking Yorkshire puds and pies! Open six days a week

Try the following too:

BRADFORD MARKET open Fri, Sat.

DEWSBURY MARKET Wed and Sat

GARFORTH MARKET Sat

LEEDS OPEN MARKET held Tues, Fri, Sat, with a fleamarket on Thursdays.

HALIFAX Market Fri, Sat

YEADON Mon, Fri

SHOPPING AND TOURIST INFORMATION

BOND STREET SHOPPING CENTRE INFORMATION POINT
Phone 0532-445701.

LEEDS TOURIST INFORMATION CENTRE
19 Wellington Street, Leeds 1. Phone 0532-462454.

BRADFORD TOURIST INFORMATION CENTRE
City Hall, Channing Way, Bradford. Phone 0274-753682.

TRANSPORT

BRITISH RAIL PASSENGER TRAIN ENQUIRIES
Leeds 0532-448133. *Bradford* 0274-733994.

METRO TRAVEL INFORMATION TELEPHONE ENQUIRIES
Phone *Leeds* 0532-457676. Phone *Bradford* 0274-732237.
Mon-Sat 8am-8pm, Sun 10am-8pm. (Free timetables on request).

METRO TRAVEL CENTRES
Open Mon-Fri 8.30am-5.30pm, Sat 9am-4.30pm. Closed Sundays and Bank
Holidays. There are centres at:

LEEDS CENTRAL BUS STATION , New York Street. Phone 0532-428888.

BRADFORD INTERCHANGE, Bridge Street, Bradford. Phone 0274-724839.

NATIONAL EXPRESS COACH SERVICE INFORMATION
Leeds 0532-460011.

AIRPORT

LEEDS BRADFORD AIRPORT
Yeadon LS19 7IZ (just under 9 miles from Leeds). Phone 0532-509696.

TAXIS

Taxi ranks at entrance points to bus and train stations, airport.

BLUE LINE TAXIS
59 Westfield Road, Leeds 3. Phone 0532-445566 or 0532-445052.
One of the Leeds' 24-hour firms.

Check the telephone directory for full list of local services.

CHAPTER 7

Liverpool

'Liverpool has such Celtic influences, from Ireland, Scotland and Wales and because of this, it has a different feeling to all the other cities in Britain. There's a great attitude in Liverpool to the arts, to music and telling stories and you have the same type of characters here as you have in Dublin. It's a very lively city, very warm. I've always felt very much at home here.'

Dublin Musician Shay Black

Liverpool means different things to different people. It's Soccer City to football followers. It's the Mersey sound for Beatles fans. It's Garden City to the greenfingered and to comedy fans it's the Scouse-dry wit of Alexi Sayle or Kenny Everett. For seafaring folk, it was the great sea port and trading centre of its time and for the millions of Irish who made their way to Merseyside since famine times, it was Ireland's other capital.

Merseyside, the product of the industrial revolution and sea-trade, has been hard hit in recent times, since the economic tide turned and shipping-related industries declined in importance. The population of Liverpool and the other Merseyside boroughs of Sefton, Knowsley, St Helen's and Wirral is one-and-a-half million and unemployment, at over 14 per cent, is the highest in the northwest region of Britain.

But the area is fighting back. There has been a revival of the city's waterfront, and the restoration of the Albert Dock complex, with its Maritime Museum, art gallery, restaurants and shops, has made it Britain's second most popular tourist attraction.

Other initiatives include the Wavertree Technology park (sixty-five acres of high technology industry), housing schemes and the international garden festival. There are plans for various construction projects around Merseyside, totalling more than £50 million.

Liverpool is also an academic centre, with over 22,000 students attending the city's university and polytechnic. And it has a thriving cultural life. There are half-a-dozen theatres, a wide range of art galleries and museums. It's the home of the Royal Liverpool Philharmonic Orchestra and more than thirty different groups are involved in dance, music, photography, sculpture and theatre.

Media groups in Liverpool include two city newspapers, *The Daily Post* and *The Liverpool Echo*, two TV stations and two radio stations. The city has also become a popular base for TV series and film-makers.

The Liverpool community, as Shay Black noted, has strong Celtic influences and most particularly an Irish influence. Scouse folk say that its high percentage of people with Irish origins should qualify Liverpool for the title 'Emerald of the East'!

An Irish community had already settled in the city before famine times, but it was since the 1840s that the Irish came to Liverpool in huge numbers. It is estimated that 500,000 arrived in the city between 1847 and 1851. Many thousands more followed in succeeding years and another great wave arrived between the 1940s and 1960s. In recent years, there has been a swing towards London as the main destination for Irish emigrants, and the number of Irish-born in Merseyside has declined: the figure is estimated at about 22,000 today.

However, there is still a tremendously strong Irish community spirit in Merseyside and a huge range of Irish social and cultural activities. The Irish Centre in Mount Pleasant, which celebrated its twenty-fifth anniversary in 1990, is the heart of community life, with dance nights (céili and modern), classes, seisiúns and other functions. It also has an Irish Community Care Group and acts as a base for GAA and soccer teams, for Comhaltas and pipe-band activities and an Irish Studies group. The Institute of Irish Studies in Liverpool University is the major centre for the development of Irish Studies in Britain and both the university and Liverpool Polytechnic have thriving Irish societies, with over 600 members between them.

EMPLOYMENT

The employment scene in Merseyside has been very poor and although there are signs of returning confidence in the job market, the picture is still fairly bleak. Redundancy figures for January to June 1989 show that 1,284 manufacturing jobs and 393 service industry jobs were lost and the overall unemployment figure for the area is 14.1 per cent and higher in some localities. Liverpool has the highest proportion of long-term unemployed in Britain, at 51.4 per cent (Regional Trends Survey, published 1990).

Recruitment agencies in Liverpool say that there are some job openings in the region, *but not for unskilled and inexperienced young people looking for casual or full-time work*. So if you are in this category, there is little point in trying Merseyside for work.The jobs simply aren't there.

However, according to the Liverpool Chamber of Commerce and recruitment agencies, there are some openings in the following areas for suitably skilled and qualified people: engineers, computer programmers, computer analysts and operators, fitters, welders, electricians, skilled production machinists etc. Tourism is Merseyside's fastest growing industry (almost twenty million people visit the area each year), and hotel and catering is a good source of work; but again, only if you have training and experience. Some secretarial and clerical work is also available, according to Manpower Agency in Liverpool, for those with good skills. There is also some demand for sales and marketing personnel and managers/administrators in a range of occupations. Going to a high unemployment area like Merseyside, (despite the work that may be available in your line of business) is always a risk and you need to think very carefully before you make a decision.

FINDING A JOB: WHERE TO LOOK

*Check the local newspapers. *The Daily Post* and *The Liverpool Echo* (Thurs for jobs), published by the same group: Liverpool

Daily Post and Echo Ltd, PO Box No 48, Old Hall Street, Liverpool L69 3EB. Phone 051-227-2000.

*Visit employment agencies and Job Centres in Liverpool.

EMPLOYMENT AGENCIES

ACCOUNTANCY PERSONNEL
16 Cook Street, Liverpool 2. Phone 051-236-3530.
Open Mon-Fri 9.15am-5.30pm.

ALFRED MARKS
Oriel Chambers, Water Street, Liverpool L2 8TD. Phone 051-227-3003.
Secretarial, technical, sales & insurance, accountants, engineers. Temp work in clerical/computer work/catering.
Open Mon-Fri 9am-5.30pm.

ASB RECRUITMENT LTD
Corn Exchange, 19 Brunswick Street, Liverpool 2. Phone 051-236-9373.
Accountancy, sales and marketing, engineering, part-time clerks financial positions. Open Mon-Fri 8.30am-6pm.

MANPOWER PLC
9th Floor, Concourse House, Lime Street, Liverpool 1. Phone 051-708-7828.
Mostly secretarial and related. Temporary and full-time work.
Open Mon-Fri 8.30am-5.30pm.

PER LTD (PROFESSIONAL & EXECUTIVE RECRUITMENT)
St Nicholas' House, Old Church Yard, Liverpool 2. Phone 051-236-2444.
Technical, sales, computer, engineering etc.
Open Mon-Fri 9am-5pm.

HOTEL WORK

Dubliner Dominic McVey, manager of St George's Hotel in Lime Street says that there are regular vacancies in Liverpool's hotel trade for receptionists, restaurant and bar staff with training and experience. Many hotel managers seek their staff from *The Williamson Square Job Centre,* 20 Williamson Square, Liverpool L1 1PW. Phone 051-708-5675.

JOB CENTRES

BELLE VALE
Unit 1, Belle Vale Shopping Centre, Liverpool L25 7AB.
Phone 051-498-4788.

BOOTLE
Stanley Road, Liverpool L20 3NP. Phone 051-933-8383.

CROSBY
117 South Road, Waterloo, Liverpool L22 0PN. Phone 051-920-7007.

EVERTON
Unit 1, The Mall Breck Road, Liverpool L5 6SS. Phone 051-260-4777.

GARSTON
Speke Road, Liverpool L19 9AB. Phone 051-494-9222.

LIVERPOOL (COMMERCIAL) JOB CENTRE
18/20 Lord Street, Liverpool 2 1TA. Phone 051-708-8455.

CAREERS OFFICE

You can get some information and advice on employment and training from *Liverpool Central Careers Office*, Merseyside House, South John Street, Liverpool L1 8BN. Phone 051-709-5400.

BENEFITS

If your job arrangements in Liverpool have somehow fallen through and you have no money to live on while you are looking for another job, or if your income is too low to survive on, then you should go to your Unemployment Benefit Office and claim Income Support. (See Ch 3, 'London', p.78 for details of signing on.)

LIVERPOOL UBO
1 Silkhouse Lane, Liverpool L2 2QE. Phone 051-227-2066.

For locations of other local UBOs contact above office.

Social Security Offices

STEERS HOUSE
Canning Place, Liverpool L1 8HS. Phone 051-709-0150. To apply for income support and other benefits. (For locations of other local DSS offices, contact above office.)

ACCOMMODATION

TEMPORARY

While you are looking for long-term accommodation in Liverpool, you'll need somewhere temporary to stay. Here are some low-priced options

CHRISTIAN ALLIANCE
Mildmay House, 6 Blackburne Place, Liverpool 8. Phone 051-709-1417.
Single rooms. Charge: stg£7 per night. Weekly rates from stg£23.00. Phone in advance to check vacancies (busy during college term times.)

LIVERPOOL YMCA
60 Mount Pleasant, Liverpool L3 5SH. Phone 051-709-9516.
Over eighteens, mixed hostel. Charge: stg£9 per night.
Phone or write in advance to check vacancies.

UNIVERSITY OF LIVERPOOL
Conference Office, Greenbank House, Greenbank Lane, Liverpool 17 1AG.
Phone 051-794-6440. Single rooms. Charge: stg£13 + VAT.
Accommodation during vacation times. Call or write to check vacancies.

YWCA
1a Rodney Street, Liverpool 1. Phone 051-709-7791.

Females over sixteen. Charge: stg£5.50 single room per night.
(Weekly rate works out cheaper.) Phone or write in advance to check vacancies.

RELATIVES

If you have relations in the Merseyside area, they may let you stay with them until you find your own place.

LIVERPOOL IRISH CENTRE

If you haven't any relatives living locally and there are no vacancies at the university or hostels, then you could check with the Irish Centre, Mount Pleasant. Manager Phil Farrelly or welfare workers Mavis O'Connor or Breege McDaid may know of lodgings within the Irish community.

Call or write in advance to *The Irish Centre*, 127 Mount Pleasant, Liverpool L3 5TG. Phone 051-709-4120.

ACCOMMODATION: RENTING A FLAT, A BEDSIT, A HOUSE

(Average prices)

Bedsit – from stg£80 per month
One-bedroomed flat – from stg£160 per month.
Two-bedroomed flat – from stg£200 per month.
Three-bedroomed semi-detached house – from stg£250 per month

WHERE TO LOOK

*Check the local newspapers, *The Daily Post* and *The Liverpool Echo*. Some Merseyside boroughs also have their own weekly paper.

ACCOMMODATION AGENCIES

Bailey & Neep is one city-centre agency. They have furnished and unfurnished flats and houses. They require one month's rent in advance, plus deposit. Contact them at 24 Mount Pleasant, Liverpool 3. Phone 051-708-5877.

You can get a list of landlords and agents with accommodation in Liverpool from '*The Basement*', Young Persons Advisory Service (YPAS). Phone 051-236-0871.

Ask at the YPAS for their 'HIPPOFAX' booklet. And remember! before signing tenancy agreements get advice from your local Citizens' Advice Bureau, or an advice agency like YPAS.

If you are seeking accommodation through the commercial agencies, you shouldn't pay a fee until the agency has actually found you a place.

HOUSING ASSOCIATIONS

Housing associations are non-profit making organisations which let property at reasonable rates. There are more than a dozen major housing associations in the Liverpool area.

One association, *Co-Operative Development Services Ltd* (CDS) also assists in the setting up of housing co-ops. CDS has 2,000 accommodation units for letting. For more details contact CDS Ltd, 39 Bold Street, Liverpool 1, phone 051-708-0674, *or* 19 Devonshire Road, Liverpool 8, phone 051-727-0707 *or* 102 Wellington Road, Liverpool 15. Phone 051-734-2224.

Young Person's Housing Association Ltd has 1,000 units of property. You'll find them at 1 Victoria Street, Liverpool 2, phone 051-227-3716. or 71 Upper Parliament Street, Liverpool 8, phone 051-709-0488.

Remember that housing associations make it a condition that you first register with the council for housing before they will consider your application. You should also apply to a number of housing associations, rather than just one.

COUNCIL HOUSING

Liverpool Council has a housing stock of 63,000 units: 46 per cent in flats and maisonettes and the remaining 34 per cent in houses and bungalows. There is a hefty waiting list but you should apply anyway, particularly if you are going to register with a housing association (see above). See Ch 2 p.52 for regulations on being accepted for council housing. *The Council Housing Department* is based at 43 Foster House, Canning Place, Liverpool 1. Phone 051-227-3911.

You can also get advice from your local Citizens' Advice Bureau on council housing regulations and a wide range of other areas, from legal problems to social security benefits. *Liverpool City CAB* is at 3rd Floor, Hepworth Chambers, 2 Church Street, Liverpool L1 3AA. Phone 051-709-8989. Open Mon-Fri 10am-3pm.

BUYING A HOUSE OR FLAT

Merseyside house prices range from stg£20,000 for a two-bedroomed terraced house in Liverpool 4 to stg£100,000 for a large semi-detached in Crosby. An average price for a three-bedroomed semi in Liverpool would be stg£50,000. A two-bedroomed flat in the Liverpool area ranges from stg£20,000 to stg£35,000 plus.

For more property information, write to *The Liverpool Echo* for its Thursday evening property edition, and to *The Daily Post* for its Saturday issue which contains a 'Property Post Homemaker' section. Both papers are published by the Liverpool Daily Post and Echo Ltd, PO Box No 48, Old Hall Street, Liverpool L69 3KB. Phone 051-227-2000.

Many estate agencies also have their own property newsheets. You'll get their addresses and phone numbers in the *Thomson Local Directory*.

ACCOMMODATION PROBLEMS: WHO CAN HELP

If you are having problems with your present accommodation (bad conditions, difficulties with the landlord), or if you have nowhere to stay, contact the following groups for information and help:

IRISH COMMUNITY CARE MERSEYSIDE
The Irish Centre, 127 Mount Pleasant, Liverpool L3 5TG. Phone 051-709-4120. Community care workers Breege McDaid and Mavis O'Connor give help and advice on benefits, social services, housing problems etc. They are at the centre Mon-Fri 10am-1pm (contactable through the centre after these hours for urgent matters, crisis situations).

LIVERPOOL COUNCIL SOCIAL SERVICES
26 Hatton Garden, Liverpool 3. Phone 051-227-3911.

HOUSING AID CENTRES

ANFIELD HOUSING AID CENTRE (FOR NORTH LIVERPOOL AREA)
115 Anfield Road, Liverpool 4. Phone 051-260-9855.

THE GRANBY HOUSING AID CENTRE (FOR SOUTH LIVERPOOL AREA)
101 Mulgrave Street, Liverpool 8. Phone 051-708-8746.

The Housing Aid Centres are open Mon, Tues, Wed, Fri 10am-4pm, Thurs 11am-6pm.

THE BASEMENT: YOUNG PERSONS' ADVISORY SERVICE
34a Stanley Street, Liverpool 1. Phone 051-236-0871. YPAS is a free and confidential counselling and information service for 16-26 year olds. Advises on wide range of issues from homelessness to careers, jobs, DSS problems, drugs, sexuality, legal matters etc. Open Mon-Thurs 11am-5pm; and Fri noon-4pm. (Answer-phone machine after usual opening hours).

YPAS also have a free 'HIPPOFAX', an advisory booklet containing up-to-date detailed information on flat seeking, DSS entitlements, landlord problems, local advice services etc.

LIVERPOOL COUNCIL FOR VOLUNTARY SERVICES

14 Castle Street, Liverpool L2 0NJ. Phone 051-236-7728.
Advice on housing, social services etc. Open Mon-Fri 9.30am-4.30pm.

WHITECHAPEL DAY CENTRE

Langsdale Street (off Swan Street), Liverpool 38. Phone 051-207-7617

Day-centre for over sixteen-year-olds. Advice on housing problems, benefits etc. Open Mon-Fri 9am-5pm (Sun also).

MERSEYSIDE ACCOMMODATION PROJECT (MAP)
Provides family accommodation for teenagers between the ages of sixteen and nineteen who, through no fault of their own, find themselves homeless. The teenagers must be referred by social service departments, probation offices or specialist youth work agencies. (MAP is part of Merseyside Council for Voluntary Services). Phone 051-709-0990.

GENERAL ADVICE AND INFORMATION SERVICES

CATHOLIC SOCIAL SERVICES
150 Brownlow Hill, Liverpool 3 5RF. Phone 051-708-0566.

COMMUNITY HEALTH COUNCIL
(Liverpool Central & Southern), 57/59 Whitechapel, Liverpool L1 6DX. Phone 051-236-1176.

COMMUNITY HEALTH SERVICE
Liverpool District Health Authority, Liverpool Clinic1 Myrtle Street, Liverpool L7 7DE. Phone 051-709-9290.

COMMUNITY RELATIONS
Merseyside CR Council, 64 Mount Pleasant, Liverpool L35SH. Phone 051-709-6858.

FAMILY ADVISORY CENTRE
Chatsworth Street, Liverpool 7. Phone 051-709-6664.

FAMILY PLANNING ASSOCIATION
104 Bold Street, Liverpool 1. Phone 051-709-1938.

GINGERBREAD
(Birkenhead), Family Centre, Brandon Street, Birkenhead. Phone 051-647-9333.

GINGERBREAD TRUST ADVICE CENTRE
9 Fleet Street, Liverpool 1. Phone 051-708-8848.

LIFE LINE PREGNANCY CARE SERVICE
Phone 051-708-9288.

LIVERPOOL RAPE CRISIS CENTRE
Phone 051-727-7599. Mon 7pm-9pm, Thurs and Sat 2pm-5pm.
24-hour answering service.

RELATE (MARRIAGE GUIDANCE) MERSEYSIDE
7 Copperas Hill, Liverpool 35LB.
Telephone for an appointment 051-709-2058.

SOCIAL SECURITY
Freephone Social Security Advice, phone 0800-666555.

TEENAGE ADVISORY CENTRE (NHS)
Abercromby Health Centre, Grove Street, Liverpool 7. Phone 051-708-9370.
Open Mon 5pm-7pm. Wide range of health services & GP referrals.
Community psychiatric nurse and health visitor. Confidential.
Not solely a service for teenagers; will see anyone needing advice and help.

WOMEN'S AID LIVERPOOL
Phone 051-727-1355.
For women seeking a refuge from physical/mental/sexual abuse

LEGAL ADVICE

LIVERPOOL 8 LAW CENTRE
34/36 Prince's Road, Liverpool L8 1TH. Phone 051-709-7222.

VAUXHALL LAW CENTRE
Silvester Street, Liverpool 5. Phone 051-207-2004.

GAY SERVICES

FRIEND MERSEYSIDE
Phone 051-708-9552. Daily from 7pm-10pm.
Phone 051-708-0234. Tues & Thurs 7pm-10pm (for women). A befriending,
counselling and advice service for gay people.

GAY SWITCHBOARD
(London) 071-837-7324 (24-hour service).

CRISIS HELPLINES

DRUGS

MERSEYSIDE DRUGS COUNCIL
25 Hope Street, Liverpool 1 9BU. Phone 051-708-6626.

SHADO FAMILY SUPPORT CENTRE
120 Stonebridge lane, Liverpool L11 9AZ. Phone 051-546-1141 or 546-6556.
Open Mon-Sun 9am-5pm. Self-help group for parents, friends, partners of
drug misusers.

ALCOHOLICS ANONYMOUS LIVERPOOL
Phone 051-263-8839.

MERSEYSIDE COUNCIL ON ALCOHOLISM
Phone 051-236-1372.

SAMARITANS
25 Clarence Street, Liverpool L3 5TN. Phone 051-708-8888 (24-hour service
for suicidal and despairing).

SEXUALLY TRANSMITTED DISEASES

Special Clinics
ROYAL LIVERPOOL HOSPITAL
Prescot Street, Liverpool. Phone 051-709-0141.
Check by phone for clinic hours & appointments.

THE WOMEN'S HOSPITAL
Catherine Street, Liverpool. Phone 051-709-5461.

AIDS
LIVERPOOL BODY POSITIVE GROUP
The Marylands Centre, Marylands Street, Liverpool 1 9BX.
Phone 051-709-3511.

MERSEYSIDE AIDS SUPPORT GROUP
PO Box 11, Liverpool L69 1SN. Phone 051-709-9000.
Mon, Wed, Fri 7pm-10pm. 24-hour answering service.

HEALTH MATTERS

DOCTORS

To register with a doctor, go to the surgery and ask to be placed on
the GPs list of patients. Fill in a form at the surgery for your medical
card, or you can get one from the Family Practitioner Committee. This
is located at *Refuge Assurance House*, Lord Street, Liverpool 2.
Phone 051-709- 5666.

The FPCs can give you a list of doctors in your area. You'll also
find a list in the *Thomson Local Directory*.

HOSPITALS

If you need emergency treatment, you can go to The Royal Liverpool
Hospital, Prescot Street, Liverpool 7. Phone 051-709-0141

PRESCRIPTIONS

You may be entitled to free prescriptions (see Ch 6 Leeds/Bradford
p.141 for conditions). Check with an advice centre on how to apply
if you think you qualify for this.

LATE NIGHT CHEMISTS

EM ESS CHEMIST LTD
68/70 London Road, Liverpool 3. Phone 051-709-5271. Open 9am-11pm,
seven days a week.

DENTISTS

LIVERPOOL DENTAL HOSPITAL
Pembroke Place, Liverpool 3. Open Mon-Fri 9am-5pm.

Check the *Thomson Local Directory* under dentists for weekend/emergency
services.

EDUCATION

Merseyside has a broad range of children's schools and colleges. You
can get brochures and general information on local authority schooling in Liverpool, from *The City Council Education Department*, 14
Sir Thomas Street, Liverpool 1. Phone 051-227-3911.

For information on independent schools in the area, write to *The
Independent Schools Information Service,* 56 Buckingham Gate,
London SW1E 6AG. Phone 071-630-8793/4.

Local playgroups and day nurseries are listed in the *Thomson
Local Directory*, but you can get information also from the *Pre-*

School Playgroups Association, 61/63 Kings Cross Road, London WC1X 9LL. Phone 071-833-0991.

HIGHER EDUCATION

Institute of Irish Studies (University of Liverpool): The IIS is a teaching and research institute, offering a broad range of degrees and courses including a three-year undergraduate programme. For further information, write to The Director, Institute of Irish Studies, University of Liverpool, PO Box 147, Liverpool L69 3BX. Phone 051-794-3831

Liverpool Institute of Higher Education, PO Box 6, Stand Park Road, Childwall, Liverpool L16 9JD. Phone 051-722-7331.

Liverpool Polytechnic: Art & design, construction, education & community studies, engineering humanities and social studies, law, social work, business, science. Contact Liverpool Polytechnic, Rodney House, 70 Mount Pleasant, Liverpool 3. Phone 051-207-3581.

.University of Liverpool: Large urban university on 85-acre site close to city centre. Broad range of subjects over seven faculties. Write to The University of Liverpool, PO Box 147, Liverpool L69 3BX. Phone 051-794-2000.

ADULT EDUCATION: CLASSES AND COURSES

You can find out about the range of adult education courses and classes available in Liverpool from Community Education, Administration, 14 Sir Thomas Street, Liverpool 1. Phone 051-236-5480, or from the Adult Education area offices.

North Area
PRIORITY COMPREHENSIVE SCHOOL
Breckside Park, Liverpool 6. Phone 051-263-2403.

ROSCOMMON ADULT CENTRE
Roscommon Street, Liverpool 5. Phone 051-207-0824.

Birkenhead
WIRRAL ADULT GUIDANCE SERVICE
63 Hamilton Square, Birkenhead. Phone 051-647-7000.

St Helen's
COMMUNITY HOTLINE
Room 204, St Helen's College, Water Street, St Helen's WA10 1PZ. Phone 0744-33766.

NURSE TRAINING INFORMATION

RECRUITMENT DEPARTMENT
Liverpool College of Nursing and Midwifery, Thomas Drive,
Liverpool 14 3LB.

EMPLOYMENT TRAINING IN HEALTH CARE
The Employment Training Centre in Liverpool offers a range of health care
courses. For details contact *The Recruitment and Placement Department*, ETC
Employment Training, South Sefton (Merseyside) Health Authority, Fazaker-
ley Hospital, Longmoor Lane, Liverpool L9 7AL. Phone 051-530-1466.

THE OPEN UNIVERSITY

To enquire about Open University courses in Liverpool, contact the
nearest regional centre, Manchester. Write to *Open University*, The
North West Region, Chorlton House, 70 Manchester Road, Chorlton-
Cum-Hardy, Manchester M21 1PQ. Phone 061-861-9823.

TIME OFF AND THINGS TO DO

Merseyside makes the most of its natural attractions, from its maritime heritage and its soccer teams, to the unique Mersey beat scene
of the sixties that produced the Beatles and a music style for a whole
generation of pop fans.

But of course the Scouse character has bred much more than the
Beatles and soccer stars. There are also the writers, the politicians,
the actors and the comedians. Liverpool is a strong 'personality' city
and Liverpudlians like to mix their cultural activities with good
entertainment events.

There are summer-time carnivals and parades, comedy festivals
and Beatles conventions, Aintree's Grand National for race goers,
garden and river festivals, arts centres and local markets, theatre
productions, exhibitions and a very broad range of music events.

To get information on most activities in Merseyside, call into the
Tourist Information Centre at *Atlantic Pavilion*, Albert Dock, Liver-
pool 3. Phone 051-708-8854. (Ask for the quarterly publication called
Mersey Wide which is a free events guide.)

Local newspapers also list arts and music activities and there is a
free 'What's On' paper, *Quiggins News*, which covers music and the
arts around Liverpool. You'll find it in music stores, The Albert Dock
and various arts venues. Or it can be obtained from the Quiggins News
Office, 12-16 School Lane, Liverpool 1. Phone 051-709-1051.

MUSIC: POP, ROCK, TRAD AND ALL THAT JAZZ

The sixties in Liverpool produced The Fab Four, The Pacemakers,
The Merseybeats, Cilla Black, and The Scaffold. Out of the seventies
came Elvis Costello, Frankie Goes to Hollywood, and the eighties

brought The Christians. Tipped for the nineties are bands like The Real People and The Preachers. But go along to the music venues and check out the up-and-coming bands for yourself.

MUSIC VENUES

THE CAVERN
Cavern Walks, Mathew Street, Liverpool 2. Phone 051-236-1964. This is not the actual club where the Beatles belted out their early songs (that closed in the late sixties) but a reconstruction job on the original site. Live bands on Mondays and Thursdays. Disco nights for the rest of the week. Danny the doorman says the new Cavern is as good as the old version – and we take his word for it. Open from early evening through to 2am.

THE CUMBERLAND TAVERN
18 Cumberland Street, Liverpool 1. Phone 051-236-0236.
Heavy rock Thurs nights and weekends.

FLANAGAN'S APPLE
18 Mathew Street, Liverpool 2. Phone 051-236-1214.
Irish music most nights

HARDMAN HOUSE HOTEL
15 Hardman Street, Liverpool 1. Phone 051-708-8303.
Mon nights: Irish folk. Sun & Tues nights: Jazz and blues

IRISH CENTRE
127 Mount Pleasant, Liverpool 3. Phone 051-709-4120.
Irish bands on weekend nights; regular Comhaltas sessions and supper céilis. Irish dancing classes Tues nights. (Call centre for monthly programme)

MA EGERTON'S
9 Pudsey Street, Liverpool 1. Phone 051-709-3621.
Weekends: Irish musice.

HARTLEY'S WINE BAR
Albert Dock, Liverpool.
Weekends live jazz sessions.

LIVERPOOL EMPIRE (THEATRE)
Lime Street, Liverpool 1. Phone 051-709-1555.
Varied music tastes catered for from opera to chart sounds.

LIVERPOOL POLYTECHNIC
The Haigh Buildings, Maryland Street, Liverpool 1. Phone 051-709-4047.
Regular gigs Tues, Thurs, Sat, Sun.

LIVERPOOL UNIVERSITY
2 Bedford Street North, Liverpool 7. Phone 051-794-4115.
Local bands. Thurs-Sun + disco nights.

KELLY'S WINE BAR
Smithdown Road, Liverpool 8. Regular Irish music sessions.

THE MAGAZINE
Magazine Road, New Brighton, Wirral, Liverpool.
Traditional music (singing more than instrumental).

THE NEWSTEAD
Smithdown Road, Liverpool 8. Thurs nights Irish music sessions.

PLANET X
19/23 Hanover Street, Liverpool 1. Phone 051-709-7995.
Wed-Sat nights alternative music for hard core new wavers.

THE ROYAL COURT (THEATRE)
Roe Street, Liverpool 1. Phone 051-709-4321.
Varied rock and pop.

THE SWAN
Wood Street, Liverpool 1. Mainly heavy metal music.

WILSON'S
Wood Street, Liverpool 1. Popular heavy metal music venue.

IRISH MUSIC GROUPS AND OTHER ACTIVITIES

COMHALTAS
Northern Regional Sec Margaret Nicholas, 225 City Road, St Helen's, Merseyside.

COMHALTAS
Liverpool Branch Sec Joan Hayden, c/o Liverpool Irish Centre, 127 Mount Pleasant, Liverpool L3 5TG. Phone 051-709-4120. Formed in '57, the Liverpool branch of Comhaltas is one of the most active in Britain. Traditional music and dancing classes at the Irish Centre. Music sessions on third Monday of each month.
Irish Dancing Classes at the centre take place every Tuesday evening and Saturday morning. Contact Maureen Bolger, c/o The Irish Centre.

IRISH STUDIES GROUP
Meets in the Irish Centre, every Tuesday evening. Contact Greg Quiery, c/o The Irish Centre.

LIVERPOOL CÉILI BAND
Supper céilis on the second Tuesday of each month. Details at the centre.

LIVERPOOL POLYTECHNIC IRISH SOCIETY
For details of activities contact James McVeigh. Phone 051-709-4047.

PIPE BAND
Practice and tuition at Liverpool Irish Centre, Monday nights.

UNIVERSITY OF LIVERPOOL IRISH SOCIETY
Contact Sec Catherine Sheran, or Soc President Max Tsu. Phone 051-794-2000.

SPORT

GAA ACTIVITIES

John Mitchel's Gaelic Football Club operates from The Irish Centre. Contact Chairman Chris Johnston, c/o The Centre.

Cricket
AIGBURTH CRICKET CLUB
Buckland Street, Liverpool 17. Phone 051-727-1665.

LIVERPOOL CRICKET CLUB
Aigburth Road, Liverpool 19. Phone 051-427-2930.

Football
EVERTON FOOTBALL CLUB
Goodison Park, Goodison Road, Liverpool 4. Phone 051-521-2020

LIVERPOOL FOOTBALL CLUB
Anfield Road, Liverpool 6. Phone 051-263-2361. (The club has a visitor centre museum. Call for details of times.)

Golf
Irish Centre Golf Society. Sec Dick Leahy c/o The Irish Centre

Golf Courses
ALLERTON GOLF COURSE
Allerton Road, Liverpool 18. Phone 051-428-7409.

Horse Racing
AINTREE RACECOURSE
(Home of the Grand National) Liverpool L9. Phone 051-523-2600..

LIVERPOOL MUNICIPAL GOLF COURSE
Ingoe Lane, Kirkby, Liverpool 32. Phone 051-546-5435.

Rugby
SEFTON RUGBY UNION FOOTBALL CLUB
Thornhead Lane, Liverpool 12. Phone 051-228-9092.

Soccer
Finn Harps Football Club, formed in '76, is a popular Merseyside team. For details of fixtures contact Irish Centre.

SPORTS AND LEISURE CENTRES

BOOTLE STADIUM
Maguire Avenue, Bootle. Phone 051-523-4212.

CROXTETH SPORTS CENTRE
Altcross Road, Liverpool 11. Phone 051-548-3421.

EVERTON SPORTS CENTRE
Great Homer Street, Liverpool. Phone 051-207-1921.

LODGE LANE RECREATION CENTRE
Lodge Lane, Liverpool 8. Phone 051-709-3148.

PARK ROAD RECREATION CENTRE
Steble Street, Toxteth. Phone 051-709-9050/5395.

QUEEN'S DRIVE RECREATION CENTRE
Queen's Drive, County Road. L4. Phone 051-525-3563.

WALTON SPORTS CENTRE
Walton Hall Avenue, Liverpool 4. Phone 051-523-3472.

LIVERPOOL WATERSPORTS CENTRE
Phone 051-207-4026. Tuition in sailing, canoeing, windsurfing etc
Phone for further details of activities.

MUSEUMS AND GALLERIES

Place	Phone	Times	Collections
BLUECOAT GALLERY Bluecoat Chambers, School Lane, Liverpool 1.	051-709-5689	Tues-Sat 10.30am-5.30pm	Modern artists , also holds etching and life classes.
BLUECOAT DISPLAY CENTRE Address as above	051-709-4014	Mon-Sat 10.30am-5.30pm	Continuous exhibitions of British design and craft work, ceramics, glass, jewellery etc
LIVERPOOL MUSEUM AND PLANETARIUM William Brown Street, Liverpool 3	051-207-0001	Mon-Sat 10am-5pm, Sun 2pm-5pm	Planetarium and Natural History Centre
MERSEYSIDE MARITIME MUSEUM Albert Dock, Liverpool 3.	051-207-0001	7 days a week 10.30am-5.30pm	Focus is on emigration, shipbuilding and other aspects of Liverpool's maritime heritage
MUSEUM OF LABOUR HISTORY William Brown Street, Liverpool 3.	051-207-0001	Mon-Sat 10am-5pm, Sun 2pm-5pm	Displays on housing, employment, health, education 150 years of Merseyside working-class life
TATE GALLERY Albert Dock , Liverpool 3.	051-709-0507	Tues-Sun 11am-7pm	Changing displays from the national collection of modern art; exhibitions, reading room, videotheque
UNIVERSITY OF LIVERPOOL ART GALLERY Abercromby Square, Liverpool 3	051-794-2347	Mon, Tues, Thurs noon-2pm, Wed/Fri noon-4pm (free admission)	Paintings, English porcelain and Greek and Russian icons
WALKER ART GALLERY William Brown Street, Liverpool 3.	051-207-0001	Mon-Sat 10am-5pm Sun 2pm-5pm (free admission)	Early Italian art; Rembrandt, Turner and modern art. Sculpture gallery with 18th/19th century displays.

THEATRES AND CONCERT HALLS

EVERYMAN THEATRE
Hope Street, Liverpool 1. Phone 051-709-4776.
Informal, welcoming theatre, renowned for its productions.

LIVERPOOL EMPIRE
Lime Street, Liverpool 1. Phone 051-709-1555.
Opera, ballet, musicals, plays and concerts.

NEPTUNE THEATRE
Hanover Street, Liverpool 1. Phone 051-709-7844.
Civic theatre, staging amateur and professional productions.

PHILHARMONIC HALL
Hope Street, Liverpool 1. Phone 051-709-3789. Home of The Royal Liverpool Harmonic Orchestra. Season includes concerts featuring international performers and conductors.

PLAYHOUSE THEATRE/STUDIO
Williamson Square, Liverpool 1. Phone 051-709-8363.
Britain's oldest repertory theatre. Varied programme, ranging from popular theatre to the classics.

ROYAL COURT THEATRE
Roe Street, Liverpool. Phone 051-709-4321. Rock, pop, musicals.

UNITY THEATRE
Hope Place, Liverpool 1. Known as the little theatre with the big heart, it's the venue for major national and international small-scale touring companies. Recently refurbished.

Film

MERSEYSIDE FILM INSTITUTE
Merseyside has more than a dozen cinema houses and it also has a thriving film society: The Merseyside Film Institute, First floor, The Bluecoat Chambers, School Lane, Liverpool 1. Membership is only stg£5.00 a year (stg£3.00 for unwaged). For more information call 051-709-4260.

OUTINGS

ALBERT DOCK
Once-derelict dock near the pier head, the buildings now houses the Maritime Museum, the Tate Gallery and Granada TV, a range of specialty shops, bars and restaurants. Open seven days a week from 10am. For more information phone 051-709-9199.

CALDERSTONES PARK
Liverpool. Phone 051-724-2371. Covers 125 acres, with lake. Old English and Japanese gardens. Open daily from 8am.

CROXTETH HALL AND COUNTRY PARK
Muirhead Avenue East, Liverpool. Phone 051-228-5311. Meet the Hall's Edwardian characters. Also has farm, adventure playground, café and garden. Open daily 11am-5pm, April to mid-Sept.

LADY LEVER ART GALLERY
Port Sunlight Village, Wirral. Phone 051-645-3623. One of the most beautiful art museums in Europe, permanent displays include English 18th-century

paintings, Pre-Raphaelite works, pottery. Open Mon-Sat 10am-5pm, Sun 2pm-5pm.

NESS GARDENS
(University of Liverpool Botanic Gardens), Neston, Wirral. Phone 051-336-2135. Displays of shrubs, rock and herb gardens etc. Open daily 9am-sunset.

SPEKE HALL
The Walk, Liverpool. Phone 051-427-7231. Half-timbered Elizabethan mansion, fully furnished, with Great Hall and panelled rooms, kitchen and servants' quarters. Open daily (except Mon) from 1 April to end of October, 1.30pm-5.30pm. Also weekends in Nov/Dec.

WIRRAL COUNTRY PARK
Station Road, Thurstaston. Phone 051-648-4371. Sited on an old railway route, there is a twelve-mile footpath through the park and lovely views over the Dee estuary. Open at all times.

MARKETS

Traditionally Liverpool has always been a city to visit for some weekend shopping. It still attracts many thousands of 'regulars' from Ireland and Wales, who like to browse in the Clayton Square Shopping Centre, St John's Centre, and around the Church Street/Lord Street areas. There are also several local markets: St Martin's Market (known as Paddy's Market), Garston Market in Island Road, Monument Place Market near London Road, and Toxteth Market on Park Road. For more information on market days and locations, contact the *Tourist Information Centre:* 051-708-8854.

TOURS

Beatles fans can take a range of magical mystery tours in the footsteps of the Fab Four. Daily Beatles tours are organised by Merseyside Tourism Board, covering the band's birthplaces, the clubs they played, the pubs they frequented etc. Phone 051-708-8854 for details.

Cavern City Tours also run Beatles tours ('tailored to suit your requirements') and a range of other events including Beatles Anniversary Weekends, and The Annual International Beatles Convention (August). For information call to Cavern City Tours, Fourth Floor, 31 Mathew Street, Liverpool L2 6RE. Phone 051-236-9091.

Ferry 'Cross The Mersey! Ferries have crossed the Mersey for over 800 years and you can't claim to be a real Scouser unless you take a ferry tour at least once! Sailings every twenty minutes from Pier Head. Call Merseytravel: 051-236-7676.

TRANSPORT

RAIL

LIME STREET STATION
Liverpool. Phone 051-709-9696. Intercity services run to Merseyside from all over Britain. Citysaver fares are available from most of the main cities. Phone for timetables, fares and special reductions.

MERSEYRAIL
The local rail network takes you from Chester to Southport, West Kirby to St Helen's.

BUSES

Bus services run thoughout Merseyside, operated by a number of bus companies, including Merseytravel's own service.

The Merseytravel Saveaway Tickets are money-saving one-day tickets that can be used on most buses, trains and ferries in Merseyside at off-peak times. To find out more about the above services, visit one of the Merseytravel shops.

The main Merseytravel shop is at 24 Hatton Garden in Liverpool city centre. Open office hours Mon-Fri. Phone 051-227-5181 or call the Merseytravel line: 051-236-7676, from 8am-8pm, 7 days a week.

MERSEYBUS INFO LINE
051-254-1616, Mon-Fri 8am-6pm, for routes and times.

COACH SERVICE

NATIONAL EXPRESS CITY CENTRE TERMINUS
Brownlow Hill, (opposite the Adelphi Hotel, City Centre). For phone enquiries about this inter-city service, call the Manchester office: 061-228-3881

AIRPORT

LIVERPOOL AIRPORT
Speke. Phone 051-486-8877 (just seven miles from the city centre)

TAXIS

MERSEY CABS
171 Lodge Lane L8. Phone 051-733-3393. One of the biggest firms in Liverpool.

You'll find a complete list of taxi firms in the *Thomson Local Directory*.

Shay Black: Touching Home in Liverpool

Shay Black is a member of the well-known musical Black family from Dublin. Shay works as a health visitor in Liverpool, sings with the city's sea shanty group, 'Stormalong John' and returns to Dublin regularly to tour and record with the rest of the family. The Black family's most recent recording was the November '89 album Time for Touching Home, *featuring Frances, Michael, Martin and Shay, produced by Declan Synnott and assisted on backing vocals and production by Mary Black.*

My mother was born and reared around Donore Avenue. She worked in Rowntree's sweet factory on the packers' line. They didn't have piped music or Radio 2 in those days, so they used to sing on the line.

My mother was a great singer and she often told me of how a chocolate-stained piece of paper would be sent up the line to her with a request written on it and she'd start the song off and everyone would sing. And when she came to the end of that song, another piece of sweet paper would be passed up to her and she would start the next one. It was all the popular tunes of the time, songs from the shows as well as the Irish 'standards', like 'The Old Bog Road'.

My father Kevin came from a very musical family on Rathlin Island and he was a great musician. He was a box player, mandolin and fiddle player and he had a go on the pipes as well. His father and grandfather before him were musicians and so my dad and his brothers could play a range of instruments too.

It's only relatively recently that Rathlin got electricity and when my father was young, they didn't have radios for music, so they couldn't hold a dance there without getting the Blacks to provide the music. They had a great wealth of material even though Rathlin was so isolated, because the men used to go over to work in the Clydeside shipyards and they would bring new tunes back with them to the island.

My dad left the island in the thirties to serve his apprenticeship as a plasterer in the Glens and then came on down to Dublin, where he met my mother. They started a little grocery shop in Charlemont Street and sold all sorts of things from butter and ham to paraffin oil. My mother worked the shop until it became too much for her and then my brother Martin took it over and he has a bicycle shop there now.

I went to Kevin Street college after school, to study electronics. I took a job afterwards but two years later I decided electronics wasn't for me and I wanted to travel. I was twenty-one and I had never been abroad. So I left the job, without really knowing where I was going. I just took the haversack and headed for London, with ninety pounds in my pocket.

After a while in London, I wanted to go further afield, so I hitched down to Paris, then Germany, Switzerland, Yugoslavia and spent some time in Greece. I arrived back in Dover four months later with two pounds in my pocket. I'd had a great time on the continent and I came back to England to work, but I wanted to do some studying too. I went to Canterbury, booked into a hostel there and lived on tick until I got a job in a quarry nearby. You were only allowed stay in the hostel for a few weeks and then you had to move on. So I slept on friends' floors while I worked in the quarry. This was about the time of the

Old Bailey bombs and Canterbury is a very English city, so I came in for a lot of abuse during that time, but I took it in my stride. I just kept my head down and worked all the hours that God sent me, for a very low wage.

Then I decided to do teacher training. I was accepted by the college in Canterbury, but I had to find the money to pay the full fees. I knew I wasn't going to make that kind of money in Canterbury, so I moved to London and worked on the building sites.

It was tough, because I was on the lump [working off the books] and it was very dangerous work. There were no health and safety regulations, no unions and a lot of lads were killed on sites then. I saw some pretty terrible incidents during this time – I met Irish lads who were crippled in site accidents, working as tea-boys and message-carriers because they couldn't do heavy work any longer. These were big strapping lads, kept on by decent-hearted gangers, even though they couldn't do real work any longer. And of course, there were no pensions for them. It was awful to see the men reduced like this.

In '74, with the miners' strike on in England, we were all put on three-day weeks and then at Christmas we were all laid off. I decided that I might as well be unemployed down in Canterbury as unemployed in London. There was no work in Canterbury while the strike was on. But after a while, I got offered a job as a porter in a psychiatric day hospital. I was lucky because the sister in charge was Irish and I was well in. The job was pretty basic, some cleaning and domestic work, fetching and carrying. I really warmed to the patients and they got on with me because I was honest and open with them. It was a small unit and all the staff got on very well together. It was during this time that I began to have second thoughts about my plans for teacher training.

I knew I was going to have difficulty finding the fees for the course and in the end I decided on nursing as a career. It helped that in nursing you were employed while training so you had a salary, even if it was basic.

About that time, I decided to go to Liverpool. I'd had enough of Canterbury and I didn't want to return to London. So I arrived in Liverpool on an old BSA Bantam bike that I'd bought for sixty pounds. I found a cheap hotel in the Mount Pleasant area of the city until I found a flat. I got work in one of the largest psychiatric hospitals in the region, Rainhill. This was where I trained over three years and after I became a registered psychiatric nurse I stayed on as a staff nurse for about a year.

In 1980 I completed my general training and became a state

registered nurse. After working on the wards for a few years I was then seconded by the health authority to Liverpool University and I trained as a health visitor. Nursing is the ideal job for me, because it involves working in very close contact with people, which I enjoy – and as a health visitor I'm working with people in their homes, within the community. It means you are somebody special in the area and it gives a great sense of self-esteem. More important, it gives me a real say in helping to bring about changes in people's lives. I work through many different networks, not just social workers, doctors, other health visitors and nurses, but politically too. I have had an input into the council's health-care strategy.

I believe that people should have access to the best possible health care, regardless of class or cost. I'm concerned with the current changes in the NHS which will make it increasingly difficult for people to get good quality care in their community. Health, after all, is a basic right.

Liverpool is a very easy city to like. When I arrived first in the early seventies, it was still pretty much in the shadow of Beatles music and the Mersey sound. But then bands like Frankie Goes to Hollywood came on the circuit and the live music scene took off again. There has always been a tradition of folk clubs in the city. I started singing in a pub near the docks called 'Oily Joes' and got to know a lot of the local musicians and singers. My own music background gave me an entrée to the folk and traditional scene and now I sing with a sea-shanty group called 'Stormalong John'.

I also play regularly with a céili band, Call Dances, and I sing and perform with a traditional-style band called 'Garva'. There's a lot going on in the arts generally; it's a very active city.

Liverpool has such Celtic influences, from Ireland, Scotland and Wales and because of this, it has a different feeling to all the other cities in Britain. There's a great attitude in Liverpool to the arts, to music and telling stories and you have the same type of characters here as you have in Dublin. It's a very lively city, very warm and I've always felt very much at home here.

A lot of this has to do with the sheer number of Irish people living in the city. Not just the Irish-born and the second generation. It goes all the way back to famine times. There are also a lot of young Irish students coming to the city polytechnic and university now. I meet them at local music sessions.

Liverpool felt like home for me very shortly after moving here. In fact, it sometimes got a little bit upsetting for my mother. When I'd be over in Dublin doing some gigs with the family and I'd tell her

'I'm going home on Friday' – meaning that I was returning to Liverpool – it took quite a while for her to come to terms with the fact that Dublin wasn't my home any more.

I do feel settled here. I've got a house and my daughter is now thirteen and she's happy in Liverpool. I'm working as a health visitor, with my own little patch to look after in the city. And I feel that I have a future in the NHS, or in the health field generally. I'm content with the people I work with and they accept me. My colleagues know about my background and interest in Irish music and they are interested in that; not just tolerant, but genuinely interested in what I know about the music. There is still that kind of warmth in English people

After sixteen years here I still feel positive about England. I still see it as an opportunity for people, although sometimes when you come back to Ireland, you can run into very negative reactions to this kind of outlook. I remember the first couple of times I came back from England, I had remarks like: 'You're a West Brit now,' and that sort of thing thrown at me.

I stuck it out because I feel that England is a melting pot. There has been such ebb and flow of emigration between the two countries for countless generations and that's going to continue. And as we go into Europe, I still see England as a place where Irish people can go and can settle and be happy.

CHAPTER 8

Birmingham and Coventry

Relaxing on the steps of Coventry Cathedral.

In the Saxon 6th century, Birmingham was simply a small settlement surrounded by deep forest. Yet by the 14th century it was one of the wealthiest places in Warwickshire and by 1900 the city had grown into a major manufacturing centre. Birmingham had turned itself into the industrial and capital city of the Midlands by dint of hard work and hot metal, forging a name for itself through engineering, metal work and skilled craftsmanship in jewellery and weaponry.

Birmingham's position at the centre of the canal network, with easy access to coal, iron and timber, helped its development, as did the talents of local innovators like James Watt, the steam engineer, Matthew Boulton, the industrialist, and printer John Baskerville.

Rapid development of the car, cycle, motorcycle and related industries fuelled the employment boom in Birmingham and nearby

Coventry and by the 1950s only London had a higher growth rate of jobs than these two cities.

But Birmingham and Coventry were over-dependent on big manufacturing firms as employers and when manufacturing all over Britain was badly hit in the seventies and eighties the West Midlands suffered the greatest jobs fall-out. By '83 the regional rate of unemployment was 23 per cent above the rest of Britain.

Today unemployment remains high: 10.6 per cent in Birmingham, 9.5 per cent in Coventry (and a great deal higher in some localities), and although service sector jobs are growing in the region, there is still a huge core of long-term unemployed.

The Victorian fathers of Birmingham might find it difficult to recognise their home city today. Redevelopment after the second world war replaced many of its finest buildings. People were moved out of the city to low-density housing schemes and in the fifties and sixties the centre gave way to ring roads, car parks and covered shopping centres.

But if its physical appearance is radically different, much of its industrial heart remains intact and the city is still a centre for manufacturing and craftsmanship, albeit on a reduced scale.

In recent years Birmingham has also become a big conference centre, with rapidly developing facilities such as the National Exhibition Centre, the vast International Conference Centre and the National Sports Arena.

Media wise, the city has two daily papers, *The Birmingham Post* and *The Evening Mail*, as well as *The Sunday Mercury* and a range of other local papers. Pebble Mill, the BBC Radio and Television centre, Central Independent Television and a number of other radio stations are based in Birmingham.

Culturally, the city has the Hippodrome Theatre – now the home of the Sadlers Wells Royal Ballet – several other theatres, arts centres, museums, galleries and the Birmingham Symphony Orchestra.

Birmingham has a number of major arts festivals each year, including a film and television festival, a jazz festival and a readers' and writers' festival. There are two universities, Aston University and the University of Birmingham.

The population of Birmingham is well over one million and it embodies a range of communities, from the West Indies, India, Vietnam, China, Pakistan and Bangladesh, as well as from Ireland, Scotland, and Wales. The Irish are one of the longest-established groups in Birmingham – by 1961 almost 60 per cent of the migrant community in the city had Irish origins.

Today, there are some 70,000 Irish people living in Birmingham. There is a flourishing Irish Centre in High Street, Deritend, which has a great range of social and cultural activities. There is also an Irish Welfare and Information Service, whose present director is Fr Joseph Taafe. Until September 1990 the service was located in Plunkett House, Shadwell Street, but it has now relocated to the Irish Centre in Deritend.

Birmingham has a number of Irish dancing schools, two branches of Comhaltas, several GAA clubs and county associations and over half-a-dozen parish social centres. Fr Taafe, who first came to the city from Mayo over twenty-one years ago, says of the Irish community in Birmingham: 'They are very friendly, good and helpful in every way. As a community, we have made a great contribution to the city. Our people have worked hard and provided manpower for the construction industry, transport, the professions and local government. We've played our part in every aspect of the city's development and we've become part and parcel of the life of the city. Birmingham is an inter-cultural city and we have integrated, while also retaining our Irish identity.'

EMPLOYMENT IN BIRMINGHAM

The job scene in Birmingham has begun to recover from the worst levels of job losses in the manufacturing industries and there has been growth in the service sector, which is expected to continue. But like Liverpool, Birmingham's unemployment levels are still very high and Alice Davis of the Irish Welfare and Information Centre warns: 'There may be positions for those who have specialised skills, but other than that it is not easy to get work in Birmingham.' The recruitment agencies in Birmingham bear this out. Where there is work, it's mainly found in areas such as financial services, the high-tech sector, hotel and catering, tourism and other services.

In other words, it is work for those who have skills, training, professional qualifications and/or a fair amount of on-the-job-experience.

If you don't have these requirements, then Birmingham is not the city in which to seek employment. And even if you *do* have the relevant skills, you should consider your employment chances very carefully before deciding to make it your destination. Below, you'll find the addresses of local newspapers you can send for, to check out the job scene in your field.

FINDING A JOB: WHERE TO LOOK

Birmingham's two daily newspapers, *The Birmingham Post* and *The Evening Mail* are published by Birmingham Post and Mail Ltd, 28 Colmore Circus, B4 6AX. Phone 021-236-3366.

EMPLOYMENT AGENCIES

ALFRED MARKS BUREAU
84 New Street B2 4BA. Phone 021-643-2656.
Secretarial work, clerical, accounts, sales, PR work. Open Mon-Fri 9am-5.30pm.

ALFRED MARKS (CATERING)
Essex House, Temple Street B2. Phone 021-633-3868.
Open Mon-Fri 8am-5.30pm.

BLUE ARROW PERSONNEL SERVICES
61 New Street B2. Phone 021-632-4477.
Secretarial, accounts, VDU work, catering. Open Mon-Fri 8am-6.30pm.

BRITISH NURSING ASSOCIATION
1st Floor, 37 Carr's Lane B4. Phone 021-643-9686.
Nursing and related jobs.

BROOK STREET BUREAU
119 New Street B2. Phone 021-643-7404.
Commercial: office, secretarial, computer work. Open Mon-Fri 9am-5.30pm.

BROOK STREET BUREAU (INDUSTRIAL)
20 Bennett's Hill B2. Phone 021-633-3888.
Catering, industrial. Open Mon-Fri 9am-6pm.

COMPUTER PERSONNEL CONSULTANTS LTD,
18th Floor, The Rotunda, New Street B2. Phone 021-632-6848.
Specialists in computer staff.

HMS RECRUITMENTS
25 New Street B2. Phone 021-643-2444.
Clerical, secretarial, accounts etc.

HMS NURSING & PARAMEDICAL
1st Floor, The Rotunda, New Street B2. Phone 021-643-5675.
Nursing and related jobs.

JOB CENTRES

BIRMINGHAM JOB CENTRE
150 Corporation Street B4. Phone 021-236-7354. For job vacancies/advice.

For location of other job centres in Birmingham, call above centre.

CAREERS OFFICE
Ground Floor, Snowhill House, 10/15 Livery Street, B3 2PE.
Phone 021-235-2647. Information/advice on careers and training.

For location of other careers offices in Birmingham, contact above office.

BENEFITS

If your job plans in Birmingham have come to nothing and you have no money, or if your income is too low to survive on, then you should go to your unemployment benefit office (UBO) and claim income support. See Ch 3 'London' p.78 for details of signing on.

UNEMPLOYMENT BENEFIT OFFICES

ASTON 30 Beacon Hill B6 6JL. Phone 021-327-3397

BIRMINGHAM CITY 281 Corporation Street B47DR. Phone 021-359-3051

HANDSWORTH 28 Soho Road B21 9YU. Phone 021-551-4561

SPARKBROOK 1 (A&B) Armoury Road B11 2RL. Phone 021-766-6464

WASHWOOD HEATH 295 Washwood Heath Road, B8 2XX. Phone 021-327-1510

SOCIAL SECURITY OFFICES

DSS LADYWOOD
65-77 Summer Row B3 1LB. Phone 021-236-3322. Open Mon-Fri 9.30am-3.30pm. This is the Central Birmingham DSS office, covering postal code areas of 1, 2, 3, 4, 5, 9, 10, 18 & 25.

For details of other DSS offices covering remaining postal areas, call this DSS office.

HOUSING BENEFIT

If you are a tenant in the private sector, this is dealt with at *The City Treasurer's Department*, 120 Edmund Street B3 2ET. Phone 021-235-9944 (Ask for private housing benefit section). Council tenants' housing benefit is dealt with at *Louisa Ryland House*, New Hall Street B3.

You may also be entitled to a number of other benefits. (See Ch 3, 'London' p.75 for details of these.) You can check whether you qualify for various benefits at:

The Irish Welfare and Information Centre (until end of September 1990) Plunkett House, Shadwell Street, B4, phone 021-236-9312. After September 1990, this service is based in *The Irish Centre*, 14-20 High Street, Deritend B12 0LN. Phone 021-622-2332. Open Mon-Fri 9am-10pm. Welfare worker: Alice Davis. Irish Centre Manager is Patrick McGrath.

The welfare service also deals with enquiries about accommodation, employment, health, legal referrals and a wide range of other issues.

Citizens' Advice Bureaux can also advise about benefits and legal and consumer problems. The main city centre office is based at Colmore Circus Subway B4 6AJ. Phone 021-236- 0864. This bureau can also tell you the location of other CAB branches.

ACCOMMODATION

Birmingham is a big convention city and it also has two universities, so the demand for rented accommodation is very heavy. While you are looking around for a flat or bedsit, here are some temporary options:

HOSTELS

Call or write in advance to check vacancies. Some hostels require a deposit.

Hostel	Age Group/Sex	Cost	Phone
ALEXANDRA RESIDENTIAL CLUB 27 Norfolk Road, Edgbaston, B16	18+	stg£5.50 per night	021-454-8134
YWCA AUDREY ACHURCH WING 5 Stone Road, Edgbaston, B16	18-25 male/female	stg£7 per night Self-catering facilities	021-440-2924
YMCA ERDINGTON 300 Reservoir Road, Erdington, B23 6DB	18+ male/female	stg£11.25 per night Evening meal stg£2.30 extra	021-373-1937
YMCA NORTHFIELD 200 Bunbury Road, Northfield, B31	18-30	stg£11.25 per night (plus £10 deposit)	021-475-6218

UNIVERSITY ACCOMMODATION

During vacation times write to:

ASTON UNIVERSITY
The Accommodation Office, Aston Triangle B4 7ET. Phone 021-359-3611

UNIVERSITY OF BIRMINGHAM
The Conference Office, High Hall, Church Road, Edgbaston 15 3SZ. Phone 021-454-6022.

ACCOMMODATION: RENTING A FLAT, A BEDSIT, A HOUSE

Renting in Birmingham ranges from reasonably cheap but poor standard accommodation, to expensive, upmarket places. Average rents in Birmingham (Spring 1990):

181

Bedsit – from stg£80-£140 per month
One-bedroomed flat – from stg£160-£220 per month
Three-bedroomed semi-detached house – from stg£280-£350 per month.

Private rented accommodation, furnished and unfurnished, is in short supply.

WHERE TO LOOK

*Check daily newspapers, *The Birmingham Post*, *Evening Mail* for 'to let' adverts.

*Birmingham Central Library, Chamberlain Square, (close to the town hall) should stock a good number of local papers. Phone 021-235-4532.

ACCOMMODATION AGENCIES

Remember! If you are seeking accommodation through commercial agencies, you shouldn't pay a fee until the agency has actually found you a place. And get advice before signing a tenancy agreement, (CAB Bureau / Irish Centre).

ROBERT ASTON AND COMPANY
87 Alcester Road, Moseley, B13 8EB. Phone 021-4494411. Open Mon-Fri 9am-5.30pm, Sat 9am-4pm. This agency deals with rentals. You'll find a full list in the local telephone directory.

What to look for when flat seeking: See advice on p. 50, Ch 2. The city council offices stock 'A Guide to Accommodation Agencies' leaflets.

HOUSING ASSOCIATIONS

There are at least fifteen major housing associations, societies and trusts in the Birmingham area and quite a number of smaller groups as well. Some have specialist areas of concern, such as housing for the elderly. Others cater mainly for families. To find out which association might best suit your needs, you can obtain a booklet from the National Federation of Housing Associations, Suite 70, Albany House, Hurst Street, B5. (Enclose stamped addressed envelope.) The booklet contains addresses and details of local associations.

Family Housing Association (Birmingham) Ltd is one well-known association in the city. It has about 1,500 housing units on its books, but there is a very large waiting list. You can reach them at 44-46 Coventry Road, Birmingham.

The Catholic Housing Aid Society (based in the same building as above) can advise you about housing possibilities, rent or housing problems.

COPEC Housing Association, 35 Paradise Circus, Birmingham B1 2AJ is another housing association. Open 9.30am-1pm and 2.30pm-5.30pm Mon-Fri (except Thurs pm). Phone 021-631-2525.

Most housing associations require you to register with the local council before they will accept your application.

COUNCIL HOUSING

There are well over 20,000 names on Birmingham Council's housing waiting list and in recent years there has been very little building of new council accommodation. So the chances of getting this kind of housing are slim. The waiting list, however, is open to everyone over eighteen years who lives or works in Birmingham and has a housing need. And as we've mentioned, you should register with the council if you are applying to a housing association, because the council has nomination agreements with most associations. Under these arrangements, the council can nominate tenants to almost 50 per cent of housing association lettings.

Application forms from *Birmingham Council Housing Dept*, Louisa Ryland House, 44 New Hall Street B3, phone 021-235-9944, or from the neighbourhood offices situated around the city.

BUYING A HOUSE OR FLAT

Birmingham house prices have been described as coming 'somewhere between Liverpool and London prices'. And this pretty well describes the range:

A two-bedroomed flat – from stg£35,000 (Erdington) to stg£56,000 (Harborne)

A three-bedroomed pre-twenties villa – stg£39,000

A three-bedroomed semi-detached – stg£50,000

A four-bedroomed detached house (Solihull) – stg£170,000.

*Check the *Evening Mail* property pages for current prices in all areas. You'll find estate agents listed in the *Thomson Local Directory*.

*Get advice before you buy. Consider carefully whether you can afford mortgage repayments.

ACCOMMODATION PROBLEMS: WHO CAN HELP

If you are having problems with accommodation (bad conditions, difficulties with the landlord), or your temporary accommodation has come to an end and you have nowhere to stay, then contact one of these groups for help and advice:

THE CATHOLIC HOUSING AID SOCIETY
44-46 Coventry Road, Birmingham.
(Contactable at Plunkett House until end Sept '90. Phone 021-236-6321.)

HANDSWORTH SINGLE HOMELESS ACTION GROUP
173 Lozelle Road B19. Phone 021-551-2760.
Temp and permanent accommodation for 16-25s who are homeless in the Handsworth area. Also gives general welfare advice.
Open Tues 10am-noon and 2pm-5pm, Thurs 1pm-7pm.
(Emergencies dealt with where possible at other times).

THE IRISH WELFARE AND INFORMATION BUREAU
c/o The Irish Centre, High Street, Deritend. Phone 021-622-2562.
Welfare worker: Alice Davis, Manager Patrick McGrath.
Open Mon-Fri 9am-10pm (office).

LINK INFORMATION BUREAU
74 Dalton Street B4. Phone 021-233-1508.
Advises 16-25-year-olds on accommodation, welfare rights.
Open Mon-Fri 9am-5.30pm. Call for appointment if possible.

NEW BOOT HOSTEL (ST BASIL'S)
110 St Andrew's Road, Bordesley Green, Birmingham B94NA.
Phone 021-772-3098. Caters for young men: 16-25. Emergency hostel stg£7.40 per night. Usually full but will give advice and information. Open 24 hours a day.

SHELTER HOUSING AID AND ADVICE CENTRE
West Midlands Housing Aid, Room 30, Second Floor, Ruskin Chambers, Birmingham 4. Phone 021-236-6688.

GENERAL ADVICE AND INFORMATION SERVICES

COMMUNITY HEALTH SERVICES
Central Birmingham Health Authority CHS, Centre for Community Health, St Patrick's Highgate Street B12 0YA. Phone 021-440-6161.

COMMUNITY HEALTH COUNCIL
Central Birmingham CHC, 2nd Floor, Ringway House,
45 Bull Street B4 6AF. Phone 021-233-1810.

Community Relations
BIRMINGHAM COMMUNITY RELATIONS COUNCIL
St George House, 32/34 Hill Street B5 4AN. Phone 021-235-4305/9.

Legal Advice
BIRMINGHAM LAW SOCIETY
(Emergency help, if outside solicitor's office hours.) Phone 021-643-5445.

Also contact your local Citizens' Advice Bureau for legal advice.

Marriage Guidance
RELATE
Bishopsgate House, Bishopsgate Street B15. Phone 021-643-1638.

One-Parent Families
GINGERBREAD
Call 021-631-2103

Other
BIRMINGHAM RAPE CRISIS AND RESEARCH CENTRE
Birmingham 3. Phone 021-233-2122.

EMERGENCY SOCIAL SERVICES
VIA City Council Switchline. Phone 021-235-9944.

FAMILY PLANNING ASSOCIATION
5 York Road, Edgbaston. Phone 021-454-8236.

FAMILY PLANNING SERVICES
Edgbaston Clinic, 14 Frederick Road B15. Phone 021-454-0146.

FR HUDSON'S SOCIETY
(Pregnancy counselling and adoption agency), Coleshill B46 3ED.
Phone 0675-463187.

NCH (NATIONAL CHILDREN'S HOMES) CARELINE
Phone 021-456-4560. Confidential advice and support service for relationship/emotional problems and abuse in the family.

WOMEN'S ADVICE AND INFORMATION CENTRE
15a Devonshire House, High Street, B12. Phone 021-773-6952.
Open Tues, Wed, Thurs, 10am-4pm.

Gay Services
LESBIAN LINE Phone 021-359-3192

GAY SWITCHBOARD Phone 021-622-7351

CRISIS HELPLINES

ALCOHOL ADVISORY SERVICE
Phone 021-622-2041.

ALCOHOL ADVICE AND INFORMATION
Phone 021-471-1361.

ALCOHOLICS ANONYMOUS
Phone 021-773-3449 (7pm-10pm and 24-hour answering service).

DRUGLINE:
Dale House, New Meeting Street B4 7SX. Phone 021-632-6363. Mon-Fri
10am-5.30pm and 24-hour answering service.
Confidential counselling service for drug users and their families.

MISSING PERSONS
Message Home (confidential service). No need to say where you are, just dial
and give your message and it will be passed on to home. Phone 021-426-3396.

SAMARITANS
13 Bow Street B1 1DW. Phone 021-643-8001 or 666-6644.
24-hour emergency service for suicidal and despairing.

SEXUALLY TRANSMITTED DISEASES

AIDS LIFELINE
Phone 021-235-3535 (10am-7.30pm) for facts, advice and counselling confidential helpline.

AIDSLINE WEST MIDLANDS
Phone 021-622-1511.

BIRMINGHAM GENERAL HOSPITAL (SPECIAL CLINICS)
Ward 19, Whitehall Street (off Steelhouse Lane) B4. Phone 021-2368611. (Women ext 5231. Men ext 5230). Call for appointment.

NATIONAL AIDS HELPLINES
Phone 0800-567 123 to talk to advisors. Phone 0800-555 777 for free leaflets.

HEALTH MATTERS

DOCTORS

To register with a doctor, go along to the surgery and ask to be placed on the GP's list of NHS patients. You can get a medical card application form at the surgery or from the Family Practitioner Committee: Phone 021-200-1681. If you don't know any local doctors, the FPC can give you a list of GPs in your area.

HOSPITALS

24-hour Accident & Emergency
BIRMINGHAM ACCIDENT HOSPITAL
Bath Row B15 1NA. Phone 021-643-7041.

BIRMINGHAM GENERAL HOSPITAL
Steelhouse Lane, B4 6NH. Phone 021-236-8611.

DUDLEY ROAD HOSPITAL
Dudley Road, Winson Green B18 7QH. Phone 021-554-3801.

EAST BIRMINGHAM HOSPITAL
Bordesley Green East, B9 5ST. Phone 021-772-4311.

LATE-NIGHT CHEMISTS

BOOTS
16/17 New Street B2. Phone 021-631-2322.
Open Mon-Fri 8.45am-10pm, Sat 8.45am-6pm, Sun 10am-2pm.
Details of other late-duty chemists can be obtained from the Family Practitioner Committee 021-200-1681.

DENTISTS

Check the *Thomson Local Directory* under 'dentists' (NHS and private patients).

EDUCATION

To get information and brochures on Birmingham's several hundred schools and colleges, write to the *City Council Education Dept,*

Council House Extension, Margaret Street B3 3BU. Phone 021-235-2590.

For information on independent schools in the area, write to *The Independent Schools Information Service,* 56 Buckingham Gate, London SW1E 6AG. Phone 01-630-8793.

Local playgroups and day nurseries are listed in the *Thomson Local Directory*, but you can also get information from *The Pre-School Playgroups Association*, Third Floor, Piccadilly Arcade, New Street B2. Phone 021-643-0063.

HIGHER EDUCATION

ASTON UNIVERSITY
Aston Triangle B4 7ET. Phone 021-359-3611. Forty-acre green city centre campus. Faculties: engineering, science, management and modern languages.

BIRMINGHAM COLLEGE OF FOOD, TOURISM & CREATIVE STUDIES
Summer Row B3 1JB. Phone 021-235-2774.

BIRMINGHAM POLYTECHNIC
Six sites. Over 4,000 students. Write to City of Birmingham Polytechnic, Perry Barr B42 2SU. Phone 021-331-5000.

BIRMINGHAM SCHOOL OF MUSIC
Paradise Circus B3 3HG. Phone 021-359-6721.

UNIVERSITY OF BIRMINGHAM
Edgbaston site. Five faculties. Write to The University of Birmingham, PO Box 363, B15 2TT.Phone 021-414-3344.

NB: If you are thinking of studying in Birmingham remember that only tuition fees are paid, *not* your maintenance costs (and with some colleges, you won't even get tuition fees reimbursed). See Ch 1 p.25 'Student Grants' for details. *The Department of Education & Science* also has a leaflet on this.

ADULT EDUCATION: CLASSES AND COURSES

Birmingham has a broad range of adult education classes and courses, held in local colleges and adult education centres. You can find out more about the kind of courses that are available from *The Education Department,* Council House Extension, Margaret Street B3 3BU. Phone 021-235-2590 or from *The Education Guidance Services*:

Solihull
SCOT EDUCATIONAL ADVICE CENTRE
Solihull College of Technology, HUT 1, Blossomfield Road, Solihull B91 1SB. Phone 021-705-6376 (ext 257).

Dudley
DUDLEY EDUCATION ADVICE SERVICE FOR ADULTS
Education Dept Westox House, Trinity Road, Dudley. Phone 0384-452239.

FIRCROFT COLLEGE OF ADULT EDUCATION
1018 Bristol Road, Selly Oak B29 6LH. Phone 021-472-0116.

THE OPEN UNIVERSITY

WEST MIDLANDS REGIONAL OU CENTRE
St James' House, 66 High Street, Harborne B17 9NB.
Phone 021-426-1661.

TIME OFF AND THINGS TO DO

Birmingham has its fair share of good theatres, galleries, music and other arts activities and the city's industrial heritage provides the focus for a huge range of outings.

Birmingham's car manufacturing tradition is reflected in the Patrick Collection at King's Norton, exhibiting over eighty cars dating from 1913. Railway enthusiasts can return to the days of steam locomotives at the Railway Museum, Warwick Road, Tyseley. The National Motorcycle Museum is based in Bickenhill and The Museum of Science and Industry, Newhall Street, is a haven for fans of old aircraft, locomotives and other machinery.

Then there are the Brummagem boats, traditional narrow craft that can be hired to explore the Birmingham canals (Birmingham has more miles of inland waterway than Venice!), the Jewellery Quarter, where Birmingham craftsworkers continue to work, the Redhouse Glassworks in Stourbridge and the Cadbury chocolate factory at Bournville.

You'll find details of leisure activities listed in Birmingham's *What's On* magazine, published every fortnight, available from arts venues and information centres around the city. *What's On* phone 021-456-6600. *The Evening Mail* also lists arts events.

Birmingham Convention & Visitor Bureau, Information Centre, is based at 2 City Arcade (off Corporation Street), phone 021-643-2514. There is also a 24-hour information hotline: phone 0839-333999

MUSIC: POP, ROCK, TRAD AND ALL THAT JAZZ

Birmingham's music scene brought forth bands like The Wonderstuff and Pop Will Eat Itself and who knows what the nineties will bring in Brum? Check out the local circuit for yourself. Some venues are:

THE BELL AND PUMP
Edgbaston, Phone 021-454-0212. Folk/roots music.

BIRMINGHAM TOWN HALL
Victoria Square, B3. Phone 021-236-2392. Concert venue.

BURBERRIES
220 Broad Street B15. Phone 021-643-1500. Rock/pop sounds.

CANNONBALL
Digbeth. Phone 021-7721403. Jazz/blues.

THE HIBERNIAN
Pershore Road, Selly Park, B30. Phone 021-472-0136.
Folk and trad sessions Wed: Pop/country weekends.

THE HUMMINGBIRD
Dale End B4. Phone 021-236-4236. Trendy venue club-nights with resident &
visiting DJs plus live bands.

IRISH CENTRE
14 High Street, Deritend. Phone 021-622-2332.
Thurs night R&B club plus current pop sounds, Irish traditional etc. Call for
details of weekly programme or check *The Irish Post* music listings.

JOHN MITCHEL'S 32-COUNTY SOCIAL CLUB
Stratford Road B11. Phone 021-772-4555. Live music weekends.

MIDLANDS ARTS CENTRE
Cannon Hill Park B12. Phone 021-440-3838. Jazz/blues.

NATIONAL EXHIBITION CENTRE (NEC)
Birmingham B40. Phone 021-780-4133. Big names of pop/rock world.

OUR LADY OF LOURDES SOCIAL CENTRE
Trittiford Road, Yardley Wood. Phone 021-443-2199.
Pop/country bands Wed to Sun.

THE PORSCHE CLUB
Regents Park Road, Small Heath. Phone 021-773-5958.
Jazz/blues plus club nights.

THE RED LION
Kings Heath. Phone 021-444-7258. Folk music.

ST ANNE'S CENTRE
Alcester Street. Phone 021-772-7375.
Irish pop/country bands weekends/Sun lunchtime.

ST DUNSTAN'S CENTRE
Kingsfield Road, King's Heath. Phone 021-444-5033.
Irish pop/country bands weekends.

ST FRANCIS CENTRE
Wretham Road, Handsworth. Phone 021-554-6708. Irish pop/country bands.

ST MARY'S AND JOHN'S SOCIAL CLUB
Gravelly Hill North, Erdington. Phone 021-384-3076.
Disco and bands on weekends.

ST TERESA'S CENTRE
Wellington Road, Perry Barr. Phone 021-356-7134 or 356-2179.
Pop/country bands Sat, Sun.

UNIVERSITY OF BIRMINGHAM
Edgbaston B15. Phone 021-414-3344.
Regular pop and rock gigs. Check with students' union office for details.

Comhaltas Groups
There are two Comhaltas groups in the city, the Birmingham Branch and the
South Birmingham Branch. Contact PRO Frank Caulfield: 021-430-3993

(South Birmingham Branch) or M Regan, 318 Harborne Park Road B17.

Irish Music Classes/Dancing Classes
Contact Pat McGrath for details at The Irish Centre, 14-20 Deritend. Phone
021-622-2332.

Conradh na Gaeilge
Very active branch, based in The Irish Centre, High Street, Deritend. Irish language courses run in the centre, and also at Bournville College of Further Education, Birmingham B31. (Phone 021-411-1414). Also at Great Barr School
and Leisure Centre, Aldridge Road B42. Phone 021-360-2521. Call these
venues for details.

County Associations
The Irish Centre, Deritend, is the base for all the associations' meetings,
dances and other functions. Indeed, it is the County Associations' elected rep-
resentatives that form the governing body of the Irish Centre. The Irish
Centre, which first opened in '67, offers a home-from-home for new arrivals
in Birmingham. It is the focus for local Irish organisations' functions, activities and services. Phone 021-622-2332.

SPORT

GAA ACTIVITIES

The tradition of GAA sporting activities in Birmingham goes back to
1907 and at present there are seventeen teams affiliated to the Warwickshire County Board. They have their own pitch, Páirc na
hÉireann. Dennis Neenan, Sec Warwickshire County Board, 27 Har-
rison Road, Erdingtonrn B24 8AT, can give you details of all fixtures
and activities.

Amateur Boxing Club
C/O THE IRISH CENTRE Deritend. Phone 021-622-2332.

Cricket
WARWICKSHIRE COUNTY CRICKET CLUB
County Ground, Edgbaston Road, Birmingham. Phone 021-440-4292.

Football
ASTON VILLA FOOTBALL CLUB
Villa Park, Trinity Road, Aston, Birmingham. Phone 021-327-6604.

BIRMINGHAM CITY FC
St Andrew's Street, Birmingham. Phone 021-772-0101.

WEST BROMWICH ALBION FC
The Hawthorns, Halfords Lane, Birmingham Road, West Bromwich.
Phone 021-525-8888.

Golf
There are many private and municipal courses in the Birmingham area. Call
Professional Golfers Association HQ, Lichfield Road, Wishaw, 0675-70333,
for details of affiliated private courses. Call the council's recreations and community services for details of municipal courses. Phone 021-235-3022.

Horse Racing
WARWICK RACE COURSE
Hampton Street, Warwick. Phone 0926-491553.

Rugby
BIRMINGHAM RUGBY FOOTBALL CLUB
Foreshaw Heath Lane, Portway, Wythall. Phone 0564-822955

MOSELEY RFC
The Reddings, Moseley, Birmingham. Phone 021-449-0048

OLD EDWARDIANS RFC
Streetsbrook Road, Birmingham. Phone 021-744-6831.

Tennis
EDGBASTON PRIORY CLUB
Home of the Dow Classic Tennis Cup. Phone 021-440-2492.

SPORTS AND LEISURE CENTRES

ASTON VILLA SPORTS & LEISURE CENTRE
Aston Hall Road, Aston B6. Phone 021-328-4884.

BIRMINGHAM ALEXANDER STADIUM
Stadium Way, (Off Walsall Road), Perry Barr B2. Phone 021-356-8008.

BIRMINGHAM SPORTS CENTRE
201 Balsall Heath Road, Highgate B12 9DL. Phone 021-440-1021.

GEM SPORTS CENTRE
Aston University Campus, Aston Triangle B4. Phone 021-359-3611.

HANDSWORTH LEISURE CENTRE & POOL
Holly Road, Birmingham 20 2BY. Phone 021-523-6336.

SALFORD SPORTS STADIUM
Salford Park, Aston. Phone 021-327-1419

SMALL HEATH COMMUNITY CENTRE
Muntz Street, Small Heath B10. Phone 021-773-6131.

For a full list of local sports centres/swimming pools phone 021-237-3022

MUSEUMS, ART GALLERIES

Place	*Phone*	*Times*	*Collections*
BIRMINGHAM CENTRAL LIBRARY Paradise Circus, Birmingham	021-235-4511		Vast reference library. Its Shakespearean collection alone comprises some 40,000 books. Collections of maps, historical printed material etc
BIRMINGHAM CITY MUSEUM & ART GALLERY Chamberlain Square, B3	021-235-2834	Mon-Fri 9.30am-5pm. Sun 2pm-5pm (free admission)	Pre-Raphaelite collection/stained glass, ceramics and costumes (tea rooms/ museum shop)

BIRMINGHAM MU-SEUM OF SCIENCE & INDUSTRY New Hall Street B3	021-236-1022	Mon-Fri 9.30am-5pm. Sun 2pm-5pm (free admission)	All aspects of science, engineering & industry, including transport
BIRMINGHAM RAIL-WAY MUSEUM Warwick Road, Tyseley	021-707-4696	Daily 10am-5pm	Houses a wealth of working railway exhibits. Paradise for locomotive-lovers
IKON GALLERY 58-72 John Bright Street, Birmingham	021-643-0708		Regular exhibitions of contemporary art, sculpture, photography
NATIONAL MOTOR-CYCLE MUSEUM Coventry Road, Bickenhill, Solihull	021-704-2784		British-built motorcycles, spanning period from 1898-1980 (restaurant & shop)
THE PATRICK COL-LECTION 180 Lifford Lane, King's Norton B30	021-459-9111	W/ends, Hols 10am-5.30pm 2pm-5pm other days	Victorian paper mill houses 'Autoworld' collection of classic vehicles.

THEATRES

ALEXANDRA THEATRE
Station Street, Queensway B5. Phone 021-643-1231. National touring companies. Drama, comedies.

BIRMINGHAM REPERTORY THEATRE
1 Broad Street B1. Phone 021-236-4455. 'In-House' and touring productions. Main auditorium, plus rep studio.

THE CAVE
Balsall Heath. Phone 021-440-3742. Fringe theatre: music/drama.

CRESCENT THEATRE
Cumberland Street B1. Phone 021-643-5858. Drama/musicals.

HALL GREEN LITTLE THEATRE
Pemberley Road, Acocks Green. Phone 021-706-9645.

HIPPODROME
Hurst Street B5. Phone 021-622-7486. Musicals/opera.

MIDLANDS ARTS CENTRE
Cannon Hill Park B12. Phone 021-440-3838. Contemporary plays, mime, dance.

OLD REP THEATRE
Station Street, Birmingham 5. Phone 021-235-4682. Amateur/fringe.

OUTINGS

ASTON HALL
Trinity Road, Aston, Birmingham. Phone 021-327-0062. Jacobean house standing in its own park. Tapestries, furnishings, pictures 16th-19th century.

BIRMINGHAM BOTANICAL & HORTICULTURAL SOCIETY
Westbourne Road, Edgbaston. Phone 021-454-1680. Ten acres of beautifully maintained gardens.

BOURNVILLE
Phone 021-433-4334. The Cadbury factory is four miles SW of Birmingham City set in model estate surroundings. Open all year round. It is hard to resist a visit to Chocolate Village!

BRUMMAGEM BOATS
Sherborne Street, Wharf, Birmingham 16. Phone 021-455-6163/0691. Boats for hire; passenger trips; guided cruises along canalways.

STUART CRYSTAL
Redhouse Glassworks, Stourbridge. Phone 0384-71161. Guided tours around the glassmaking factory.

Parks
Birmingham's parks include *Cannon Hill Park* (eighty acres), *Small Heath Park, Calthorpe Park, Highgate Park, Handsworth Park, King's Heath Park.* Brochures and more information from Recreation & Community Services: 021-235-3022.

MARKETS

Birmingham's council markets are in the vicinity of the Bull Ring, the site of the city's original market, dating back to 1166.

BIRMINGHAM RAG MARKET
New, secondhand goods. Open Tues, Fri, Sat.

THE BULL RING OPEN-AIR MARKET
150 stalls; open every day, except Sun.

THE BULL RING CENTRE MARKET HALL
Fish, poultry, household goods. Open six days (except Wed pm)

FLEA MARKET AND THE ROW MARKET
From arts & crafts to clothes. Open same times as Rag Market.

ST MARTIN'S ANTIQUES MARKET.
In St Martin's Market, Edgbaston. Open Mon.

GENERAL SHOPPING

BULL RING SHOPPING CENTRE
Open Mon-Sat. 150 shops and market.

CITY PLAZA
Mainly a fashion centre, beside traditional department stores.

THE PALLISADES
Enclosed centre, built over New Street Station. Mon-Sat.

THE PAVILIONS
Three-level High Street shopping centre. Mon-Sat. Normal shopping hours are
Mon-Sat, 9am-5.30pm with late-night opening on Thurs – 8pm.

TRANSPORT

RAIL

NEW STREET STATION
Phone 021-644-4288. The hub of the National Intercity network and the Midline local rail services, with trains to and from all major cities. Train time
enquiries phone 021-643-2711.

BIRMINGHAM INTERNATIONAL
Station for the National Exhibition Centre, served by Intercity electric trains
from London and through-services from Manchester, Liverpool, the Thames
Valley and the south coast.

All British Rail timetable, fares enquiries, phone 021-643-2711.

CENTRO

The governing body for all the West Midlands area bus services and Midline
trains. Address is 16 Summer Lane B19. All travel enquiries bus services and
local trains: 021-200-2700 (7.30am-10pm).

WEST MIDLANDS TRAVEL
Address as above. Phone 021-236-8313 (to 7.30pm).

WEST MIDLANDS TRAVEL SHOP
Colmore Row B1. Enquiries 021-200-3334.

CENTRO TRAVEL SHOP
New Street. Phone 021-632-5909.

DIGBETH COACH STATION
Digbeth B5. Phone 021-632-6742.

NATIONAL EXPRESS COACH SERVICE INFORMATION
Phone 021-622-4373

AIRPORT

BIRMINGHAM INTERNATIONAL AIRPORT
Airport Way, Birmingham B26 3QJ. Phone 021-767-5511.

TAXIS

TOA TAXIS
Vivian Road Harborne. 24-hours a day radio cabs. Phone 021-427-8888. (This
is one of the city firms. A full list of taxi firms in the *Thomson Local Directory*.)

TRAVEL HOME

There is a travel shop in the Irish Centre. Phone 021-622-2562.

Coventry

Coventry's name comes from its Anglo-Saxon meaning: Cofa's tree. This was possibly a landmark or object of worship, planted at a crossroads of tracks leading to other parts of the Midlands.

Not many people recall Cofa's tree every time the city is mentioned: what does come to mind, however, is the image of Lady Godiva riding her horse through Coventry back in the 11th century, wearing nothing more than her long trailing tresses to cover her bare body.

This historic horse-streak was part of Lady G's campaign to free the local people from high taxes imposed on them by her husband, the Earl Leofric. The old earl pledged that he would give in to her pleas only if she accepted his wager of a stark trot through the town.

When Lady Godiva competed her unclothed *tour-de-Coventry*, Leofric kept his word and lifted the taxes, granting the townspeople a charter.

Coventry, for all its modest size, was one of the most important cities during the Middle Ages. Wood was the city's main trade, along with leather and metal, and later on it became a big cloth manufacturer.

The mechanisation of the 19th century brought the making of sewing machines and bicycles to the city and The Daimler Company produced the first English motor car there, and from this followed the production of aircraft. Coventry's industry drew workers from many parts of Europe and by 1941 the population had grown to 190,000.

The city was devastated in World War II air raids, but the targeted car and aircraft-producing factories resumed manufacturing and a rebuilding programme began in the razed city centre. Coventry emerged from wartime destruction as a modern industrial city with just a few medieval buildings left as a reminder of its past.

Today the population of Coventry is 304,000. The city has suffered heavily over the past two decades due to job losses in the manufacturing industries. The unemployment figure is 9 per cent, with areas like Foleshill and St Michael's Ward hitting 20 per cent. And although local firms like Jaguar and Peugeot Talbot have reported business increases, other firms have had to cut their workforce to survive.

Coventry's employment programme is attracting new investment and jobs on the commercial front and developments like the Westwood Business Park and the University of Warwick Science Park will create more work locally. But long-term unemployment is still very high: about 25 per cent of Coventry's unemployed have been out of work for over three years.

THE IRISH IN COVENTRY

The Irish community in Coventry has been established since the 1840s. Within the space of a couple of decades, 3 per cent of the population in Coventry were Irish and in the 1950s and sixties many thousands more came to the Midlands from Ireland. Today, there is an Irish community of almost 50,000 in Coventry, and in '89, the city elected its first Irish-born Lord Mayor, Kildare man David Cairns.

There is a thriving Comhaltas branch in the area, several GAA clubs affiliated to the Warwickshire county board; Irish social centres like St Brendan's and St Finbarr's; cultural groups including eight Irish dancing schools, a theatre group and Conradh na Gaeilge. There is also an annual Irish festival in Coventry, held in August.

You can get information on all Comhaltas activities from Mrs Maureen Dolan, 20 Heathfield Road, Coventry. Phone 0203-714320.

ST BRENDAN'S CLUB
Hartford Place, The Butts, Coventry. Phone 0203-687635 is the venue for Comhaltas classes and other music and social activities.

ST FINBARR'S CLUB
Stoney Stanton Road, Coventry. Phone 0203-258086 for GAA activities, music and social nights.

THE HEART AND HUMOUR THEATRE COMPANY
Run by Maurice Dee, can be contacted through The Arts Exchange, Unit 15, The Arches, Spon End, Coventry 1.

David Cairns, who achieved a great deal during his term as Lord Mayor in the promotion of Irish activities in the area (and initiated the annual Irish Festival in Coventry), can be contacted for information on Irish community activities via *The Council House,* Earl Street, Coventry. Phone 0203-853333.

EMPLOYMENT

Work opportunities in Coventry are mainly in specific areas such as the car industry (skilled manual work, managerial or professional jobs) or office-based work in the commercial, technical fields.

Employers are interested only in suitably qualified and skilled personnel. If you are in this category and you want to make enquiries about job possibilities in your field, then write to *Coventry Chamber of Commerce & Industry*, St Nicholas' Street, Coventry CV1 4FD (phone 0203-633000) for more information.

You can check out the current job scene by writing away for copies of *The Coventry Evening Telegraph* (main job vacancies, Thursday). Coventry Newspapers, Corporation Street, Coventry, phone 0203-633633), *The Coventry Citizen*, Corporation Street, Coventry, phone 0203-634343 and *The Coventry Weekly News*, 16a Queen's Road, Coventry, phone 0203-552001.

EMPLOYMENT AGENCIES

ACCOUNTANCY PERSONNEL
4a Copthall House, Station Square, Coventry. Phone 0203-257202.

BERTRAM PERSONNEL GROUP
3rd Floor Coventry Point, Market Way, Coventry. Phone 0203-252171.

CAREERS CENTRE/JOB LIBRARY
Greyfriars Lane, Coventry. Phone 0203-831714.

COVENTRY JOB CENTRE
Bankfield House, 163 New Union Street, Coventry CV1 2QQ. Phone 0203-555133.

PROFESSIONAL & EXECUTIVE RECRUITMENT
Bankfield House, New Union Street, Coventry. Phone 0203-223265.

BENEFITS

UNEMPLOYMENT BENEFIT OFFICES

For surnames A, B, E-G, M-R, W-Z:

CHEYLESMORE UBO
Coventry CV1 2HE. Phone 0203-633200.

For surnames C, D, H-L, S-V:

PARK COURT UBO
Warwick Road, Coventry CV3 6QP. Phone 0203-252145.

SOCIAL SECURITY OFFICES

For people living in postal code areas CV1, CV2 or CV3:

94 Gosford Street, Coventry CV1 5DB. Phone 0203-632022.

All other codes:

APOLLO HOUSE
The Butts, Coventry CV1 3GF. Phone 0203-634500.

ADVICE

THE BENEFIT SHOP AND LAW CENTRE
2nd Floor, Broadgate House, Broadgate, Coventry. Phone 0203-223051. Guidance on social security appeals, employment law, landlord/tenant problems and other issues. Call for times of advice sessions.

CITIZENS' ADVICE BUREAU
2nd Floor, Fleet House, Corporation Street, Coventry. Phone 0203-227474. Open Mon, Wed, Fri 10am-2pm; Tues noon-2pm; Thurs 5.30pm-7pm.

ACCOMMODATION: HOSTELS/UNIVERSITY

UNIVERSITY OF WARWICK
(During college vacation times) Gibbet Hill Road, Coventry. Phone 0203-523523. Write for details of vacancies to the university's conference office.

YMCA II
The Quadrant, Warwick Road, Coventry. Phone 0203-229184.
Male/female. Rate per night: stg£10. Busy: Write or call in advance.

YWCA SHERBOURNE HOUSE
The Butts, Coventry. Phone 0203-221681. Male/female. Rate per night:
stg£5.60. Very busy hostel: Write or call in advance to check vacancies.

ACCOMMODATION: RENTING A FLAT, A BEDSIT, A HOUSE

Average prices

Bedsits – from stg£80 per month

Two-bedroomed flat – from stg£200 per month

Three-bedroomed house – from stg£250-£350

Accommodation is not easy to find, as Coventry has a high student population. But check *The Coventry Evening Telegraph* and other local papers for lettings. Also check with *The Council Housing Dept* for lists of reputable letting agencies. (Spire House, New Union Street, Coventry. Phone 0203-833333.)

HOUSING ASSOCIATIONS

COVENTRY CHURCHES HOUSING ASSOCIATION LTD
Highfield House, St Nicholas Street, Coventry. Phone 0203-555433.

You'll find a full list of other associations in the *Thomson Local Directory*.

COUNCIL HOUSING

Before you apply for council housing, check with local advice agencies on council housing regulations and how best to present your case. You can go to your local citizens' advice bureau, or to the benefit shop. Phone 0203-223051.

BUYING A HOUSE OR FLAT

For current prices, check *The Coventry Evening Telegraph*'s property pages. *George Lovett & Sons* is one of the largest estate agents in the Coventry area. Address: 29 Warwick Row, Coventry. Phone 0203-258421.

You'll find a full list of local estate agents in the *Thomson Local Directory.*

ACCOMMODATION PROBLEMS: WHO CAN HELP

If you are having problems with your present accommodation (disputes with the landlord, bad conditions), then contact *The Benefit Shop and Law Centre* for help and advice. Phone 0203-223051.

Coventry Young Homeless Project can advise you if you've nowhere to stay. Unit 15, Arches Industrial Estate, Spon End, Coventry CV1 3JQ. Phone 0203-715113.

GENERAL ADVICE AND INFORMATION SERVICES

The Coventry Unemployed Workers Project has published an information booklet (*Everything You Want To Know About Unemployment*). It gives comprehensive advice on entitlements, job-seeking and training/education opportunities. It also contains a vast range of information on support groups, crisis agencies, health services etc, as well as listing local arts, cultural and sports amenities.

For more information on this booklet, call 0203-714082. They are based at Unit 15, Arches Industrial Estate, Spon End, Coventry CV1 3JQ.

EDUCATION

COVENTRY LOCAL EDUCATION AUTHORITY
Education Offices, Civic Centre 1, Coventry. Phone 0203-833333.
For enquiries about all levels of education.

COVENTRY POLYTECHNIC
Priory Street, Coventry CV1 5FB. Phone 0203-631313.

COVENTRY TECHNICAL COLLEGE
The Butts, Coventry CV1. Phone 0203-257221.

UNIVERSITY OF WARWICK
Gibbet Hill Road, Coventry CV4 7AL. Phone 0203-523523.
(Social science, arts & science subjects).

TIME OFF AND THINGS TO DO

Coventry offers a broad range of cultural activities and leisure attractions. It has the renowned Belgrade Theatre, the Herbert Art Gallery and Museum, Coventry Cathedral, medieval Spon Street and The Museum of British Road Transport, as well as The Midland Air Museum.

The town of Warwick has its medieval castle, and a few miles away is Kenilworth, immortalised by Sir Walter Scott. Stratford-Upon-Avon, Shakespeare territory, is just a car-drive away.

Coventry Tourist Information Centre, Smithford Way CV1, can tell you about places to see and things to do. Phone 0203-832312.

SPORTS AND LEISURE FACILITIES

Coventry City Council's Sport and Recreation Centre, Fairfax Street, Coventry, can give you information on a wide range of leisure facilities. Phone 0203-228601.

TRANSPORT

COVENTRY TRAVEL SHOP
Pool Meadow Bus station, Coventry CV1 5EZ. Phone 0203-525689.

WEST MIDLANDS TRAVEL LTD
Passenger enquiries phone 0203-223116.

All travel enquiries – bus services and local trains: Call Centro in Birmingham: 021-200-2700.

BRITISH RAIL
Phone 0203-555211 (Coventry) or 021-643-2711 (Birmingham).

COVENTRY AIRPORT
Baginton, Coventry CV8 3AZ. Phone 0203-301717.

Packie Bonner: The Big Man from The Rosses

We grew up in The Rosses in Donegal, in a small fishing village called Burtonport. There were my twin brother Dennis, myself and five sisters, my Mum and Dad and my grandmother, so it was a hive of activity at home all the time.

We had a little croft and a few cows and chickens. We set potatoes and vegetables and cut turf every year and hay and corn. This was about 200 yards from the sea and my dad was a fisherman in his younger days, so we owned our own boat.

We lived off the sea, pulled dulse and cut rack [seaweed] and the summer was spent out fishing with my brother and my Dad. It was a fantastic upbringing that I suppose helped me along to where I am today.

I remember when we were kids at Loughanure School, my Dad

used to cut the turf. And at that time they used to have 'squads' to do it. My Dad would go to three or four different houses in the locality to help out and then they would all come to our place to cut our turf. It was always a big, big day when the squad came to us. And when my Dad, who was building houses locally, decided he didn't have time to go out around all the other houses cutting turf, we did it in the evenings ourselves.

Dad used to pick us up from school and we would go off with him to the bog. This is how it works – they cut the turf and then somebody catches the sods, throws them up to the bank and out from there. We were only ten years old at the time, so my dad used to cut away ahead and we'd catch just one sod at a time between the two of us; that's all we could manage!

It could be Easter-time when we were cutting the turf and freezing up on the bog. Tough when you're wee kids. And when my dad had a house contract on, Dennis and myself would go working with him for the summer. And we learnt a lot from that …Well, enough to be able to do a few jobs around the house anyway!

There were fantastic characters in our community then. At home, I knew everyone around from about the age of ten. And because we were twins, we were known to everyone. My Dad was a great character around the place because he was a storyteller. People use to call in and he would tell tremendous stories, they were great evenings.

My Dad wasn't into sport really at all, until we started. But he used to tell us, when we were wee kids and very impressionable: 'I played with Sligo Rovers. I used to play at weekends with them when I was fishing up there!' And we believed him for a long, long time, you know! But although he couldn't really play football at all, he loved the sport. He loved hurling and football, though he never played.

We played Gaelic football and soccer and my Dad travelled everywhere with us and encouraged us in every single way. I played Gaelic from the age of eight or nine right up until I left for Glasgow at all levels, including senior, with the county.

I played out field. I could catch the ball and I was fast. I really enjoyed it. It's a fast game, a great game. I'd love to be playing it now and every time I go home in the summer, I always train with the local team.

I started playing organised soccer when they set up an under-six-teen Keadue team, when I was about fourteen. We had a very good team and we went on to win the league that year. I got in to the senior team, more or less right away, because I was quite good in goal at that stage – I was about fifteen then.

I was scouted for the Irish Youth Team during an inter-provincial tournament final up in Mosney. Declan McIntyre, who now plays with Galway United, got injured and I had to play. This was against Leinster. All the top FAI officials from Dublin were down for the game and I happened to have one of my better games that particular day – only for Declan's ribs injury, I wouldn't have played at all and I might not be where I am today.

It was a wonderful feeling to be selected and I remember we went to St Malo in France to play. That was my first trip abroad and I recall the feeling of fear, wondering what it was going to be like. Obviously, when you are young, you're not as outward-going and I was just sixteen, young enough to be going away.

Then Celtic scout Seán Fallon got in touch with Keadue Rovers and I went over to Glasgow for a trial. That particular week, the ground was covered with frost and snow and I ended up playing one game for a junior club, just so they could see me playing. I did quite well, but then I went home and thought that was it, there was no chance, even though they said to me, 'We'll be in touch.'

In the meantime, Leicester City wanted me to go over on trial. And that was a good experience. They had a youth hostel connected with the club and all the players from outlying areas used to stay there, even some of the first team boys. It was amazing for me, meeting the senior players and I learnt a lot from them.

I went over there a couple of times and I remember, one night, I wanted to phone home. Now back home then, we didn't have dialling phones, you just got onto the operator. Well, I couldn't work out how this phone worked. I was actually dialling the wrong way and I had to get the landlady to show me how to make the call. I felt so stupid! But it's these simple things that seem so big a problem and they can build up on you at that age, when you're away from home.

Then Celtic got in touch with me again. They invited me over and we went on a tour of France, an Easter tournament – and that was great, my first time away with the team.

I came back home and I was studying for my Leaving Cert and then I got this phone call just before my exams, to say that the famous Jock Stein, Celtic's manager, was coming over and he wanted me to sign. I couldn't believe it! So my Mum and my Dad went out to meet him in a hotel in Letterkenny. All I wanted to do was to sign at this stage – money didn't really come into it at all.

So I signed and I remember I started getting the odd wee wage-packet in the post, maybe £20 or £30, the schoolboy rate, you know.

And I thought this was fantastic – getting wages, actually earning while I was still at school doing my Leaving Cert!

Bound for Glasgow

I left home for Glasgow in July '78 and everyone at home was in tears because I was leaving for good. I was sick for three days before that, maybe it was nerves about going, but anyway, off I went in a coach bound for Glasgow. I remember the coach picking up a girl passenger around Lifford area and she was bawling crying, the poor girl. She was only young and she must have been away to work in Scotland. Well, she was starting to get over it a bit after a while and next thing the coach driver sticks on this tape. It was one of those sad Irish songs 'Leaving home for Americay' – that kind of thing – and then I was crying too and the poor girl was bawling the whole way down to Larne. Dreadful it was!

Well I arrived at Celtic for the start of pre-season training and, at that time Jock Stein had gone, and Seán Fallon had left. Seán was the fatherly type to me because he was from Sligo and I was devastated when he left. It was a big shock to me.

On the first day there, I was walking down into the reserves dressing-room and Billy McNeill, the new manager, was passing by with somebody. 'Who's that?' he said to the fellow with him, referring to me, and God, I was away into the dressing-room so fast! But in one way, it probably helped that he was new and didn't treat me as the new boy in the club, because he was finding out who everybody was. So I was the same as everybody else there in his eyes.

I was lucky with the Donegal connections in Glasgow. I stayed with an aunt and uncle for the first two years or so and it was great in one way – that I was with people I knew. But there were no young kids in the house and I really missed my own family and friends.

I found the first year very, very hard. I'd really nobody to go out with and the younger guys in the team stayed with their parents in other parts of the city and they had their own friends. So I never really went out anywhere for the first two years.

And I was so homesick, I must have written half a dozen letters a week, to all the family and my school pals. The best moment was when you got a letter in the morning. I'd wait till I got on the bus for Parkhead and then open it on the journey. It was a great feeling, to hear from home. I think I wrote all those letters not so much to give information on what I was doing myself, but to hear back from them. I just wanted so much to get letters.

I must admit there were times when I went upstairs about six or seven o'clock in the evening to lie in bed and have a cry to myself. It was living in the city that was completely alien to me. In Donegal, you could go out, walk over to the next-door neighbours and have the crack, but you couldn't do that in the city. I don't think I ever met the next-door neighbours in Glasgow for those two years. I didn't know them. My aunt and uncle knew them, but they would just say 'hello', that's all. This is something I have tried to do in my own household now. Anybody who comes in is welcome. I invite them in to have a cup of tea, and be a bit Irish about it. I like to do that.

I also missed my twin brother Dennis – that was one thing that made it very hard to leave Donegal, because the two of us were buddies since we were born and we played football and did everything together. The split came when I left for Glasgow and he went to college in Letterkenny and he couldn't just pop over to Glasgow any time that he wanted, so we were apart.

I made my debut on St Patrick's Day, against Motherwell at Parkhead and the unfortunate thing was that there was a postal strike on and I couldn't send a letter to my family, or even phone them, to tell them about it. So they didn't know until they got the Scottish papers in Donegal that Sunday. And we had won 2-1 that day.

I was lucky in the sense that I got into the team so quickly. If I had struggled in the reserves for two or three years, or got into the team but hadn't done well, things might have been a lot harder for me.

When my aunt and uncle moved back to Ireland, I was lucky because I had another aunt and uncle on my mother's side living down the road. So I spent another two years or so there. And I used to go out more, after I got to know a guy who lived nearby. The social life in the city is very different from home. You had to have the flash gear, you had to have a bit of money on you and you'd be asked if you had a car, that sort of nonsense. If you chatted with any of the girls, they thought, that was it, they were getting off with you! Maybe I'm in a different social life because I'm a footballer. But that was one thing I hated about the city. In Donegal, or anywhere around Ireland for that matter, I think you could go out socially and talk to anybody and it doesn't have to mean any more than that.

I met my wife Anne, who was born and reared in Glasgow, through the guy I used to pal around with. He knew Anne and her friends from school. I asked her out and we've been together ever since. We're married now for over seven years and we've a boy and a baby girl.

Life at the Top

It's far more enjoyable in the sense that you know far more people, but at this stage, it gets harder. You're in the public eye and you're under pressure with important games. You have to try and cope with it. And the attitude to the game is very different over in Glasgow. They tend to take you for granted and they sort of feel, 'Well, you're playing for Celtic, and my God you *should* be winning.' Whereas at home in Ireland, it's more like, 'You're doing brilliant, good on you.' And it's very nice to be appreciated at times, you know!

I adored football as a kid and I still do, but it's more a working thing now. And at times, you just want to get away from it, to get away from the pressure, just for a while.

If I get a break for a couple of days, I just jump on the plane and head down home to Donegal. My Dad's dead now, but my brother Dennis is back home. He emigrated to America, but now he's back, playing football for Finn Harps and working at home.

There's also a gentleman called Tony, a fisherman, who is very close to my family and surroundings. And when I go back, the first place I go is up to him. He looks after our little boat now. And we go fishing. We were out last night in the boat and we caught about twenty small fish and I got quite a nice pollock. And that's the 'crack', that's what we do. And going home for the few days helps me relax. I think it helps me play well.

It was a great feeling to play in the World Cup. We felt it was absolutely brilliant just to have qualified. The Romanian game was the highlight for me, obviously. Up till then there hadn't been a great deal for me to do. I felt I needed a good game behind me.

And I enjoyed the whole game. It was a challenge and I was pleased with how I played. When it came to the penalties I knew that if I saved one we had a chance of qualifying [for the quarter finals]. But there was no pressure on me, even though it was the World Cup. I was just looking forward to the challenge and I had nothing to lose.

It was only later on, back in the hotel in Genoa, that it sank in – we were through to the quarter finals and meeting Italy. A stage further along and on to Rome. For a small nation like ourselves to be playing against the host team in the World Cup was a lovely feeling.

The day after the match in Rome, when word filtered back to us via the media from home, we realised what it meant to everyone: the Irish were happy people. We'd done everybody proud. The Irish could hold their heads up. We are a very proud nation, you see, and I'm glad that we did something that everyone could take pride in.

The Homecoming – Dublin

The homecoming was overwhelming. We knew there would be an enormous crowd waiting in Dublin because a quarter of a million people turned out after the European Championships to greet us. I enjoyed every moment of the journey from the airport until we got to

O'Connell Street. But then I must admit that I was scared: the place was jam-packed and the crush was unbelieveable. All the way from O'Connell Street to College Green, I was afraid somebody would be seriously hurt. I was so pleased afterwards that nothing like that had happened.

Home to the Rosses

Then going back to the Rosses – when I touched down in Carrickfinn Airport, coming into my home place, it meant so much to me. Going to Keadue, to Dungloe and on to Burtonport, everywhere you looked, every house and shop window, there was a green, white and gold flag and a picture of myself. It was a lovely feeling that I had done something for the people of the Rosses, something that everyone could relate to. They had a little part of themselves in the World Cup because I was from there. And the local community is great – they gave me a fantastic homecoming. It meant more to me than anything.

I think, when you live in another country you become more Irish, you know. I listen to RTE every single day, going in to Parkhead in the car every morning. I'm into Irish music now, the way I never was when I was a kid. Anything Irish I love.

What I would love to do now would be to get something going so that I would have time here in Ireland, to be in the position where I had a business going that brings me over, so I could spend a month or two at a time here. That's the way I would like to be. I love coming back home.

CHAPTER 9

St Albans

There are many interesting remains from Roman times in St Albans.

On the outskirts of St Albans by the banks of the River Ver, lay the city of Verulamium, which was the third largest Roman city in Britain. In AD 209, Alban, a soldier of the time, became Britain's first martyr, executed there for his beliefs. And so the district in Hertfordshire was named in memory of Alban's unhappy fate.

St Albans' proximity to London made it an important coaching stop and by the 16th century it had its own craft guilds and cottage industries. The advent of the railway link from London in the early 19th century brought industry to the area. Printing became important to the city (several of William Caxton's works are said to have been printed there) and other manufacturing industries followed. By the end of the 19th century the population had grown to 16,000.

Today, the city and district of St Albans is the largest in Hertfordshire and the population is 128,000. Printing continues to be its prime industry, but it is also the home of big firms like Marconi Instruments and Schweppes. Situated just twenty minutes by rail from London, St Albans has a thriving business community, with a variety of work opportunities. It has a very low unemployment rate: just under 2 per cent.

THE IRISH IN ST ALBANS

St Albans has an Irish population of over 4,000 and there is a range of regular community activities. The base for these social and cultural events is *St Albans Irish Club*, Cotlandswick, North Orbital Road, London Colney, Herts AL3 5TR. Phone 0727-22251.

ST ALBANS IRISH ASSOCIATION
(Chairman: John Doyle) c/o 35 Elm Drive, St Albans.

COMHALTAS CEOLTÓIRI ÉIREANN
(Chairman: Pat Judge) c/o 16 Sunderland Avenue, St Albans, Herts. Phone 0727-51418. The Comhaltas branch has weekly music and céili dancing classes, monthly céilis, monthly traditional sessions and an annual dinner event (Nov). Most activities take place at *The Irish Club*, London Colney.

ST COLMCILLES HURLING & FOOTBALL CLUB
Playing fields at St Albans Irish Club grounds. Chairman Jim Moss. Phone 0727-62870.

GALWAY ASSOCIATION FOR HERTFORDSHIRE AND BEDFORDSHIRE
9 Foxcroft, St Albans, Herts. Chairman: Tom Miskell. Phone 0727-65634.

EMPLOYMENT

Most local employment is in the service sector: professional and scientific posts, distributive trades, transport and communications, insurance, banking and public services.

In the manufacturing sector, most employment is in engineering, printing and publishing; and in the rubber, plastics, clothing, timber and furniture businesses. High technology production and research work is expanding. There are some shortages in skilled labour, but unskilled people will find it very difficult getting work in St Albans district.

FINDING A JOB: WHERE TO LOOK

*Check out the local newspapers. You can order copies of: *The St Albans & District Observer*, St Georges House, Adelaide Street, St Albans, phone 0727-41133 or try *The Review*, 115 London Road, St Albans AL1 1LR. Phone 0727-46323/34411.

EMPLOYMENT AGENCIES

BLUE ARROW PERSONNEL SERVICES LTD
Clockhouse Street, 5 London Road, St Albans. Phone 0727-41433.

COMPUTER PEOPLE GROUP PLC
38 The Maltings, St Albans. Phone 0727-41351.

JOB CENTRE
54 Victoria Street, St Albans. Phone 0727-38326 or 0727-40121.

MANAGEMENT PERSONNEL
Eclipse Court, Half Moon Yard, 14b Chequers Street, St Albans.
Phone 0727-35116.

REED EMPLOYMENT
11 Market Place, St Albans. Phone 0727-43410.

ST ALBANS CAREERS OFFICE
Hertfordshire House, Civic Close AL1 3JZ. Phone 0992-556944.

UNEMPLOYMENT BENEFIT OFFICE
Beauver House, 6 Bricket Road, St Albans. Phone 0727-40161.

Advice

CITIZENS' ADVICE BUREAU
29 Upper Lattimore Road, St Albans. Phone 0727-55269.
Open Mon-Fri 10am-4pm, Sat 10am-12.30pm.

ACCOMMODATION: TEMPORARY

Hatfield Polytechnic has holiday flats in vacation times. Enquiries:
to the Deputy Housing & Conference Manager, *Hatfield Polytechnic,*
College Lane, Hatfield, Herts, A1 I0 9AB. Phone 0707-
279631/279064.

There are no YMCA hostels in St Albans, but you should contact
the tourist information centre for advice and information on bed-and-
breakfast accommodation in the area. The tourist information centre
is at the *Town Hall,* St Albans. Phone 0727-64511.

ACCOMMODATION: RENTING A HOUSE, A BEDSIT, A FLAT

*Check the local newspapers for accommodation vacant columns.
Accommodation can be both costly and hard to find in St Albans
because it is within the London commuter belt. For a list of
agencies, check with *The Council Housing Dept,* Civic Centre, St
Peter's Street. Phone 0727-66100.

HOUSING ASSOCIATIONS

ALBAN HOUSING ASSOCIATION LTD
22a Hall Place Gardens, St Albans. Phone 0727-55562.

PRAETORIAN HOUSING ASSOCIATION LTD
5 Holywell Hill, St Albans. Phone 0727-58003.

COUNCIL HOUSING

Local authorities are the largest class of landlords offering rented accommodation and in the St Albans district there are over 8,000 houses and flats, with an ongoing building programme. The council operates a points scheme to assess the priorities of potential tenants, mainly based on residence, current living conditions and need. But there are other factors as well, and you should check with the Citizens' Advice Bureau before you apply to the council.

THE COUNCIL HOUSING SERVICE
Civic Centre, St Peter's Street. Phone 0727-66100.

SHELTER HOUSING ADVICE CENTRE
The Civic Centre, St Peter's Street, can also advise you. Phone 0727-64010 (Mon-Fri 9.30am-12.30pm)

BUYING A HOUSE OR FLAT

House prices are very high, due to proximity to London. Check with local estate agents and the district newspapers.

Paul Camp, 48 London Road, St Albans, phone 0727-69181 is one estate agent in St Albans. You'll find a full list in the *Thomson Local Directory*.

ACCOMMODATION PROBLEMS: WHO CAN HELP

If you are having problems with your rented accommodation or disputes with landlords, then contact *The Housing Advice Centre,* St Peter Street, (phone 0727-64010), or the *Citizens' Advice Bureau.*

Marlborough Five Hostel, 5 Marlborough Road, St Albans. Phone 0727-65970. A local hostel for homeless people. (Males from sixteen years/females from eighteen years). The nightly charge is stg£7. But check with above advice centres first.

Check with *St Albans Irish Association.* There may be lodgings within the local Irish community. Contact The Irish Club, phone 0727-22251.

GENERAL ADVICE AND INFORMATION SERVICES

THE ST. ALBANS CITIZENS' ADVICE BUREAU
29 Upper Lattimore Road, phone 0727-55269, can give you advice and information on benefits, money problems, legal matters and so on. They can also tell you of other local organisations, support groups and crisis services. Open Mon, Tues, Wed, Fri.

Social Services (Council)
DIVISIONAL OFFICE
Catherine Street, St Albans. Phone 0727-60141.

211

Counselling for Young People
YOUTH AND COMMUNITY SERVICE
Alma Road, St Albans. Phone 0727-55374.

EDUCATION

The area has a good range of educational services, mostly administered by Hertfordshire County Council. For details contact *The Education Office*, Hertfordshire House, Civic Centre, St Albans.

Polytechnic: *Hatfield Polytechnic*, PO Box 109, College Lane, Hatfield, Herts AL10. Phone 0707-279000

Adult Education – Advice: *EGA (Educational Guidance for Adults)*, PO Box 109, Hatfield AL10 9AB. Phone 0707-279499.

TIME OFF AND THINGS TO DO

There is no shortage of cultural and leisure activities in the St Albans area. You can visit the city museum of St Albans, the home of the famous Salaman collection of trade and craft tools, or the Verulamium Museum, with exhibits from four centuries of Roman occupation. The Royal National Rose Society, on the outskirts of St Albans, contains one of the most important rose collections in the world. And there's The Maltings Arts Centre and The City Hall venue for arts activities.

St Albans Tourist Information Centre can give you more details. Contact the centre at Town Hall, Market Place, St Albans. Phone 0727-64511.

SPORTS AND LEISURE FACILITIES

The City and District's Council Directorate of Community Service is the area's major provider of leisure, sports and entertainment facilities. The directorate has published a fifty-page leisure directory, packed with information. For more details contact the *Sports and Leisure Services*, Civic Centre. Phone 0727-66100 (Mon to Fri).

TRANSPORT

LONDON COUNTRY BUS SERVICE
St Peter's Street, St Albans. Phone 0727-54732.

BRITISH RAIL PASSENGER TRAIN SERVICE INFORMATION
Phone Luton 27612.

LUTON AIRPORT
Phone Luton 0582-405100 and see next chapter!

CHAPTER 10

Luton

Commuting to London from Luton is very common, but there is also a growing local industry.

Luton, the Bedfordshire town famed for its straw plait, hat and brewing industries, as well as Vauxhall cars, was a pioneering force in the use of strong marketing strategies to lure new industries to its area.

As far back as the turn of the century, Luton's local authorities sent out promotion brochures, selling itself as a good location for industrial development. This marketing technique brought companies like Vauxhall, Laportes Chemicals and Electrolux to the area and by the fifties, Luton had grown from a country town to a booming manufacturing centre.

Its high employment record, however, was hit by the recession of the early eighties, as the manufacturing sector shed jobs. But Luton recently launched another big promotions drive: the 'Luton Initiative', brainchild of local Irish business-man Derek Ludlow. And today, the growth of small-firm employment in Luton is amongst the fastest in the country. Unemployment figures have come down from 13.8 per cent in '86 to the current level of 4.9 per cent.

Luton's good location in the southeast gives it natural advantages. It is just thirty minutes by train from London and has its own international airport. Hi-tech business parks and office developments are bringing in more companies.

Although manufacturing employment has fallen and two in three jobs are provided by the service sector, old stalwarts like Vauxhall continue to be major employers in the area.

The population of Luton today is just under 170,000 and even with increasing local work opportunities, many people commute to work in London. Part of the Luton Initiative programme is aimed at improving the image of the town. There are plans for a cultural centre, to include a theatre and art gallery. A fifty million pound leisure centre is also in the pipeline, as well as more attractive shopping facilities, redevelopment of the railway station and a new civic hall.

THE IRISH IN LUTON

There are over 20,000 Irish people in Bedfordshire, with about 13,000 based in the Luton area.

Comhaltas

The Luton Leagrave Comhaltas branch, with over 70 members, has regular sessions at St Joseph's Parish Centre, Gardenia Avenue. For more information, contact Branch Sec John Maguire, 4 Whitefield Avenue, Sundon Park, Luton.

GAA

There are three GAA football teams and a hurling team in Luton (Erin Gaels, St Dymphna's, St Vincent's and Eoghan Ruadh). Contact *Hertfordshire County Board* Sec Michael O'Regan for details at 54 Gordon Road, Harrow, Middlesex.

There are Irish social activities (dances, Comhaltas nights etc) at: *St Joseph's Parish Centre*, Gardenia Avenue, Luton, and Holy Ghost Parish Centre, Westbourne Road, Luton.

The Luton Irish Advice Bureau and Day Centre, 229 Brook Street, Luton LU3 1DU, phone 0582-28416. Open Monday to Friday from 9.30am-5pm. The centre provides advice and information on accommodation, jobs, entitlements etc. There is also a medical care service, a clothing store and furniture store. Low cost meals are also available. Ask for Sr Eileen O'Mahony.

Bedford Comhaltas: The Ard Rí branch in Bedford has over fifty members. Details of sessions from E Byrne, 102 Acacia Road, Bedford.

EMPLOYMENT

The job scene in Luton ranges from car-manufacturing to hat-making firms, with the greatest number of jobs in the service sector. The local recruitment newspaper, *Jobscan*, reports skill shortages in the professional and technical areas, and skilled manual workers are also in demand. Vacancies for sales and advertising staff, engineers and accounts personnel, computer programmers, and some temporary catering and construction workers are advertised in the local press.

FINDING A JOB: WHERE TO LOOK

NEWSPAPERS

JOBSCAN
Delivered free in Luton and Dunstable. Phone 0582-29683, fax 0582-29741 to obtain copies.

THE LUTON AND DISTRICT CITIZEN
Citizen Group of Newspapers, 31 Manchester Street, Luton LU1 2QG. Phone 0582-404444/404111.

LUTON HERALD & POST
Herald House, Church Street, Luton LU1 3JQ. Phone 0582-401234.

EMPLOYMENT AGENCIES

ALFRED MARKS
Aldwyck House, Upper George Street, Luton. Phone 0582-400300.

BLUE ARROW PERSONNEL SERVICES LTD
5 The Gallery, Arndale Centre, Luton LU1 2TG. Phone 0582-401636.

CAREERS OFFICE
Link House, 49 Alma Street, Luton. Phone 0582-28654.

LUTON JOBCENTRE
4 Chapel Street, Luton. Phone 0582-37551.

MANPOWER
54 George Street, Luton LU1 2AZ. Phone 0582-30471.

BENEFITS

Unemployment Benefit Offices

LUTON A
26-30 Cardiff Road, Luton LU1 1PW. Phone 0582-400701

LUTON B
Phoenix House, Mill Street, Luton LU1 2NE. Phone 0582-31241

Advice on Entitlements

THE LUTON-IRISH ADVICE BUREAU
(Sister Eileen O'Mahony) 229 Brook Street, Luton. Phone 0582-28416.
CITIZENS' ADVICE BUREAU
Grove House, High Street, North Dunstable. Phone 0582-661384
LUTON ADVICE CENTRE
Grosvenor House, 45 Alma Street, Luton LU1 2PL. Phone 0582-32629

ADVANCE ACCOMMODATION: HOSTELS/B&Bs

Luton doesn't have YMCA-type hostels in the area. There is the Luton Hostel, on Dunstable Road, but this is supposed to be emergency accommodation. Admission by interview only.

To book some temporary advance accommodation, contact the Tourist Information Office and ask for a list of local B&Bs. *Luton Tourist Information Centre*, Grosvenor House, 45-47 Alma Street, Luton. Phone 0582-401579

ACCOMMODATION: RENTING A FLAT, A BEDSIT, A HOUSE

Good-quality rented accommodation is very hard to find at a reasonable price in Luton.

Bedsits – can be stg£40 per week.
One-bedroomed small furnished flat – stg£300 per month.
Unfurnished three-bedroomed houses: – start from stg£350 per month.

There isn't a shortage of housing in the area, it's just that much of what is available in the low-to-medium price range is poor quality, so be prepared to spend a bit of time looking for somewhere suitable.

WHERE TO LOOK

The local newspapers, *The Herald and Post* and *The Luton Citizen*. Check with The Irish Advice Bureau for names of reputable landlords or accommodation agencies.

HOUSING ASSOCIATIONS

Aldwyck Housing Association, Aldwyck House, Upper George Street, Luton, (phone 0582-33722) is one local housing association. You'll find a full list in the *Thomson Local Directory*, or check with *Luton Council's Housing Dept* for advice, phone 0582-31291, ext 2231/2239.

COUNCIL HOUSING

There isn't a great deal of council housing in Luton and there's a big waiting list for what's available. There is also a one-year residency ruling but you can still put your name down on the waiting list. (And you should, particularly if you are thinking of applying to local housing associations.) *Luton Borough Council* is based at The Town Hall, Gordon Street, Luton LU1 2BQ. Phone 0582-31291.

BUYING A HOUSE OR FLAT

Housing in Luton is not cheap. A modern three-bedroomed semi can cost between stg£68,000 and stg£74,000 and a two-bedroomed flat can be stg£46,000+. One estate agent in the area is *Holmes Commercial*, 16 King Street, Luton. Phone 0582-41077. You'll find a full list in the *Thomson Local Directory*.

ACCOMMODATION PROBLEMS: WHO CAN HELP

If you are having problems with your accommodation or a dispute with the landlord, then contact *The Irish Advice Bureau* for help and information at 229 Brook Street, phone 0582-28416 or *Luton Council Housing Dept*, phone 0582-31291 ext 2231/2239.

If you are homeless there is an emergency hostel *The Luton Hostel*, 280-282 Dunstable Road, Luton. Phone 0582-22629. This is run by Signpost, a charitable organisation. It caters for 16-25-year-olds, but is usually fairly full. Admission is by interview.

GENERAL ADVICE AND INFORMATION SERVICES

LUTON ADVICE CENTRE
Grosvenor House, 45 Alma Street, Luton. Phone 0582-32629.

LUTON LAW CENTRE
2a Reginald Street, Luton LU2 7QZ. Phone 0582-481000.
For problems with housing, employment, welfare benefits, discrimination etc.

EDUCATION

To enquire about local schools, write to *Bedfordshire County Council*, Education Dept, 111 Stuart Street, Luton. Phone 0582-402500.

HIGHER EDUCATION

BARNFIELD COLLEGE
New Bedford Road, Luton LU3 2AX. Phone 0582-507531.

BEDFORD COLLEGE OF FURTHER EDUCATION
Cauldwell Street, Bedford MK42 9AH. Phone 0234-45151.

DUNSTABLE COLLEGE
Kingsway, Dunstable LU5 4HG. Phone 0582-696451.

LUTON COLLEGE OF HIGHER EDUCATION
Park Square, Luton LU1 3JU. Phone 0582-34111.

TIME OFF AND THINGS TO DO

Bedfordshire has many historic homes, good museums, parks and gardens. Information and brochures from *The Tourist Centre,* Grosvenor House, 45-47 Alma Street, Luton. Phone 0582-401579. Open Mon-Fri 10am-4pm, Sat 9am-1pm. Regular arts and music events are listed in the local newspapers.

TRANSPORT

Buses
LUTON AND DISTRICT TRANSPORT LTD
Luton Bus Station, Bute Street. Phone 0582-404074 (Open 10am-3pm)

Rail
BRITISH RAIL ENQUIRY SERVICE
Phone 0582-27612.

Airport
LUTON AIRPORT
Luton LU2 9LY. Phone 0582-405100.

CHAPTER 11

There is Always a Point of Return

For everyone who goes away, there exists the possibility of coming back home again to settle in Ireland.

There are several reasons why you might want to come home. You may be homesick, or things may not be working out as you expected or hoped in Britain. Or you may just decide that having experienced life in Britain, you would prefer to live in Ireland.

Try and sort out in your mind which of these reasons are behind your need to come home and whether coming back to live in Ireland would be a good decision for you in the long term. And if you do really want to come home again, then by all means do so. At least, having lived in Britain for a while, you have taken the time to compare the different cultures and lifestyles and all this experience will stand to you.

But keep in mind that it is important to check out the work scene in Ireland and what there might be for you to return to. Give a bit of time to thinking about the reality of day-to-day living at home again. When you are away, it's the memory of good times with friends and family that stay in the mind: the grey bits in between tend to get erased.

But by taking the time to think about how you'll do in Ireland and how you'll feel about the lifestyle, you are giving yourself a better chance of being content with your decision. Staff in the Emigrant Advice Service in Dublin emphasise that coming back home is at least as big a step as leaving Ireland in the first place. And the more you can check out and organise for yourself in advance, the happier the homecoming.

We hope that this guide has been of some help to you – and remember while you are away do keep in touch with home.

So keep listening, and good luck!
Aonghus McAnally, Cés Cassidy, Peter Browne
and Tom McGrane

IRISH CENTRES IN BRITAIN

Birmingham
IRISH DEVELOPMENT CENTRE BIRMINGHAM

14/20 High Street, Deritend, Birmingham B12 0LN. Phone 021-622-2332/2562. Secretary: Patrick McGrath. *Also* (at same address) **IRISH WELFARE AND INFORMATION CENTRE** Chairperson: Rev. Fr J.A. Taaffe

Corby
CORBY IRISH CENTRE

Patrick Road, Corby, Northants NN18 9NT. Phone 0536-743068. Chairperson: Michael Doherty

Haringey
HARINGEY IRISH COMMUNITY CARE CENTRE LTD.

72 Stroud Green Road, London N4 3ER. Phone 071-272-7594/272-9230. Chairperson: Bill Aulsberry.

Leeds
LEEDS IRISH CENTRE

York Road, Leeds 9. Phone 0532-480887/480613. Manager: Tom McLoughlin.

Liverpool
LIVERPOOL IRISH CENTRE

127 Mount Pleasant, Liverpool L3 5TF. Phone: 051-709-4120. Manager: Phil Farrelly.

London
IRISH SUPPORT AND ADVICE CENTRE HAMMERSMITH

55 Fulham Palace Road, Hammersmith, London W6 8AU. Phone 081-741-0466/7. Director: Fr Jim Kiely.

LONDON IRISH CENTRE

50/52 Camden Square, London NW1 9XB. Phone: 071-485-0051. Director: Rev. Fr T Scully OMI.

Luton
LUTON IRISH ADVICE BUREAU

229 Brook Street, Luton. Phone 0582-28416. Social worker: Sr Eileen O'Mahoney.

Manchester
IRISH WORLD HERITAGE CENTRE

10 Queens Road, Cheetham Hill, Manchester M8 8UQ. Phone 061-205-4007. Chairperson: Michael Forde.

Newcastle-upon-Tyne
TYNESIDE IRISH CENTRE

43 Stowell Street, Gallogate, Newcastle-upon-Tyne NE1 4SG. Phone
091-261-0384. Manager: John McGonagle. Chairperson: Terry McDermot.

Northampton
NORTHAMPTON IRISH CENTRE

32-34 Abington Square, Northampton. Phone 0604-32375.
Chairperson: Dennis Flynn.

Nottingham
NOTTINGHAM AND EAST MIDLANDS IRISH SOCIAL CENTRE

2-4 Wilford Street, Nottingham NG2 1AA. Phone 0602-475659/473424.
Chairperson: M. Geraghty.

St Albans
ST ALBANS IRISH ASSOCIATION

Cotlandswick, North Orbital Road, London Colney, Herts AL3 5TR.
Phone 0727-22251. Chairperson: J Doyle.

Sheffield
SHEFFIELD IRISH SOCIAL CENTRE

151 Brunswick Road, Sheffield. Phone 0742-731578.
Chairman: Pat Naughton.

Stafford
STAFFORD IRISH CENTRE

Fancy Walk, Stafford. Phone 0785-42752. Chairperson: Vincent Ward.

For information on other Irish societies and associations in Britain contact:
THE FEDERATION OF IRISH SOCIETIES

London Irish Centre, Murray Street, Camden NW1. Phone 071-267-5514.
Chairperson: Seamus McCormack. Secretary: Cathy Conroy.

Other books from The O'Brien Press

Pictorial Ireland
Yearbook and Appointments Diary
Superb full colour photographs of Ireland's wonderful
landscapes, towns, people. Each year a new diary, available
every summer in advance. *Wiro bound £6.95.*

Irish Life and Traditions
Ed. Sharon Gmelch
Visions of contemporary Ireland from some of its most
well-known commentators — Maeve Binchy, Nell McCafferty, Seán Mac Réamoinn, Seán MacBride. Deals with nature, cities, prehistory, growing up in Ireland (from the
1890s in Clare to the 1960s in Derry), sports, fairs, festivals,
words spoken and sung. 256 pages, 200 photos.
£6.95 paperback.

Old Days Old Ways
Olive Sharkey
Entertaining and informative illustrated folk history, re-
counting the old way of life in the home and on the land.
Full of charm. *£5.95 paperback.*

Kerry
Des Lavelle and Richard Haughton
The landscape, legends, history and people of a beautiful
county. Stunning full colour photographs. *£5.95 paperback.*

Sligo
Land of Yeats' Desire
John Cowell
An evocative account of the history, literature, folklore and
landscapes, with eight guided tours of the city and county,
from one who spent his childhood days in the Yeats
country in the early years of this century. Illustrated.

A Valley of Kings
THE BOYNE
Henry Boylan
An inspired guide to the myths, magic and literature of this beautiful valley with its mysterious 5000-year-old monuments at Newgrange. Illustrated. *£7.95 paperback.*

Traditional Irish Recipes
George L. Thomson
Handwritten in beautiful calligraphy, a collection of favourite recipes from the Irish tradition. *£3.95 paperback.*

Consumer Choice Guide to Restaurants in Ireland
With the Consumer Association of Ireland
About 300 restaurants assessed by consumers from all over the country. An essential guide for the traveller.
£4.95 paperback.

THE BLASKET ISLANDS — Next Parish America
Joan and Ray Stagles
The history, characters, social organisation, nature - all aspects of this most fascinating and historical of islands. Illustrated. *£7.95 paperback.*

SKELLIG — Island outpost of Europe
Des Lavelle
Probably Europe's strangest monument from the Early Christian era, this island, several miles out to sea, was the home of an early monastic settlement. Illustrated.
£7.95 paperback.

DUBLIN — One Thousand Years
Stephen Conlin
A short history of Dublin with unique full colour reconstruction drawings based on the latest research.
Hardback £9.95, paperback £5.95.

Exploring the
BOOK OF KELLS
George Otto Simms
For adult and child, this beautiful book tells when, how and why the famous Book of Kells was made, and gives a simple guide to its contents. Illustrated in colour and black and white. *£6.95 hardback.*

Celtic Way of Life
The social and political life of the Celts of early Ireland. A simple and popular history. Illustrated. *£3.95 paperback.*

The Boyne Valley Book and Tape of
IRISH LEGENDS
More than an hour of the very best stories from Irish mythology read by some of Ireland's most famous names: Gay Byrne, Cyril Cusack, Maureen Potter, John B. Keane, Rosaleen Linehan, Twink. Illustrated in full colour.
£6.95 (book and tape).

The Lucky Bag — Classic Irish Children's Stories
'Long stories, short stories - all good stories' - *The Irish Times.* 204 pages of the best for children from Irish literature, with sensitive pencil drawings by Martin Gale. *£4.95 paperback.*

The above is a short selection from the O'Brien Press list. A full list is available at bookshops throughout Ireland. All our books can be purchased at bookshops countrywide. Prices are correct at time of printing, but may change. If you require any information or have difficulty in getting our books, contact us.

THE O'BRIEN PRESS
20 Victoria Road, Rathgar, Dublin 6.
Tel. (01) 979598
Fax. (01) 979274